Highway to Hell

The Hell Fire Series, Book 1

By Lydia Anne Stevens

Dedication

This book is dedicated to the seven men and women
from the Jarheads Motorcycle Club who lost their lives in
the New Hampshire crash on June 21, 2019, the three
injured members of the motorcycle club, the other
surviving members of the motorcycle club, and all of the
family and friends impacted by this devastating tragedy. I
didn't know you personally, but your charity work is
appreciated, as well as your service in the Marines. Rest
easy and may your ride to Heaven bring you peace.

Acknowledgements

I would like to acknowledge my Mom and Dad, whose passion for motorcycle riding helped craft this book. It has been a blast asking about how bikes work, riding habits and developing an interest in the activity myself.

I would also like to acknowledge Juli Beck, whose book trailer helped promote interest in Highway to Hell. You graphic design abilities helped me out when I was floundering trying to create my own. I appreciate the work you put into the video and I love it so much!

Another acknowledgement is due to Paige Wheeler. I thoroughly enjoyed my time as an intern with your literary agency. Your expertise and guidance were invaluable, and something I will cherish moving forward with my career.

Additional Works

The Ginger Davenport Escapades

Why Me? The Ginger Davenport Escapades, Book 1
Why Should I? The Ginger Davenport Escapades, Book 2
Why Not? The Ginger Davenport Escapades, Book 3

CONTENTS

Chapter 1.. 1

Chapter 2.. 15

Chapter 3.. 37

Chapter 4.. 52

Chapter 5.. 65

Chapter 6.. 80

Chapter 7.. 91

Chapter 8.. 101

Chapter 9.. 122

Chapter 10... 153

Chapter 11... 167

Chapter 12... 190

Chapter 13... 202

Chapter 14... 214

Chapter 15... 229

Chapter 16... 241

Chapter 17... 258

Chapter 18... 276

Chapter 19... 289

Chapter 20... 303

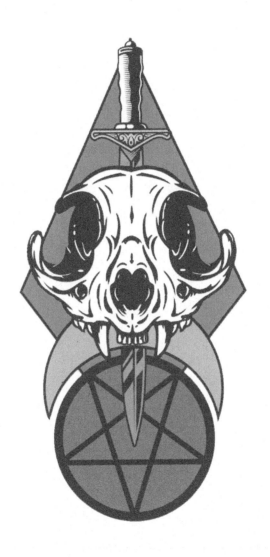

Highway to Hell

The Hell Fire Series, Book 1

CHAPTER 1

"Hey, any of you able to connect?"
The weight of Sugar, my Harley Davidson FXR3, settles from the custom-crafted, raked-out front end, onto the kickstand. Balancing a motorcycle while wrestling with a cellphone in the pocket of skin-tight leather pants isn't easy. Green flames lick up the side of Sugar's tank and settle back from live fire into the custom paint job, her growls kick down to a low purr. Stroking the side of the tank warms my fingertips. A text notification buzzed in my pocket half an hour ago, but now the buffering circle of pain-in-my-ass on the screen is spinning merrily away and won't let me open it.

Limbo, the first circle of Hell, is home sweet home and also where the wi-fi doesn't auto reconnect. For real, why does eternal torture have to suck so bad? In Heaven, the password would be handed out on gilded placards with a calligraphy font, but whatever.

"Hell has wi-fi?" Tora dismounts from the back of Leona's ride. The new pledge's #Cutie t-shirt is as out of place here as her skinny jeans. She'll be rocking the leather and lace in no time.

The rattling sounds of the rest of the motorcycle engines echo off the football field-sized room, causing her to have to shout above the noise. Floor lights run up each aisle of parked vehicles in the grey cement. The black stone, cavernous room emits an eerie yellow glow. They look like eyes glinting up from the other eight levels of Hell below. Leona's black eyes flare as she pulls her bandana down off her face and her gaze slides up and down Tora's body. Leo blinks, shaking her head from her stupor, and then throttles down the engine of her bike to idle and turns it off. She flips me off and looks out over the rows of vehicles, idling her libido for a minute.

"Yeah, Baby Girl, but the network crashes all the time." Tabby pops her bubble gum and checks her phone. Her blond pigtails sway back and forth from the rumble of her bike. She didn't seem to notice Leo's lust-filled leer, but Faline did. She frowns at Leo and dismounts her camo colored 1942 Norton and begins wrestling the captured mark from the attached sidecar.

"You going to give me a hand or what?" Her grey eyes flash like storm clouds backlit by a lightning-filled sky.

Leo looks over and shrugs while Tabby puts her phone in her pocket and swings her leg over her bike. Tora's eyes glaze over and her jaw drops in a newbie, no-clue-what-to-do expression, as she watches Fae wrestle with the mark and Leo slowly dismounts her bike.

Setting my phone on Sugar's tank, the buffering circle on the screen continues to spin as it tries to open a text from Auntie J. When the error message pops up and the network continues being a bitch, pressing the black button on the side of the screen locks it out of sight, out of mind.

"Tabby, give Faline a hand with the mark. Auntie J texted so it's time to check in. Leo, show Tora where we deliver the marks."

"Aww man, Catriona, why do I have to deal with that piece of shit?" Tabby says.

Hell no. Disobeying orders in front of the new pledge? Not cool. Tabby is popping her gum only a few steps across the garage parking lot. It sounds like firecrackers as it echoes off the walls, but my leather boots clunk louder, like the sound of gunshot under the vast open sky. But as huge as the garage is, there is nothing open about it. Nothing free, not even us.

"It's the job, Tabitha. You signed on for the grunt work when you signed up for atonement." Flames flicker in the depths of her pupils, engulfing the blue irises, but she quickly tamps them out.

"You're right. Thanks for the job, boss." Her pixie face tightens, and she looks along the long row of vehicles at the pile of junk cars and accident debris. Hell's own version of a scrap heap. Memories of my first few days down here swim in my head. The frame of Sugar was in the heap. Coping with being newly dead and damned for eternity was how Sugar ended up being rebuilt from the frame out.

We're all thinking the same thing when we look out over the garage. How easy it would be to escape. We could just get in one of the working cars or hop on our bikes and drive back through the portal of Hell into the human dimension and never look back. We wouldn't really be free though. Not really. Not with all of Hell chasing us down and making us heel, and not until we finish the job. And the one after that, and the one after that, and so it goes.

I nod at Tabby and give her a shoulder bump. I can play both sides of the court. Strict versus chill. Sometimes my girls just need a reminder of who they're working for and why. It keeps them in line when the temptation of the open road is staring them in the face every day. It would be all too easy to jump ship and make a break for it, but they've learned I'll be the fair leader if they all learn to play nice. Demons sometimes kick sand at each other down here in the box. Loyalty fits a demon about as well as a conscience fits a psychopath. At least I'd gotten the cream of the crop when my girls pledged into my gang. So far, none of them have pulled a runner.

"You bitches are crazy! This can't be real!" Jeremiah, the mark, screams as Faline sinks her claws into the fleshy part of his underarm, forcing him to follow us.

The yellow fire in her eyes, tail twitching in agitation behind her, and fangs protruding from her mouth should be enough of a warning, but Jeremiah Worthington doesn't recognize the direness of his situation. Having his soul captured in the human realm and brought to Hell by a band of biker demons is not the time to get lippy. It's ironic given his previous vocation as a pushy lawyer. I turn to him. This fool has been a pain in the ass since we picked him up.

"The little girl you killed, Katie, was supposed to grow up and invent a device to utilize natural energy from the sun, the ocean, and the wind, It would have been powerful enough to turn the planet around from universal threats like global warming, animal extinction, and energy efficiency. She was going to save humanity." I don't understand all the science crap. It's more up Fae's alley, but point made here. I walk toward him and he cowers under the harshness of my heterochromatic stare. He sways closer to me a little. It's my eyes. It always captivates the marks, no need to add the demonic flames to be hypnotic. It's like they don't know which one to look at, the blue or the green; but they always look away when they realize they have been caught gawking. Jeremiah is no different. A coward to the core, he wilts under my stare and tries to back away from me.

Cowards and crooks have often been synonymous in my book and I would know, having been those things in my human days. I stand over him where he has tried to crouch down next to the sidecar and slap my palm against the metal. A deep metallic vibration rings from the side and I imagine given its vocation it would be the sound blood would make if it could scream. It certainly has seen its fair share of blood and bodies. Jeremiah is no different than the other marks and today's testament is his own blood screaming through the side panels of the car.

"Instead, she was taken too early because of your stupidity, Jeremiah. The only consolation is she has gone to a better place, but it leaves us having to deal with you." I keep my voice low. Damned or not, the marks are still sensitive, like they think they're going to wake up from the nightmare. Trying to remain calm while still instilling the reality into the situation is critical to successfully delivering the marks.

"I didn't mean for her to die!" He tries to pull himself out of Faline's grip as she hauls him back up to his feet.

"The road to Hell, Sunshine…" I let the fire in my own eyes flare up so he gets a good look into the depths of some of the Inferno. Gone are the cool tones of serenity. There's trying to ease a mark into the situation and then there is tolerating fools. Jeremiah has proven to be the latter.

He turns beside Fae's bike and vomits. It splatters across the cement floor like a water balloon popping against pavement on a hot summer's day.

"Bloody Hell!" Leo's English accent is sharp as she dances away from him, kicking the toe of her boot trying to rid the clinging effluvium from where it sprayed her foot.

Paved with the best intentions, I think as I watch him wipe his mouth on the back of his hand. I crinkle my nose as the rancid stench wafts toward me and stand. At least he didn't hit Fae's bike. She might have mopped it up with his face.

"Are you kidding me?" Fae's look of disgust mirrors not only my own, but the other Hellcats too.

Leo winds up her barbed whip, which reeled him into the veil separating the human world and ours. There are still chunks of flesh caught in it and Jeremiah's eyes widen as he watches her. He glances down at his plaid shirt where the barbs ripped out of his stomach. Blood stains spread across the shirt. Shock and adrenaline must be keeping him from feeling the full effects of the injuries. That will come later. He may have left his corporeal body smeared down Route 666 from his last sojourn as a drunk driver, but the soul is just as corporeal in this dimension and capable of being carved out like Swiss cheese. I've seen it all before in this gig.

Besides, it's not like he'd been a model citizen. He probably deserves whatever this place has in store for him. But who am I to judge? I certainly deserved it. I wince from the pain of my own mental kick. We're often our own harshest critics. I sigh, staring down at Jeremiah. There isn't anything I can do for him now. Not unless he's offered a deal with the Devil, but those contracts come up on the side of rare to almost never.

Jeremiah was the kind of lawyer to represent the worst sort of scum on the planet. Pro bono meant nothing to him. Back in my days being associated with a drug dealer, he might have been the kind of lawyer I turned to in a pinch. Down here, the souls of the shady characters in life fade in and out between light silver and ebony smoke, depending on their transgressions. Jeremiah, I'm not sure of. Me, I thought my soul was charcoal, now I'm down for being medium rare to silvery-gray. I pride myself on having the potential to be better at least, him probably not so much.

His hazel eyes crinkle at the corners as he searches the garage, looking for a way out. Even if he figured it out, the portal we just came through wouldn't open for him anyway. The giant black wall of rock is as solid as any cliffside on this side of Hell. It only opens up for those of us who have the coveted hall pass. Reapers, that is. Those who go out and mark the souls, and those who go out and collect them. We're all different kinds too. I happen to prefer riding out on Sugar as compared to the most notorious of reapers, the dreaded four horsemen of the apocalypse. I don't even think they have permission to start the apocalypse. I guess I'll have to ask. But at least Sugar is a lot prettier than the pale horse of Death. I look around the garage, expecting to see a skeletal horse with a pale coat and fiery red eyes, but the stables of Hell must be located someplace else. The world is a big-ass place after all and Hell isn't any different.

I turn my attention back to Jeremiah. Beads of sweat run down his forehead and there's a yellow stain on the front of his khaki shorts, courtesy of the gang and I arriving at the scene of the accident to collect his soul. Death is a messy business. So is terror. Soiled underwear is par for the course. Which is why Limbo stinks like the rotten ass of a dead sardine when Tora opens the atrium door. My eyes water and I cover my nose with the sleeve of my jacket.

"This is your reality now." I squeeze my eyes shut, dampening the flames burning within them, and then turn away leaving him to scream profanities at my back. As I push through the throngs of people milling about, I can feel my whiskers pressing against my cheeks, as my inner Hellcat threatens to shapeshift out. The ache in my spine is a telltale sign I need to get to the elevators and out of here before I make catnip out of some of these people.

Some days, I hate my job. Why, of all the hotspots around the continental U. S. that are named after Lucifer himself, can't we get a back-alley entrance to the Underworld; one with some privacy so we can haul the marks in and then shove them into the hordes of people? In my opinion, this is the worst circle of Hell.

"Excuse me, miss?" A dumpy looking woman with eighties-style brown hair tugs on the leather of my jacket as I glare at the woman. No one touches my colors.

"I just oiled this leather yesterday." I swat her fingers away and check my jacket for fingerprints. Possessions and pride often go hand in hand down here. There's not a lot left to live eternity for, besides the rare few things we can call our own. I was one of the lucky ones, given a shot at a second chance.

"Oh, I didn't mean to smudge. I was merely trying to tell you there has been some sort of mistake. You see, I don't belong here." The woman gazes glassy-eyed at the long lines of people cueing toward the benches of judgement. It's like organized chaos. They try to sort themselves out to go where they need to. It's what humans do; make hierarchies and order. The rules are in place down here, but no one really knows what they are or how to follow them.

I bite my lip, trying hard not to give her a false sense of hope. I wish everyone here might have a smidgen of a chance to come ride with me and the Hellcats and earn redemption for our souls, but not everyone is going to get the invitation. I guess Hell really does have gilded placards in a way. Maybe just not the calligraphy kind.

"Lady, this isn't Welcome to Disney. Take a ticket and get in line. You can dispute your claim with the Drudes." I opt for the harsh reality even though the hurt look on her face makes me flinch. I rub my palm against the leather of my pants.

"Drude? What's a Drude?" She looks at the high wooden bench at the far end of the atrium.

It sits high, like a judicial bench, because it's essentially what it is, but instead of a long line of middle-aged men in black robes and funky-looking wigs, the presiding judges, jurors, and possible executioners resemble nothing like privileged white folks, and more like nightmares wrapped in dirty-gray, and blood-splattered robes.

"A demon. Usually associated with nightmares. When Lucifer wants to get all up in your business in the witching hour, he sends them out to prey on your worst fears. They invoke nightmares in humans. Then come back, bellies full in a manner of speaking, and regurgitate the crap to feed the negative energy down here." I tap my boot, wanting to get on with my business, but this sort of hold up feels like just another pesky customer service issue for me. When I entertain my impatient and irritable nature, I can't help but think she assumes she has a coupon for get-out-of-jail-free, but she can't find it at the bottom of the endless bag of sorrow and regret. I don't have the heart to tell her the the lines in Limbo, heading for the Drudes working the table, are more like an all you can eat buffet for those demons. Only the buffet is self-delivered souls. Some of them are hauled off to the other levels of Hell for different kinds of torture, but most remain here, cast off to the sides and milling about like wayward sheep, unsure of who to follow but not aware enough to sort through their chaotic confusion.

"Nightmares? So, I'm dreaming then?" Her eyes widen and her lips twitch in anticipation of the barest hint of hope revealing itself.

I feel the tightness of irritation in my chest loosen a little. The woman is in her mid to late forties. She has the look on her face that speaks of desolation and despair. Like she'd seen too much shit in her time and decided to drink herself to death because it was the best way to escape. It saddens me, people like her always seem to find a spark of hope within themselves after it's too late. Maybe because it hits so close to home. I certainly had been like her, afflicted with the hopeless dilemma, but it didn't mean everyone got a cush deal like mine. I harden my heart, remembering the rules. There is nothing I can do for the woman now.

"Yeah, a nightmare. Who wants to spend an eternity waiting in line, right? Look, the Drudes will consider your case and decide then. I'm not the one for the job. I just bring them in."

"Them? Who is them?" The woman licks her dried-out lips, glancing around for the "them."

"The souls."

"I still don't understand."

I close my eyes and groan as I run my hand through my spikey, caramel-colored hair, wanting to tear it out. How many times have I pushed my way through the crowds of people and needed to explain this? At least once every time I bring in a new mark. So, daily. I do this crap daily.

"You know where you are?" I open my eyes and stare down at her. Her eyes don't fully meet mine. She suffers from the same affliction of nervous I-don't-want-to-stare-because-that-would-be-rude vibe. This place is rude. A daily affront to everything anyone holds virtuous. I have a hard time remembering names, so I stopped asking for them. Mostly I recognize the people here by the look on their face. The level of how much this place has worn at their soul. It ranges from the hope on hers to the look of dejected defeat.

"I...I think so." The woman's eyes water as she looks around the massive stone room.

Columns line the outer circular walls and dark crevices collect in corners like dust bunnies breeding under furniture that haven't been moved in years. Great, cue the waterworks and the denial too. I sigh and glance up at the domed ceiling. It's just as spartan and gloomy as the rest of the room. Maybe we could commission a corrupt painter to put in a skylight or something. There's my hope shining through my brain like a beacon of -- *what the shit, Catriona?* Don't forget the mission. Someday you get a one-way ticket out. No need to entertain the false idea of incorporating hope to the masses who don't get out. I switch gears in my head, downshifting to a practical speed. Nah, no skylight. We all have other stuff to do rather than watch out for Hell's version of a pervy-Picasso. I turn my face back to hers, reminding myself as much as I feel for her situation, I am not a hugger.

"My job is to collect the souls that have been marked to come here. With me so far?" Farrah hair Femme nods. "Ok, well, my crew and I," I point to the four biker chicks behind me manhandling Jeremiah into the foyer. "We drive them here into Hell on our motorcycles. We act as transport to get souls past the walls of the human realm into this one and deliver our marks to get in line with the rest of you who are waiting for sentencing."

"Yes, but I still think there has been a mistake. I came here on a boat," she insists as her fingers curl around the sleeve of my jacket.

I look down at them and feel my jaw crack. My fingers had once curled similarly, as I looked up into the eyes of my murderer. There's a defining moment in everyone's life. Some think it's the first bad decision. Some think it's the catalyst to those decisions. Some even think the defining moment is when the big crisis comes and the lesson is learned. I think maybe I was a combination of all three. My defining moment came at the end. When I blinked up into the eyes of the man holding the gun. I cried and I begged.

I often imagine what it would have been like if I were a hero. If I'd notched my chin up and said, "go ahead. Pull the trigger." I've had about two years down here to accept the fact I am not, nor was I ever, that person. I begged. And if I were to ever relive the moment, I can with the utmost confidence say, I would beg again. But what's the lesson learned from all of this? I know what moment defined me. I know my life wasn't perfect and I should have made better choices, but in the end, I would still ask for it back. I would make the changes and do the right thing. Hindsight is twenty-twenty and when my handler emerged from the shadows near the junk pile when I was making makeshift tools to fix up Sugar, and offered me the second chance, I didn't hesitate to take it. I look around for my handler to see if she will pop out of the shadows like a damn poltergeist and save this woman, but no such luck for the late-eighties lady.

I crack the cement my jaw has become and my teeth hurt as I grind out, "There's more than one way other than a motorcycle to get here. Your case is not my problem, lady. I just deliver the goods."

"You have to help me. Please!"

I wish I was immune to the begging. I have been listening to it for what feels like an eternity, although my gig only started a few years ago. It still gets to me, every damn day.

"I told you, I--" I pull her fists off of my jacket as more tears stream from eyes just as dull brown as her hair.

"Bitch!"

My head snaps to the side as something that feels like a boulder smashes into my cheek.

CHAPTER 2

I stagger back a couple of steps as pain explodes in my skull and then a copper taste floods my mouth. Sappy lady also stumbles a few steps and quickly scrambles away from us. I spit blood on the floor, convincing myself I hadn't just been shot point blank again. The black spots fade from my vision just as I see Jeremiah try to tackle me, but I'm quick to jump back to my feet, survival instincts kicked up to one hundred percent. Just because I'm dead doesn't mean I won't defend against a personal attack.

Faline tries to wrap her arms back around Jeremiah. His face is contorted into the unmasked rage of a psycho killer and he's definitely worse for wear, burnt from the sidecar's flames with scraps of flesh hanging around his waist from the barbs. The wounds will disappear in time, this being the land of the dead and all. Torture comes in daily doses around here like Percocet in a halfway house's candy dish. The current injuries he is sporting are a tickle compared to what is in store for him in the circle he is headed for.

Normally, I would have just let Jeremiah go once inside Limbo, but he'd proven to be a feisty mark on the ride between realms. He tried to push

15

through the sidecar's flames so he's one of the souls we must physically hand over to the Drudes.

I snarl, cupping my throbbing cheek, and then tackle him. We both go down in a heap of limbs. I twist once we are on the floor and pin him down. I straddle his waist, hiss down at him, and clock him in the nose. My knuckles tingle on the impact and I shake my hand. I'm not usually the one to dole out torture around here, but the job permits me to use force when necessary. It satisfies me to hear the cartilage crunch, but then the blood spurts, spraying across my t-shirt.

"Damn it! I loved this shirt!" I want to strangle him as I look at the gray t-shirt with "Hellion" written in glittering gold lettering across the front. So maybe the new girl's #Cutie t-shirt isn't so far-fetched.

He's holding his nose and moaning, but it is a safe bet he isn't going anywhere. A couple of Drudes float in beside me as I scramble to get off him. I hate being anywhere near the Drudes if I can help it. The dense patch of fog wafting around them is like a black void. I've tried to discern a form beyond it, but there is nothing solid under the miasma. The feeling they emit is the cold terror of nightmares. It sucks me in and makes my skin crawl, reminding me my worst nightmares have already come to pass, but they can ensure I relive them, again and again.

It's momentarily paralyzing, but to keep from freezing on the spot, I rub my arms against the prickling sensation under my skin and watch as they float Jeremiah away. His screams rip through the atrium and those waiting in line around us stare as he struggles against the fog, but he is lost to it. His eyes are bloodshot from terror. Whatever terror is near the surface of Jeremiah's mind, it wasn't hard for the Drudes to find.

Newly formed Drudes give people night terrors once or twice a week. They go for the sick and elderly types, or little kids. Drudes who have been around the block a few times are the ones who have perfected the craft of night terrors. Some of them even have favorite victims.

"Trina, you're growling!" Leo has lit a cigarette as she watches the spectacle. The ember tip glows like my eyes and the smoke curls around her face like a veil. She shakes her dark head and I see her spikey black hair with white tips flash under the low torchlight.

Faline and Tabby are shifting side to side, trying to figure out how to help and settle on crowd control if need be while Tora looks on terrified.

"No shit. Always the level-headed one, you are." I stand and she hands the cigarette to me. I take a drag and cough. I've never really enjoyed smoking, but I do relish the feel of my blood pressure dropping when the nicotine hits my system.

"I thought I was the level head." Faline looks like she's ready to hand me a fire extinguisher to douse myself, but the flames die down in my soul. Her face is tight and I can't tell if it's from the severity of her hair pulled back into a tight knot at the base of her skull, or if she's genuinely worried. I blink, reminding myself of a mission. Her hair reminds me of the color of espresso and as soon as I can get to the level I'm going to, the sooner I can have a cup of caffeine, the balm to my tattered soul. Besides, it's not like I can kill anyone with my temper. Everyone here is already dead, technically. We were all given corporeal bodies when we make our deals with the Devil. I feel my claws rescind along with my fangs and whiskers.

"I don't get paid enough for this crap." I hand the smoke back to Leo.

Her dark fingers pinch the butt and she flicks the ashes on the floor. There's no such thing as Hellish housekeeping.

"We don't get paid at all." She takes a drag and the tip lights up again.

"Point made."

"You could always take it up with the Union Rep." The smoke curls out of her lips and it is mesmerizing for a moment. I pretend my temper is coiling out and escaping this place and the thought calms me down. I'm itching for a proper smack down Jeremiah had been promising, but my girls are getting so proficient, the jobs have pretty much become get in, get the mark, and get out.

"Hell has a Union? What happens to the person who complains?" Frumpy Fran who begged for my help earlier is back in my face.

I groan. I should have chased after Jeremiah. Then I consider her question. "I've never really given it much thought. I think the person would get the ax. Literally."

A shudder ripples through my girls. Tora looks just as perplexed as Fran. Picture that. Me going to Hell's HR department. The gang's handler here in Hell, Jezebel. More fondly known to us as Auntie J. I can just see Auntie J, a Gorgon demon, with her simple woodsman hatchet or rolling pin; it depends on the mood she's in, baking or breaking. She has one too many chins and smells like sulfur and baking spices. Female Gorgons are the demons of wisdom and mysteries, it makes her the best candidate to be the liaison between most of the demons and the Devil. She's also the bringer of death if necessary. Like, literal death. Death of a soul death and of the permanent kind for demons. She fought for my deal with Lucifer, but asking for a dime for this job is a stretch. Even for me. Auntie J is no pushover. Despite being able to equate her to the boisterous and irritating relative who only shows up for holiday dinners, she could rock the lumberjack hardware with the best of the woodsmen.

I continue to watch as the Drudes, bouncers of the year, drag Jeremiah off. Satisfied, I turn my attention back to the woman, not wanting to keep Auntie J waiting anymore.

"Look, lady. Your best bet is to wait in line like everyone else, ok?"

"But..."

I nod at the woman and Leona stubs out her cigarette on the floor with her boot as she grabs the woman under her arm. She knows when my patience is shot and I'm grateful my girl steps in before I overstep my role and boundaries of the job. I don't need any more smudges on my soul, and delivering undue punishment, even with whatever she deserves down here, would tarnish the offset I've been working so hard for. I can hear the woman protesting even as I make my way through the lines of gawking people.

"Come on, girls. We're going to the Dog Pound," I call over my shoulder. The rest of my crew is hot on my heels when we reach the other side of the unadorned antechamber.

The area near the far walls is darker than the pale beige stone of the rest of the room. The archways are cast into shadows where the light bulbs have burnt out. No one has bothered to replace them and why should they? It makes the whole room feel forlorn. I hit a button on the column of granite near the wall and hear the rumble of the elevator spring to life and ascend from somewhere below my feet. It's a funny place down here. There's the incorporation of modern amenities in a place as archaic as time itself. The electricity feels out of place here, like a historical building renovated for modern living. You know the toilet shouldn't be able to flush, or the kitchen to have running water, but then those little commodities have been added for the benefit of the owner. Maybe that's why I like the occasional visit to ancient ruins as a stop off before the end of a job. The character is still imbued within the walls, even if the Hell is a bit broken. At least it's untarnished with the need to make it better. Kind of like how my foster parents treated me and my sister, Fiona. I feel the hurt arc through my body. Fiona was the perky upgrade while I was the ruins.

When the little ping of the lift sounds and the doors slide open on an ear-piercing screech due to lack of oiling, I step onto the elevator and wait as everyone squashes in next to me. I hit the button for the tenth floor then close my eyes. No one realizes there is a tenth floor in Hell. It's all *"8-6-7-5-3-0-9!"* for

Hell's floor plan. Throw in a level 1, 2, and 4 and no one cares what's beyond that. Probably because they've never survived any of the levels above it.

I don't want to see through the transparent slats on either side of the doors into the next eight circles as the elevator rumbles to life. I've always been grateful I'm not on one of those floors now. I might have been if it hadn't been for Auntie J. She stepped up on my behalf and asked Satan for a deal for me. She brokered my contract so to speak. Hashed out all the details. I owe her a solid for sure. Maybe I am more like the souls in Limbo than I realize. Looking for a clan, a semblance of order, the top of the gang's hierarchy.

I open my eyes thinking we must be nearly to the Dog Pound. I've gotten good at timing it in my head, but the fight with Jeremiah and the deep thoughts have me rattled. I never knew the human body could suffer so much from torture. Crime drama on TV paints a vivid picture of what is on the insides of the human body, but it is nothing compared to the reality of the mush splahing down like raining cow viscera on a butcher's block, into a tub below the table. Anytime I catch a glimpse of intestines, it makes my own stomach roll. It takes guts to walk through Hell with my head held high and the knowledge there is a job to do. I don't like looking into the third circle of Hell, Gluttony.

"The Dog Pound?"

I forgot Tora has no idea what it is. Grateful for a distraction, I glance over and see Tabby tighten the blond ponytails on top of her head. Then she answers for me.

21

"It's kind of like a Hellhound frat house."

"Who are they?" Tora chews her fingernails.

"The gang who marks the souls we collect."

"That doesn't sound so bad." Tora looks between the three of us. She giggles, hearing the lie in her own voice none of us bother to point out.

"Cats and dogs, sweetie. This is Hell. Do you honestly think two rival gangs of demons are going to get along?" Faline checks her phone again. Ok, so apparently Fae will call her on the bullshit meter going off. Then again, Fae's bedside manner is what got her in trouble with the Cosmos in the first place.

"Oh, sorry." Tora chews on her other hand.

"Don't be sorry. That shit'll get you chewed up and spit back out down here. Hellhounds versus Hellcats. They loathe us and we loathe them. We still must work together though, but it's cool because the Cats stick together. You're one of us now." I shoulder bump her to make her feel better.

She peers up at me with pale green eyes. Her freckles blend with her whisker spots so I can't see one over the other. But it's the flaming red hair that captures everyone's attention. I can see the whole innocent look being what caught Leo's attention this morning. If opposites attract, she and Leo are polar. I just hope the beguiling face doesn't get her torn apart down here. I'll give her a minute to get accustomed then I'll have to harden her up.

I smile at her, something we rarely do down here. Redemption is a terrifying road to travel and atonement for the crap we've done is an even harder gear to grind. She's only been with us for a day. Or longer. I lose track of time in the Underworld because it moves differently than the living realm. She showed up this morning and Auntie J brought her to us just as we were about to ride out to collect Jeremiah. I don't have her full story yet, but she fits the bill stamped with Lucifer's seal of stands-a-chance so she hopped on the back of Leo's bike and away we went.

She looks around and I see the small smiles on Faline and Tabby's lips. I nod and the elevator shudders to a stop. The doors ping as they open and we step out into the Dog Pound. I look around for the five Hounds. At least, by last count, there were five. They have a tendency to get territorial and tear each other up like the rabid mongrels they are. Mostly, when their leader, Damien, isn't keeping a tight leash on them.

Sure enough, there's Damien himself, son of Satan, sitting sprawled on one of the black leather couches, watching a football game on a big plasma TV. Two of his boys are playing pool at the far end of the room with a third leaning against a pinball machine, looking on. The newest recruit is perched like a watchdog, sitting stiff and rigid in the armchair next to the couch. Damien obviously hasn't bothered to make him feel welcome, but not my problem.

The space is like a coed clubhouse for both gangs. The Hounds constantly dominate the Pound, watching whatever they want on TV and emptying the fridge of whatever is good and unspoiled. I'm not sure we have to eat, but who doesn't love stirring a French fry in the puddle of grease and ketchup at the bottom of one of those plastic dinner baskets? Some of the best food that won't ever kill me slowly anymore is in those truck stops just off the highway. I'm always down for a stop-off, knowing the fridge here is always empty. The way I see it, as long as you can stomach the sound of crackling roaches falling into the deep fryer, you're all good. It doesn't really bother me since roaches were like pets in our apartment before the state of Arizona took Fiona and I from Mum and gave us to the Andersons.

As I watch the domination seep out of every Hound in the room, I know there isn't a chance we'll get to chill and relax or veg-out on the couch with them all around. I try to think of the positive. At least we all have our own private rooms and aren't sprawled out all casual on a torture rack or something.

"Kitty Cat! You aren't going to say hello?" Damien rises from the couch, shoving his hands in his jeans as he walks over to me.

Shit. I'm caught between him and the TV. I hate being cornered by him, but my crew takes a step back behind me. I hear the leather from their clothes as they do. They aren't even going to try to help me weasel my way out of this confrontation. I'm going to have to play "beat a bitch" later.

"It's Catriona or Trina. I've told you this before. Glad we had this chat. Later." I try to walk around him, but he sidesteps, blocking my path. I can feel my whiskers and fangs again. Damn it. Now is so not the time to show off the goods. "What?"

"Did you miss me?" His cocky grin makes me want to punch him too.

I flip him off.

"You're always such a delight to talk to."

"And you're always a pain in the ass."

"Throw a dog a bone, Catriona."

I hate it when he uses my full name. Like he has a secret he is willing to tell me after he uses it, but he is waiting for me to ask. "For you or your crew?"

"You know what I meant."

I cross my arms and look past him at my bedroom door. "Never going to happen."

"Why not? We could be indestructible, you and me. Or we could destroy whatever the Hell we want, when and where we want, and do anything we want."

His black and silver eyes bore into mine and I feel like prey being hunted as he tries to wear me down. He's been trying since I joined the ranks of mercenary soul-hunters for his father. The problem is I can't figure if he is just jonesing for a tumble in the sack or if there's something else he's coming after me for. He talks like he wants to take over the world, but he has never come out and said it's his end game. I shudder to consider if he does have a personal vendetta in the tug of war between Heaven and Hell and what it means if there is a shift in the regime leadership. Damien will destroy the organized chaos that is the system down here and we can't have evil running amok doing as it pleases, can we? Hell, versus Heaven and Humanity, are still not odds I'm sure I want to bet on.

As I stare back into his dark face, I get the feeling like he is asking me for something more. He's never outright said he wants a skin on skin session. I've always just assumed he meant sex. I've had my fair share of the bad boy types and I'm done with them. Despite the fact Damien is tall dark and damn-he's-fine, there is no way I'm falling in with the likes of him. That path only leads a girl down the road of chaos and destruction.

"I told you once, I've told you a thousand times, Damien. I don't play well with others, especially you. Not interested." I wonder when my breaking point will come and I'll just haul off and deck him? Maybe around the time I have to tell him one thousand and two times not to piss in my litterbox. I really should be getting into Heaven soon. I have the patience of a saint when it concerns him. Not.

"I understand. You're all about saving the remnants of your soul. I could retrieve it for you."

Temptation, damn you look so good in those jeans.

I recoil, but don't take the bait. He has promised it before, but I recognize it for the pretty lie it is, all wrapped up in his masculine form of seduction and sin. If I was stupid enough to take him up on the offer, he would renege on his promise and work tirelessly to destroy the last vestiges of whatever remains of my soul. I watched him do it to his last two "girlfriends" here in Hell. They'd gone away after he'd had his fun. I don't know where and I've never asked, not even Auntie J.

"Who's the new rider?" I look at the kid sitting in the black leather chair. He's not looking at us but using his fingernail to scrape red paint off the wall where one of the Hounds carved last week's hockey score between the Diablo's and the Saints. I can never remember the states for the college teams, but ESPN seems to be the channel of choice on the TV all the time.

"I'm so glad you asked. This is Phil, a fallen angel." He nods to Phil, still sitting in his chair. The expressions on Phil and Tora's faces are the same; like a Grandma at the senior citizen's home when the kids come to pick her up for the family barbecue. They bite their lips in anticipation, and squint, gauging the distance between where they're standing and how far away the exit is. Grandma got game with her walker on BBQ day. She's like an Indy-500 driver and will run you the big TF over if you get in her wayn-not unlike them. They're ready to bolt out the door.

"You have a fallen angel named Phil? Scary." The poor kid is an anathema to scary. He looks like he's no older than fifteen, maybe sixteen. What sucks is Hell has no rules for underage employment. Leave it to Damien to start recruiting the young ones. Asshole. I wonder what Phil has done to fall from Heaven? With his appearance pulling a twinsy with Tora's, he looks like he could pass off as this year's prom king. I wonder if demons ever get their boogie on? If so, I've never seen it. Tabby gets another smack down for playing the pop songs in her room last week. I'm a classic rock girl and I don't need an earworm. Phil's baby-blues flick to my eyes. I want to smile at him, but I'm not sure it won't land him a beat-down by the other Hounds later on.

"I see you've got a new recruit yourself." Damien turns his attention to Tora, who takes a step closer to Leo as she walks into the room off the elevator. *Damn, girl, in this pound you need to grow a pair if you want to survive.*

"These are the two Hellhounds, Doug and Richard." He nods to the two who are playing pool, still talking to Tora. They are huge guys with way too much macho and muscle to keep track of. So not my type. Their silver collars glint under the low light above the pool table. I can never remember if Doug is the one with the nose piercing or if it's Richard. I'm pretty sure it's Richard because Doug is so simple Sam whenever I see him around. Even his name screams 'please give me a personality.' I only know him because his flat brown hair and hazel eyes are so ordinary, I almost wish he had a cooler name. At least Richard has the bullring and dyed hair so electric blue it could light up the foyer under the broken light bulbs and torches in Limbo.

"Wait, wait. I've got this one! Doug the dog and Dick the..."

"And this is a recruit who has been here for about a week. The Incubus, Charles." He points to the third guy watching the game. Charles is someone important, or at least he was when he was alive. The way he holds himself in a rigid, holier than thou stance makes me want to stick his nose in the Jeremiah juice up in the garage. Men who stick their noses in the air and use that much hair gel to grease back their ebony waves should be forced to suffer down here. His skin is pale. Too pale. Tora's is pale due to fright, and understandably so, but his is unnatural.

I shift my weight, not wanting Damien to catch the shudder as I sniff the air and figure out what Charles is. Incubus smells about as well as a four-week-old corpse and it doesn't matter how much expensive cologne he has doused himself in. There's no covering up dead and decaying. I wonder what Damien did to merit his Daddy sticking him with one of his fouler creatures of the night? Being babysat doesn't look good on Damien either. I see it now. The lines in his face. Talking about Charles stresses him out. There's so much dirt here, I can't wait to claw my way to the bottom of the pile and roll in it when I find out what Damien is hiding.

All three men stop what they are doing and turn to us simultaneously. It's creepy as shit because there is no light in their eyes. Just irises bleeding into pupils full of dead and dangerous.

"Sticking with your usual crew huh? All bottom feeders? I suppose we all knew you couldn't sink any lower." Bravado is my only recourse sometimes, but at least it gets the Hellhounds attention off Tora, the fresh meat.

"There's the pot calling the kettle, Kitty Cat. Have you helped your boy toy sell any more drugs lately?"

I stiffen, ready to pounce. I just sauntered my ass into that one, didn't I? I loathe the knowing sneer on Damien's face. Why is he looking at me with a damn secret in his eyes again? Screw it, why should I care about his games? I shake my head, clearing the fiery feline eyes and rescind my fangs. I push my way past him, walking across the sitting room to the door of my own room. My girls follow as Damien crosses his arms and grins. I'll figure his secret out someday. It'll wipe the smirk off his face and rub his nose in the litter for sure. I feel my ears turn pink.

"Come on, Trina! If you're going to come

home, claws sharpened and fangs out, you can't really expect me, my father's son, to play fair now, can you?"

"You're pathetic." I yank open the door of my bedroom and slam it shut behind Leo, the last one in the room. She'd come down not long after we did and walked into the middle of the confrontation just as Damien really got his game on.

The girls filter through my room, standing awkwardly around like they don't know if they should ask me to move so they can leave or sit and lean against any available surface.

I lean back against the door as if it will keep the wolves at bay. Breathing hard, I listen to the sounds of deep demonic laughter coming from the Dog Pound. I can't stifle the growl of anger rising in my throat as I yank my jacket off and toss it on my forest green Rattan Papasan chair sitting next to my bookshelf.

"Don't let him get to you, luv." Leo and the rest of my girls remain scattered around the room, waiting for me to cool my head. Tora gazes around the room, taking in the details on the walls and the simple furniture. The ivy and cream décor is an anathema to my persona, so it amuses me watching the confusion parade across her face. Tabby continues to thumb through her phone, snapping her gum and looking ignorant and happy. I envy her sometimes, which isn't a good thing since it seems to be one of the seven sins getting the souls bit in the ass down here.

I peek at Fae. I always know when she pinches the bridge of her nose the way she's doing, she's either planning the best possible way to take someone out with the least amount of effort, or she's running sciencey things none of the rest of us don't understand. Leo is toying with the barbs on her whip, pretending not to be sneaking glances at Tora.

"He's a douche bag." Tabby finally says and slings her own colors over her arm. The emblazoned red and black cat skull on the back of the leather is face up. I walk across the tiny five-foot expanse and fling myself onto my bed, not caring my boots are still on or the fact I still have Jeremiah's blood on my favorite shirt.

"He's such an asshole." I fling my arm over my eyes, not wanting to see how trapped I am, cowering in my bedroom.

"Yeah, but we knew that already."

I peek out from under my arm as Leo leans against the spot on the door where I just vacated.

"Umm, why did they have collars on?" Tora raises her hand.

"Sweetie, don't raise your hand. This is Hell, not third grade." Faline looks like she's going to argue Tabby's supposition. Sometimes interacting with the Hounds feels like playing nice on the playground with the class bully.

"Those are Satan's Hounds. The collars of obedience." Fae's tone is clipped and matter of fact. I half expect her to whip out a clip board and start jotting notes like in the days of yore when she was playing doctor.

"Hellhounds are obedient?" The creases on Tora's face deepen.

"Aren't all dogs? You'd be surprised by the

codes some demons live by down here. I need five," I hold up my palm and waggle my fingers, "before I go find Auntie J. Show Tora to a room."

"She can sleep with me." Leona, as my second, has her own room.

Tora doesn't catch on, but Tabby giggles. "Not sure she plays that way, Leo."

"Huh?" Tora's head is playing the Ping-Pong routine.

Leo looks disappointed, but knowing her, she won't be deterred for long. Tora will catch on to the rhythm soon enough though and then decide if she's up for some Leo-loving.

"Come on." Faline opens the door and ushers them out into the Pound, leaving me in peace.

I gaze up at my sky-blue ceiling, wishing I were anywhere else but locked up in here. I purposefully decorated my room with colors of nature. Blue and green swirl with earthy browns on the ceiling in a kaleidoscope of colors. It makes the room feel less like it is suffocating me. I trace a finger down the ivy leaves on the cream wallpaper next to my bed and close my eyes, letting my hand drop to my chest, along with the irritation and annoyance at everyone and their uncle, just as a knock sounds at the door.

I groan and jump out of bed. I cross the room in a heartbeat and open the door to tell Damien to piss off, but find Auntie J standing on the other side with her hands on her hips. She looks ripping mad, which doesn't bode well for me. *Uh oh.* I should have read her text.

"Auntie J, what's up?" I step back, holding the

door wide. When Auntie J wants to talk, there is no way anyone is going to deny her entrance to do so.

"Why do you let that boy get to you? You know he does it on purpose just to get you going." Auntie J looks around the room like it offends her, scrunching her nose up like she can smell the freshness of the vines and flowers.

"I can't help it. I mean, can he be any more blasé about who his father is? The way he flaunts it. His transparency is so friggin' aggravating." I shut the door behind her, pointedly refusing to look out into the Pound.

"You'd be surprised by the depths of Damien." She walks over to the chair.

"He's the epitome of depravity." I skulk to my bed and sit back down, folding my arms over my chest.

"I see you've been bending the rules again." Auntie J nods at the blood smear on my t-shirt. She picks up my colors and sits in the low bucket seat, folding the leather jacket over her lap. The wicker base of the chair creaks as a whoosh of air leaves the plump cushions.

"I didn't bend the rules. Jeremiah just got a little lippy." I'm not supposed to dole out any punishment to the marks, it's for the Drudes to decide, but he had it coming.

"And my wings are made of glitter." Her black eyebrows shoot up and I quaver under "the look."

"You don't have wings." I feel the tension leave her. It's like a wave of heat and I settle back against the bed. Whatever made her mad, for some reason she has always been quick to let it go whenever I piss her off, which isn't often.

"That you know of, child." She winks at me and I always get the sense she's seen a millennium of time down here when she calls me child. I've never asked her what the crime was in exchange for the time. It's an unwritten rule not to ask. And if there is even a modicum of decency in the souls down here, we don't want to know.

I sit back up and lean forward, looking over Auntie J's shoulders. "Have you been holding out on me?" How Auntie J hides her wings, I have no idea. Probably how I hide my tail and whiskers, but she does it well.

"Just don't shake them out on the carpet. I have a theory glitter spawns itself and its damn near impossible to pick up with a vacuum cleaner."

"This is Hell, Baby Girl, why do you think glitter is a favorite craft of mine?"

"Tabby could bejewel your wings for you like she does her jeans. It would be less messy and you'd be sporting the bling permanently," I offer.

"I'll pass on that nefarious business. Speaking of, you've got another mark to collect."

"Really?" *Yes!* I'll collect anyone to crawl back out of this hole. Well, almost anyone. Freedom is just a few job details away again. I can almost taste the crisp air out on the highway filling my lungs. I can hear the rush of wind and feel the heat of the sun on my face.

"Don't sound so excited about it. You would have known if you answered my text."

Something in her voice is off, but I'm too excited to be getting out of here, I ignore it. Auntie J has a lot of issues to deal with as Hell's handler. No use prying open Pandora's Box.

"Sorry, wi-fi was down. Besides, it just means the girls and I get to ride again!" I jump up and hold my hand out for my jacket. She holds it out to me.

"Anything troubling you lately, Trina?"

I look into brown eyes so dark, they almost match her hair. I think about telling her my own hope and despair is at an all-time low. How many more years of collecting souls do I have before I will be redeemed? How much longer do I have to put up with Damien and his shit? I have sins to atone for, I know, but my punishment seems eternal despite my deal, and now there is another recruit to train and build a bike for. Airing my grievances may fall on deaf ears though. She is still a demon.

"Nah, I'm good. You know how I roll, Auntie J." I know I'm not fooling my handler for one minute, judging by the ancient eyes staring back at me, but I might have stalled for some more time before I have to truthfully answer her question.

I whip my colors behind my back and shrug the leather on over my shoulders. I grab my crimson cell phone out of my pocket and sure enough, Auntie J's text finally pings through as the circle and buffer finally clear the screen. I clear her message without looking at it and send a text to my main group contact, the Hellcats.

New mark. Meet me in/garage for deets. Time 2 ride

The responses I get back are immediate.

Hell yeah! from Leo.

Already? from Tora. She just doesn't understand Hell is a busy venue. I'll let it slide. For now.

Who's the mark? from Faline. Fae is the true straight shooter of the crew. She's all business or she will mess shit up.

But I just did my hair! Tabby, my lil' Diva.

"Who's the mark?" I glance up.

Auntie J rises from the chair and comes over to me. I get the feeling she doesn't need to see my phone screen to know the responses I got. She's chuckling and shaking her dark head. Her ebony curls sway and bounce. She's rocking a blowout, apparently having lost track of time down here. So, sixties, man. Her red and black button-down bulges at the buttons and her jeans are stained with a viscous fluid making me curious, but not enough to ask about it. She places her hands on either side of my face and leans in.

At first, I'd been completely weirded out by the way the name was always given to me. I had a hard time coping with the fact it was just the way the ritual was done. I'd never been accustomed to affection or intimacy. Not from my non-existent Dad or my junkie mom and certainly not from my drug dealer ex-boyfriend who was one of the reasons I was in Hell. I hold still while Auntie J gives me a kiss on the forehead. Her lips are large and warm, and I close my eyes. It seems like such a gentle way to receive the info for a sanction from Hell, but the name slips into my mind as Auntie J exchanges the information. I have his name and location now, but I gasp, not trusting the info until his face swims up from the images of my memories. I stare at Auntie J. I knew this day was inevitable, but I'd just not expected it so soon.

"My ex-boyfriend? Zeke!"

CHAPTER 3

"You son of a bitch, you knew!" I explode through my bedroom door and slam into Damien, who is standing at the fridge. His black t-shirt does nothing to soften the blow into his hard chest, but I enjoy hitting him like I hit the portal above in the garage. It's freeing.

Bottles clink together as the entire GE white-refrigerator vibrates from the impact from our bodies. I hear growls and snarls behind me and I see colors flashing in my periphery as my crew launches out of their rooms at the sound.

Leo pounces, trying to pull me off him. A fight with Jeremiah is a far cry different than a tousle with the son of Satan. Damien's surprise has momentarily frozen his ability to react because he doesn't retaliate. I try to beat on him. My fists flail out in all directions. I'm a mass of rage and razor-sharp claws and fangs, but Faline joins Leo in holding me back. I'm panting, trying to fill my lungs with air because I knocked the wind out of myself too. Damien is rubbing his chest where I hit him.

"He was marked this morning." His nose scrunches and I want to break it. The smug S.O.B. had been taunting me earlier, knowing all along what this would do to me. I see his boys crowd around us, their eyes blazing and their collars shimmering. Charles' haughty face looks bored, but the tension in his muscles speaks volumes. Phil, yeah, no idea where the kid is. Probably cowering like Tora next to the TV. "Why?" I focus on Damien. Or try to.

Zeke. Oh man. The first of so many things. Kisses, sex, love. Well, maybe love. Who am I kidding? I loved him. I just doubt whether he ever loved me in return. Hell isn't necessarily the confines of ten floors or torture in this dimension. Zeke was my escape up above. The first time I saw him, I knew he was something more. What I didn't know was, the "more" was fate sealing itself. He was my escape, my freedom from a life of mediocrity. Even if it was slating my destiny as one of the damned.

I feel the prickling heat behind my eyes and force myself to blink it all back. Tears are rejoiced around here and I will never give Damien the satisfaction of seeing he's been the cause of mine. Zeke had been, when I first arrived down here. Betrayed. Broken. That's what I was. Maybe it's why I threw myself into rebuilding the broken motorcycle, Sugar. I needed to fix things. Anything. It had taken a few weeks to realize just because Zeke did those things to me, just because I didn't seen the downfall for the slippery landslide for what it was until it was too late, didn't mean the love hadn't been there festering in my heart. Once he betrayed me, it opened up like a fresh wound, leeching into my tattered soul. But as broken as it and I was, it was still a form of love. What's the saying, we hurt the ones we love? I try not to let myself wonder if he ever loved me. Right now though? Emotions march across my essence like ants intent on building my walls of hurt and despair back up. We've all hidden behind those walls. The path to healing lies in knowing there is something better on the other side of them. The path lay in slowly deconstructing the walls and letting myself hope for Heaven. A place where true love, or rather, untarnished love might actually exist.

"Catriona Clarke!" Auntie J's voice cuts through the tension in the room. The snarling and hissing ceased immediately because her tone is darkness itself. "Catriona, you knew his day of reckoning was coming. You can't blame Damien for carrying out the duties he's been charged with." I blink and bite my lip to keep it from trembling.

Auntie J stands between us as she speaks to me. Damien looks murderous, his shoulders tense, like he's ready to jump after me, and the lines of his face are pinched and tight, like he is straining to hold back his rage as his brain catches up with the fact he was just full on body checked by a woman half his size and weight, and in front of his boys no less.

"Can't blame him? Or shouldn't?" Sometimes my brain takes a hiatus in all the conflicting feelings because the warning look on Auntie J's face as her eyebrows lift and her lips press together, is enough to shut my smart-ass mouth the eff-up.

"Do we need to rethink the terms of your contract?" She taps a foot. My eye twitches, but I shake my head.

"That's what I thought, child. Now take your girls and go collect the mark. I tried to warn you. Remember that, Trina." Her voice softens when she says my name. She alone knows the full story behind Zeke and I. Damien has guessed at some of it. Perks of preferential treatment from Daddy, I suppose. I shrug Faline, Tabby, and Leo off, and give Damien a once over, then turn away.

"Let's ride." My voice is raw, even as hard as I have tried to hide the emotions. This is going to be the hardest mark to collect. The history slams into me and it hurts worse than anything this place could come up with for painful pastimes.

I stomp through the Dog Pound and shove my way past poor Phil. Just as I suspected, the kid looks petrified to be near any of us. I try not to, but I am already plotting ways to win over Phil as I glance one more time back at Damien. I'm surprised to see he doesn't look satisfied. I expected him to. Maybe throw down a cat got your tongue joke. Or tail. He likes to play with his prey. He even named the Dog Pound after his band of misfits. He was here long before me and it's like the Hellcats were given territory when I was brought on board, but only because he reluctantly permitted it.

His face is impassive, except the curiosity in the depths of his eyes. They flicker, observing and intuitive, across my face. It provokes my own inquisitiveness and curiosity is dangerous for my kind. Why isn't he smug? Maybe as retribution I can convince Auntie J to let Phil ride with us. Kind of a tit for tat deal. Damien marked mine so I'm taking his. Petty maybe, but it's all I've got against him right now. I'll have to bring in Zeke without issue though. I've pushed the line with Auntie J far enough today.

Tabby presses the button for the elevator and

41

doesn't crack a joke or giggle about the almost fight. My girls know me well. They may not know the story of Zeke, but they know enough to take this mark seriously.

When the elevator doors slide open, I step inside the boring tan box and stand at the front facing the metal and glass as we pass Treachery, frozen shards of sadism are imprisoned within the faces staring back at us in horror. Fraud yields a glimpse of vast ditches with the souls enticing the demons with false promises to let them out. Violence is maybe the worst level. If the history of the human race has been a malevolent one, with an infinite number of cruel acts carried out against one another, it is petty compared to the ferocity taking place on this level. This is the level where my eyes flicker, remembering the brutal ring of a gunshot in a warehouse a few years ago.

Heresy burns bright with tombs lit up like torches, burning the screaming heretics encased within. Their eternal torture produces enough light it shines through the entire level. I can't see past the brightness of the first few tombs that are alight, but the level goes on for what must be an endless amount of space if it is anything like the other levels. Souls fight one another in Anger, as the level is so appropriately named. I see them fall under the weight of the vengeful emotion, but the torture is they quickly get back up and rejoin the battle to vent their endless well of anger, but to no end. The emotion has already consumed them so they will never feel anything else. The crushing stones of Greed are thankfully the only thing I can see as we pass the level. I don't need to see the bodies, weighed down by their own over-indulged vices being squeezed out like puss from a wound. Gluttony is hard to see in. Even with the satyrs and their torture racks, there is a constant rain of sludge pouring down, a melding of all of the gluttonous components of overindulgence from each person within.

Lust is a tornado of activity. Winds so powerful throw the souls around so they will never find peace within, and they shake and rattle the elevator. The occasional body thumps against the elevator doors and I think the ancient metal box we are contained within is purposefully slow so all who seek comfort and a false sense of security can witness the horrors contained within each floor.

As I force myself to witness the flashes of punishment taking place for each floor this time and see the specific torments being doled out on each, I wonder which one Zeke will end up on. I can't help it. Sometimes the macabre has a better hold on my mind than rationale does. I can't help but think I could have ended up on one of those floors. I should have. But thanks to Auntie J, I was granted a reprieve from those tortures. Zeke won't be so lucky.

I step out into the crowd in Limbo and push past people. I ignore the indignant cries and questions this time and head straight for the garage. The atrium, like the rest of the Underworld, is dark but small torchlights in lieu of the bulbs sit next to the enclave adjacent to the garage. I hadn't seen it when I first came in because the crowd was too thick, but the souls are scattering to get out of my way now.

In the narrow space, the boatman, the man

who ferries the souls who aren't special marks, accepts some coins from those he just ferried down the River Styx. It's probably where Fran, the lady I named when I first got back, came from. It makes sense since she was raving about having come in on a boat and not a motorcycle. I stop as Tora gazes down the river to the estuary where the Acheron, Lethe, Cocytus, and Phlegethon rivers meet the Styx and dump into Oceanus, the river circling the world and leads out of Hell. What most humans don't know is the vortex of trash in the Pacific Ocean is where Oceanus becomes a portal to Hell. It's like all the bad ocean junk is swirling in a disgusting maelstrom and dumping back down here, like a toilet into the sewer.

Tora watches as the other four boatmen, shrouded figures hunched and wraith-like, paddle their way toward the dock from their respective rivers of pain, forgetfulness, wailing, and fire. She shudders as she watches the souls come in and I touch her elbow, drawing her attention away from it all. Her pale skin is covered in goose bumps, but I'm not sure if it is fear or the cold. Hell can be heat and fire, but it can also be cold fire, depending on one's own personal version of it. She must not like the cold.

"It's easier if you don't watch and try to count them," I whisper in her ear and she nods.

We make our way back to the garage and I'm grateful I don't have to use the boats. I love the freedom of the open road with the wind and the sun's heat hitting my face. It makes my situation less critically dire and more tolerable. I hold onto the feeling every time we ride out and enter the world of the living.

"Hold on to the feeling you get every chance we have to ride out of this place," I tell her. "It makes the rest of it a little less dismal."

She bites her lip. "But it won't make getting this mark hurt any less for you?"

I wince. She means well enough. The question is innocent, if not a tad personal. She needs to lose the innocence in a hurry if she's going to rock this gig. But so far, she has kept her cool, so it warrants a bit of an explanation.

"It's the price I have to pay. We messed up in life. Now we're demons. Think of it this way though, we are the lucky ones because we still have fragments of our souls to hold onto and repair."

"Yeah and being a demon doesn't mean we don't have feelings." Tabby links her arm through Tora's as we walk and Leo falls into step beside me. Faline walks a few steps ahead to open the door to the garage.

Tora doesn't comment further. The afterlife is a hard situation to process and I think as humans, we always take it for granted we will just get to the pearly gates and all will be forgiven. We don't consider there is an alternative if we mess up badly enough. It's like a festering cyst we refuse to think about. It's always there in our minds, ready to burst and spew its raunchy puss and soil the purity of our happiness, but somehow, we lance it and forget about it.

I swing my leather-clad leg over my bike and begin backing it around and out of the line of other vehicles. Reapers have unique ways of riding out to collect souls. Some of us ride in style and then there are those who take the sturdy, 'Merica approach in the rusted out green, red, and blue pickup trucks lined up at the far end of the garage. Satan has style though and his own line of cars. The one I always gawk at is the three-million-dollar McLaren P1 GTR. It's one of only 40 ever made. I try not to drool when I read the license plate, HADES.

When I turn the engine over on Sugar, the green flames spring to life from the paint. I glare across the garage at the Hounds' bikes, which are parked on the opposite side of the garage. The one that stands out the most is the homemade Gothic-style hearse attached to the back of a Harley. Their bikes are twice the size of ours and black with red accents, but at least the alley in between the park jobs gives us enough room to rev up and burst through the other side of the veil.

Tora climbs on the back of Leo's teal and cream 1973 Bonneville Triumph, which has been altered into a trike. It makes sense to have Tora ride with her because the seat is wider and more comfortable for two. I watch as Leo glances down where Tora's gray boots rest on the pegs, making sure she isn't touching the chrome.

Leo brought the bike with her from her motorcycle accident in Meridian, England, where the bikes are made and she restored it in this very garage like I did. Faline came next and she too reveled in the process of putting a scrap of junk back together. Her clinical mind found solace in the process of mechanics and systems. It was methodical, which is a comfort to her. Some people rationalize, like Leo and I, and some people compartmentalize, like Fae.

It's apparent Leo doesn't mind Tora wrapping her arms around her waist though. She gives me a wicked grin and I can't help my lips twitch. Tora presses her face to Leo's colors, breathing in, and I see Leo's eyes light up when she does.

Shaking my head, I look behind me to see Tabby mount her 1950's burgundy and ivory Chief. The bike was made before the ivory ban and Tabby, liking high end, had to have a bike with the real deal. Elevator level Greed? Yeah, I've got your girl, Tabby, if she doesn't redeem herself. She'd come in after Fae and as much as I pleaded Auntie J to take the walking, talking catastrophe in pink and glitter, I don't get to choose who a deal is made to. It took a few weeks for her to grow on me, painfully like an unwanted beauty mark. At first, I couldn't tell if she was the fake kind, like the fashion trend, glaringly obvious and unnatural, but eventually the effect is less jarring when you look at her. It took a while to see some depth under the diva. But Tabby has proven to be the balm to the banes of our existence. Her naivete is less innocent and more doing whatever the heck she wants when she wants to, but it was initially rooted in the necessity of survival. Especially given she reveled in being a prostitute and hasn't changed since she died, but at least it makes for some humorous anecdotes on a misery filled day. I think she tried to bone a Drude once. It didn't go well based on the sounds of tantrum induced by rejection the day she made her attempt. Seriously, how does a demon deny another sex-addict demon the sins of the flesh? It's kind of like a rite of passage down here, if we want.

Ethics and bikes aside, I pull a bandana up over my nose to keep the dust and bugs from hitting my face, and I rev my engine and drive at what looks like a solid black wall. It rises so high up the inky edge blends with the shadows of optical illusion. I'm not even sure the wall has an end or this place has a ceiling. Sometimes I think of the garage as a cave and other times it just seems like an industrial-sized warehouse.

I hear Tora scream as she did this morning when I hit the wall. Instead of smashing headfirst into it, sending body parts and mechanical ones into the air, I burst through the other side and the sun hits my face. The dry heat of the desert slams into me and packs more of a punch than the illusionary wall. Based on the surroundings whizzing by as I open up the throttle and take off, we are somewhere along Route 666, the Devil's Highway in Utah. I see a sign for the Devil's Garden as the gold and bronze landscape passes by. Flashes of green dot the horizon and I grin at the open road. Freedom. At least for a short while.

It's always disorienting when we transition from the Underworld to the living realm. There are thousands of what I call hot spots, named after Lucifer. They are thin enough for the magic to push us through the veil without tearing a rift in reality. The bikes are imbued with a mark of their own, enabling us to come out somewhere near the location of our marks. The souls of the damned act like homing beacons, to what I call the magical GPS, somewhere in the rides. My homing beacon is calling us west so we continue along the highway in the direction we came out on.

Leona pulls up and flanks me just behind and to my right with Tabby to my left. I can hear the distinct growls of the engines and know Fae is bringing up the rear. If anyone could see us, my bet is we look like a kaleidoscopic cloud of flames and smoke manifesting from somewhere over the rainbow from a dimension far, far away.

As we crest a hill and round a curve on the highway, another sign flashes by on the side of the road, "Devils' Garden, 30 Miles" but I know we won't be going all the way into the city. I start to downshift and here the subsequent sounds of my gang following my lead as we near our destination. The hum of Sugar's tires on the pavement reverberates up through the frame of the bike and then through the seat and into me, causing me to press my lips together and hum the tune of liberty and independence along with her. I feel the smile playing on my lips. I can't help but grin like the kid in the candy store whenever we are given a job. There have never been any time constraints placed on us, just the expectation we will bring the marks in. Maybe I push the limit sometimes, but to date, Auntie J hasn't written me up for it, whatever that might entail. I can't imagine a pink slip from Hell is going to look as official as any a corporate office's might. It's probably etched in a slab of stone and used to press the offender like the damning judgement of the heretics in charge of the Salem witch trial fiasco. Pushing pink slips and pondering the resulting punishments of Purgatory aside, I downshift a final time and turn off the highway.

We pull up to a truck stop west of Devil's Garden. There are only five cars in the driveway and no trucks. The cars range from decrepit to high-end, which is unusual for this area out in the middle of nowhere. Three of them, the dilapidated ones, look like they are held together by duct tape, and from this distance, a flash of silver tells me my hunch isn't far off. The fourth is in pretty decent shape. It's red and brown like the dust of the desert on either side of the highway.

A neon orange sign blazes in the window advertising "The Sloshed Sloth, Bar and Grill." A wooden sign with a poster of a happy, inebriated looking sloth hangs between two posts and sways, creaking in the breeze. I squint and count the bullet holes in the sign. Joy riding one-oh-one, if you can't hit the sign racing down the highway while inebriated, you're doing it wrong.

I park Sugar just as three men stumble out of the bar and trip over themselves trying to get to the luxury sedan, which is the nicest vehicle in the lot. We watch as the man in the white suit screams at the two sides of beefcake to, "Drive! Drive! Drive!"

Leona starts laughing as red dirt sprays up behind the tires and the men, beaten, retreat with their tails between their legs. Tora sneezes as red dust filters through her sinuses. We'll have to get her colors soon, as well as a bandana. When Auntie J brought her to me this morning, she only had time to give her a phone that was connected to Hell's network, so I'll have to get on getting her the rest of her gear.

Watching the men scramble like eggs makes

me wonder what's inside the bar causing them to make tracks so fast. I dismount, opting to keep my bandana on. Zeke wasn't one of the lunkheads with Mr. Threads so he must be inside. Maybe I can get away with bagging and tagging his sorry ass without him knowing it's me. There's a whole lot of hurt I am not looking to deal with right now, but I'm stalling because part of me doesn't want to know how he finally bought it. We usually show up after the mark has punched their ticket, but occasionally we have to wait around, playing the part of average biker chick babes until they do croak, then whip them into the other side of this dimension. Leo nudges my shoulder and Tora walks so close behind her, she bumps into her back when she stops.

"Hey, luv, if you're going to be right up my ass, at least buy me a cold one when we get inside."

Tora turns red in the face and I pat my pockets and pull an extra bandana out of my pocket for her to tie around her head.

"Suit up, girls. I don't want him to know it's me." Fae and Tabby pull theirs back up, but Leona never took hers off.

"Incognito, boss?"

I don't answer her. The heat of the sun bakes into the black leather of my jacket and pants, and I'm not sure if it's because of the rays or if it's the tightness in my throat making me uncomfortable as I approach the bar's wooden steps. Panic attacks have never been my bag, but I haven't seen Zeke in three, maybe four years?

The steps creak as we climb them, like they're protesting under the weight of my anxiety as I

Lydia Anne Stevens

ascend. The red door to the bar stands open, but I can't see inside. As I approach the door, my pulse pounds and I will myself not to react to whatever I see inside. I can smell the blood. All demons can. In addition to the coppery scent, it's punchy and fresh. I step inside and my girls fan out on either side of me. We stand in the entrance and let our eyes adjust to the darkness as we scan the room.

I spot the mark right away. It blazes in the dim light of the bar. Tables and chairs are upturned and a broken pool cue rolls across the floor. What agitates me more than the bar fight is the mark is so white and it shouldn't be. The darkness of the person's soul is equivalent to the darkness of the paw print marking him or her. Damien usually swipes them dead center in the chest and it's always ebony, backlit by some halo of unnatural light, which taints it red, like blood. This one is different. This one is pure. It takes me a minute to realize I'm staring at the mark, rather than recognizing the person it is imprinted on.

I look up into the face of the man Damien marked. Zeke's twin brother is staring back at me. Oh fuck.

"Lowell?"

52

CHAPTER 4

"Who the Hell are you?" Lowell demands. He's wiping blood from a cut on his forehead with the hem of his gray t-shirt. It drips down onto his jeans as he helps an older man with a bushy gray beard and mustache up from the floor. The man is dressed in leather and a rock and roll t-shirt from times past.

I move further into the bar, assessing the broken bottles and notice two men cowering behind the pool table with broken off bottlenecks in their hands. One of them is shifty-looking with dirty jeans and a gray and black flannel with a grungy looking t-shirt under it. His face is weathered like his car, I guess duct tape is his go-to because the sticky stuff is holding his boots together. The other guy is greasy. Not just his hair, but his pores ooze oil too. It appears it isn't for a lack of showering, he's the cleaner of the two, but it's like the slick substance oozes out of his soul. He's also wearing a long-sleeve shirt, which is unusual for the dead-heat of summer. They have the sniffles, but judging by the faint chemical odor mixed with their sweat, the shirts are probably to cover up the track marks.

Leo shifts a few paces to my left to cover my

flank if they attack, but I smell piss and mark them off the list of most pressing concerns. Junkies are slow to react even in between shoot-ups when they are close to sobering up. If they try to pull anything, they'll be tartar for toast with my girls at my back. I turn back to the splintered bar.

"Lowell, it's me, Catriona." I pull the bandana off my face and his pupils dilate as he sucks in a breath. *What the Hell is going on? Where is Zeke?* I look around the bar, wondering if I'm going to see a pair of legs sticking out from under a table or something, but from what I can see, the Sloshed Sloth is still sans a fresh corpse.

"Catriona?" He takes a step back like he's seen a ghost because technically, yours truly was buried a couple of years ago.

"Look, I can't explain it all now. I just need to know where Zeke is."

"You're dead."

"Only on the inside."

"Zeke buried you."

"Caskets aren't comfy, Lowell." I crinkle my nose. My own was hot and stuffy and smelled all kinds of funky from the embalming fluid. At least, I always assumed it was. I figured it was a precursor for the atmosphere downtown, but when I stepped foot into Purgatory and was given a corporeal body again, there was a feeling I've always had a hard time describing. It was neither hot nor cold. It was hungry. Hungry for freedom from the borrowed body. It gave me the shivers and made me wish for the comfy cushions of the casket.

Lowell grabs for the edge of the bar and sits on

a broken stool, which collapses under his ass. Wood chunks clunk around him and he's damn lucky he didn't get goosed with one of his own stools. Tora giggles behind me, but it is quickly silenced. I don't need to turn around to know it was either Leo giving her the hush up or Fae staring her down for disrespect and order.

Lowell grunts, then gapes up at me. I can see the shock in his honey eyes and I sigh. I'm going to get nowhere with him so I turn to the old guy instead.

"Hey, what happened here?"

The badass baby boomer looks me up and down and then reaches behind the bar and grabs a bottle of Scotch. He unscrews the cap and takes a swig then hands it down to Lowell. Lowell coughs after trying to down half the bottle and the old man slaps him on the back.

"Easy son. You got cracked on the noggin pretty hard and there's a pretty decent egg swelling up."

"She's dead, Marty." Lowell blinks as he takes another sip from the bottle and then wipes his mouth on the back of his wrist. I hold out my hand for the bottle and he hesitates before passing it over. I take a swig and feel the burn going down my throat. I may be dead, but at least I can still feel something. His face is ghostly white and I hand the bottle back to him. He needs it more than I do, even though I was expecting to find his brother here instead.

"She looks pretty solid to me with all them curves." Marty looks between us and raises a bushy white eyebrow. He reminds me of Einstein if my man genius was rocking the denim and leather.

"Grandpa got game?" Tabby takes a step forward, eyeing him up and down.

"Cap the libido. We're on a job." I can't deal with Tabby's games today. This is a screw up of epic proportions and I need a minute to think. Neither man looks ready to answer my question about the bar fight so I turn and gaze out the window, which is sporting a red film of desert dust. "What I can't figure is, what's up with the wrong markup?"

Marty strokes his beard, returning Tabby's ogle.

"I know, but I'd still do him." Tabby pouts like I took away her favorite toy. As an ex-prostitute, I don't even want to know what's in her toy box.

"Freak." Faline swats Tabby's shoulder and she growls in return. Ignoring her, Fae leans into me to whisper, "Let's just grab the mark and get ghost."

I search her anxious gray eyes. "He's not the right one and he's not dead yet. We'd have to wait it out anyway." I need to buy more time. Is this just me buying time for Zeke? In my few years of doing this gig, nothing like this has ever happened. Why has it happened now it's my ex in the mix?

"I dunno, Luv. He looks pretty peaked to me." Leo is staring at him like she's waiting for him to drop dead right there. "Besides, he's Zeke's twin-"

"We can't just take in whoever we feel like! That's not how it works. And look at his mark!" I point to it and all eyes turn to the center of Lowell's chest. Marty and the two men cowering behind the pool table squint at Lowell, unable to see what we do. They'd all seen it when we walked in, but maybe like me, they haven't processed the meaning of it yet.

"I don't get it." Tora squints at the white paw print too.

"Damien's mark rips into and imprints on the soul and the print is always black like the soul itself. Lowell's soul isn't spoiled like the others. His is white and pure."

There's a collective, "Oh!" and then all eyes turn back to me.

"What are we going to do?" I can hear the anxiety creeping into Faline's voice as it goes up an octave. Her words come out rushed and I have to strain to understand what she is saying.

"I need to think." I turn away from Lowell. The resemblance to his brother is unsettling. I convinced myself on the ride I wouldn't let seeing him affect me so much, but my stomach has been churning since I walked in the door. I walk to the old 1950's jukebox sitting in the corner and look at the selection. It has been updated with mostly classic rock, Hell's Bells is right. I groan and smack the jukebox then dig my phone out of my pocket. I flip the screen on with my thumb and a picture of a cabin set against the bank of a river backlights the screen. I hit the button on the side and then thumb through the recent contacts when the white and green screen appears. I hit send when I reach the right one.

"Auntie J, call me back. There's been a mix up with the mark." I end the call, which went straight to voicemail and look back at everyone. They're staring at the floor. Of all of the monumental screw-ups, Damien just had to screw the pooch on this one. I hit the call button on the contact, which is labeled Assface.

"Kitty Cat!" Damien is far too enthusiastic. I can count on one hand the number of times I've called him, each was worse than the last.

"You've marked the wrong man." I try to keep the irritation out of my voice then I get hit with a sneaking suspicion. What if this was intentional? What if he tried to drag this out, to revel in my misery? Would he do that? I know one of his favorite pastimes is to make the vein in my temple throb with annoyance, but can he mess with the cosmos?

"No, I didn't. I got the details of the job this morning and was told Zeke would be at the Sloshed Sloth. I showed up and did my part, then did a lonely housewife and left." He sounds sure of himself, but there's no hint of nefariousness in his voice, like he has been waiting for this call.

"Still a pig, but not the point. You marked Zeke's twin brother, Lowell. Didn't you bother to look at the print and see his soul is pure?"

"I didn't really care. I got sidetracked. The housewife was really lonely."

Will he ever have a serious conversation with me? I swallow, keeping the growl at bay as I pinch the bridge of my nose. I wish this damn headache would be the death of me. Being undead has its complications.

"I can't get ahold of Auntie J. You need to come and fix this."

"Not how it works and it's also not my problem." Here's karma coming back to bite me for adopting the not-my-problem with Fran. Well, bitch, I bite harder. This isn't right on so many levels.

"Damien! You can't be serious. His soul is pure.

He doesn't belong. You have to fix this!" I hear a low growl over the phone and goose bumps break out over my skin.

"No, I don't. When are you going to understand? All men are animals in one way or another. I'm sure he's done something shady in his pointless, miserable life. So just bring him down here like a good girl and call it a day."

I feel heat race through my veins at his "good girl" comment. I breathe through my nose to calm down before I respond, but then I hesitate, caught on the brink of a decision that could change everything for me.

"I can't do it, Damien. He doesn't deserve it. It's not right."

Again, I wonder if this is projection. Am I about to throw away everything for Zeke's brother thinking it will fix-what? Fix what? I don't know. What I do know is sometimes in life, or the afterlife, there is an overwhelming call to action. Maybe we can't explain why we do something in the unnamed conviction we have, but it doesn't mean we should stand by and not act just because we can't explain what makes it right over wrong.

"Are you serious? This coming from the woman who stood by and did nothing when her boy toy was selling drugs? Now you're going to take the moral high ground?"

I begin pacing around the bar and glass from broken bottles crunches under my feet. Forget about eggs. Hell, I'm walking Belinda Carlisle's gig on broken glass, ready to fall over into the inferno for eternity if I go against my orders. But he's not wrong.

I did stand by and do nothing. I may not have put the drugs in the hands of the buyers myself, but which sin was worse? My redemption won't come cheap and my atonement won't be a cake walk. Irony is a cold-hearted bitch who packs one Hell of a right hook. I can do nothing; turn my back on a man who doesn't deserve the fate he's been thrust into. Or I can go up against Lucifer and his entire domain. I shudder. Lucifer, the one who granted me the reprieve of eternal damnation in the first place. I'm about to throw in the towel and make a break for it, whether I am ready to or not.

The phone is silent and then Damien's low voice grates in my ear. "Are you refusing to collect a mark? My father has given you special circumstances. If you start stepping on his toes, I guarantee you are not going to like the consequences. Daddy has anger management issues."

"This isn't a joke, Damien." I look at Lowell, whose face has morphed from disbelief to confusion and now the slight hints of fear are creeping into the lines at the corners of his wide eyes. It's like watching one of those creepy baby dolls whose eyes open and shut when you pick it up and lay it down. Fiona used to have when we were kids. If the situation weren't so serious, I'd find his open-mouthed, ape-face comical. But situation is dire and I need Damien on board. "We have to fix this!"

"We can't. It's done. Bring him in, Catriona, or the Hounds will come and get him, and all of the Underworld will be very unhappy with you."

I take a deep breath and then hang up the phone. My hands are shaking so bad it makes it difficult to thumb up Auntie J's number again. Where is she? The wi-fi was back up when I hit up the girls to ride again. Why isn't she answering me?

"Auntie J, call me back immediately!" I end the call. What have I done? I've worked so hard for years now trying to right the wrongs I'd done as a human. Now I've just gone and thrown it all away because of what? Sentimentality for a man whose brother was the reason I died in the first place? Because Lowell's face resembles Zeke's so much I can't wrap my head around my heart and shut the emotions down to see reason? I look down at my phone which is vibrating in my hand again. Assface is calling pops up on the screen. I hit the ignore button, sending him to voicemail, the place where every contact goes who doesn't rate much recognition in the busy day to day life of humans and the damned as well.

I crunch my way over to the bar and push open the little half door and grab one of the unbroken bottles of whiskey and down a mouthful of courage for the nerves. It burns like I imagine I will when the Hounds catch me. But the liquid courage relaxes my limbs enough to know I've made my decision and I'm sticking to it.

"What's up, boss?" Fae begins unwinding her own barbed whip. We all have one, perks of the job. It seems more sinister now I might be on the receiving end of its sting.

"Put that away. This isn't Zeke."

Lowell has managed to stand and is leaning on Marty. The two locals are creeping to the side door and Leo steps after them.

"No, let them go. The less involved in this

mess, the better."

The men scramble and trip over one another. Get gone and stay gone is how I feel about their scrawny washed up asses.

"Catriona." Lowell's voice is steady. Damn, but the man's got some excellent shock absorbers if he's with it already. "What is going on? How are you here? Does Zeke know you're...you're here? What mark are you talking about and where are you supposed to be taking me?"

"Lowell, I can't explain everything right now, but we need to get you out of here." I figure he is going to demand explanations, but now I've hit ignore, rejecting Damien and all he stands for that I was part of, I figure it's time to make a move and do it quickly, before Damien and company show up to tell me exactly how they feel about being back-burnered in this business.

"Why?"

"You aren't safe here."

My crew busts out with the protests. Took them long enough. They overheard the convo, but remained quiet, absorbing the fact not only have I reneged on my deal, but by association, theirs as well. I have no intention of holding them to this, but right now, I don't have time to deal with the bureaucratic bullshit that comes with being a leader. I'll cut them lose later, but right now, it's time to ride.

"Enough!" I hold up my hand and they all fall silent.

Fae crosses her arms over her chest and taps her foot. Tabby snaps her gum and Leo leans back against the jukebox. Tora looks at the side door where

the townies vacated. Wistful looks good on her.
"Lowell, was Zeke supposed to be here today?"

"He stops in sometimes and I usually kick him out for dealing, but..." He scratches his sandy hair and gazes around the trashed bar.

"But what?"

"I promised Gigi I'd look after him and let him stop out here at the bar every now and then. It's how I check up on him. He never could resist a beer on the house."

I rub my chest when he mentions Gigi. Lowell and Zeke's grandmother was one of the nicest people I ever met. Zeke brought me to visit her a year before she passed and I saw a rare side of Zeke that made me believe he was a man worth loving. I was so wrong, but Gigi never gave up hope. There's a box of cards from every holiday on the Christian calendar under his bed and a few handwritten notes of "just because," a testament to that fact. After the year passed and Gigi with it, the box began to collect dust and any sense of Zeke's moral code along with it.

Lowell rubs the back of his head and winces. His hand comes away smeared with blood. He'd been more injured than I realized.

"Come on." I take a few steps toward Lowell and grab him under his arm. It has been a long time since I've felt the heat of humanity brush up against me. All my other marks were sans theirs. Heaven always stakes their claim on the good ones. The humanity is a warm feeling, like a hug. Like Gigi's hugs. I may have been the cause of the downfall of one of her grandsons, but I'll be damned if I'm not going to save Lowell for her now. I feel like somehow,

I owe her.

My crew follows behind me and I hear Marty start to bitch, until Tabby links her arm with his. I don't glance back. Tabby has some unusual proclivities, but whatever, I'm not one to judge. We make our way back outside and I look down the highway. Storm clouds move black and swift from the direction of the Nevada desert. The rumble of thunder blends with the cadence of carburetors.

"Get on." I glance at Lowell and then I swing my leg over Sugar. I hear the girls rev their engines as I reach for the key near the top of the tank. I see Fae glare at Marty, who looks like one of those gray and white-bearded collies sitting in her sidecar. If he sticks his tongue out the side, I might tell Tabby to throw him a bone and give him a treat. She'd like that. He hadn't even asked permission to tag along with our crew. He just climbed in, no questions asked.

I feel the weight of Lowell settle behind me. He gazes at the clouds and squints.

"Those aren't normal clouds."

"No. They're Hounds." There's no time to argue with Lowell about leaving Marty behind. He's coming with us, whether we like it or not.

"Who?"

"Hellhounds. They're coming after you. And now me." I turn the key on my bike and it howls to life.

"Why you?"

That's a good question. What had I ever done except exist when I was a human? Why me? Well, maybe because my defining moment taught me even though all I did was exist, I hadn't really done anything wrong and sell drugs alongside Zeke, I hadn't done anything to stop him. Maybe by saving Lowell, I am saying I am saving the soul of a person who never bought from Zeke and ended up six-feet under with the memory of a needle sticking out of their arm.

"Because I'm going to protect you until we can get the mark on your soul removed."

"How are we going to get away from them?"

Lowell's arms slip around my waist and I flip up the kickstand and pull out onto the highway. I glance over my shoulder and see five black dots emerge from the tail end of lightning bolts from the storm striking the highway. For sure, Damien likes to make a flashy entrance.

Just before I shift and open up the throttle to pick up speed I shout, "We'll figure out how to remove the mark later. First, we're going to run like Hell, from Hell."

CHAPTER 5

W e ride the highway northeast for hours until we hit Route 191. The grit from the road is stuck in the corners of my eyes and it stings. When they start to water, I decide to turn southwest to head in the direction of the borders of Utah, New Mexico, Arizona, and Colorado. I hold my hand out low and to the left so the Hellcats know to turn with me. We drive to the Colorado Plateau; it's risky rolling up on the four corners since the chance of meeting a crossroad demon is high, but I've started to form a plan. It's the mother of all stupid plans, but it just might work.

We're at a slight advantage with our head start and the Hounds would have stopped at the Sloshed Sloth to check out the situation, so I think we might be leading by half an hour. Maybe.

When we drive up on the tourist site to the meeting point, I pull my bike in and park and let my girls ride up in a semi-circle where we can face one another and hash it all out. I cut my engine and lean forward on my handlebars. I feel Lowell behind me slowly start to stretch and I swing my leg over Sugar, giving him a chance to get off and move around. He walks in a circle to my right and winces from the stiffness in his limbs. The old man, Marty, swings his leg over the sidecar and pulls the same gimp along routine, while I swing my leg back over my baby and lean forward again, checking my phone for any missed calls. There are none except the one missed from Damien. I guess that chance was all I got. Damn, where is Auntie J? I shut my phone and glance around.

There are tourist signs everywhere at the four states' corners, because no one has seen four right angles meet, but whatever. It's mostly annoying because the tourists, who are milling about, all stop to stare at us. There's a huge sign indicating exactly where the state's four corners meet. There are park benches surrounding the area with a number of tourists toting unimpressed looking teenagers and squawking toddlers who would rather be in hotel pools because of the heat. Posts with built-in cubbies hold brochures which I'm sure discuss how unusual the converging state lines are; stand next to each of the benches surrounding the courtyard. Gray slabs of stone decorate the courtyard and are embedded into the stone to mark which state is which and where the four corners meet. A sandstone rock wall curls around the courtyard and red viewing benches. Rocking a ponytail, a woman wearing black yoga pants and a blue t-shirt props herself on her hands and knees on the monument of stone slabs meeting in the corner. Her prone position makes her look like she's bent over waiting for Arizona to come up behind her so does she actually have the audacity to look at us with such incredulity? The tourists around her have the same looks on their faces, like we are the freaks and her bent over on hands and knees presenting herself head down, ass-up is nothing to be shaking my head at.

I snort. They better hope they aren't here when Damien shows up because when he figures out my plan, he's going to be ripping mad. He also might contort yoga-lady into a more twisted position if she gives him the haughty look she's casting us.

I turn my attention back to my girls. The tourists can bite me. We're going to bounce in five anyway, so they're not high on my list of priorities. It just bugs me, as much as I try not to judge, even with my temper and attitude, people are going to look at me and my lot and assume the worst.

"Trina, what the Hell?" Faline's anger quivers across her face in her twitching lips and the vein above her eyes.

I don't blame her. "Look, I have a plan." I hold up my hands. "We're going to split here and now. Each ride off in a different direction. You can all find a hotspot and check in with Auntie J. Let her know what's up, alright?" I'm not going to hold them to this. It isn't their snap decision. They've got their own deals with Satan to consider.

"Damn it, Trina. Are you insane? We can't split." Fae rarely swears at me, and when she does, Tabby pops her gum and laughs.

I grin at her. "Well, yeah. I wouldn't be sitting here if I did the sane thing, would I?" Fae rolls her eyes and I get down to the heavy. "Hey, I get it. You're all trying to atone. None of us really want to be stuck down in the pit forever. Which is why I'm shouldering this one. Go back to Auntie J."

Faline looks like she is ready to ride off and not look back. She wants to do her time and that's it. Tabby is looking at one of her bejeweled fingernails, which is chipped. She pulls a file out of her pocket and looks bored. Leo's got my back since almost the beginning when I was first put in charge of the newly formed gang. We learned our way together, got a feel for the bumps in the road. Tabby might follow Faline, if she gets to keep her kink Marty, riding shotgun in the sidecar, but Leo deadpans me with her glare and I know she's in it for the long haul.

"We aren't splitting, Trina." She lights a cigarette and glares at a couple of teenage boys who look like they're ready to pop the "Hey, what's ups?"

Tora leans around her on the bike and watches us all.

"We don't have time to argue. We need to split to throw them off for a while until I can figure out how to unmark Lowell. Then we'll hook back up. This way they'll divvy up and then we're looking at one on ones with the Hounds instead of taking on the whole damn gang."

Tabby pops her gum again and shrugs, which makes Fae flinch. "I'm game. Could be fun."

"What about sacred ground?"

It's the first time Lowell has offered any contribution to the conversation and everyone stops and looks at him; even Marty who is tapping on the sidecar, much to Fae's annoyance. It looks like he's trying to figure the custom job and the flames, but he's in for a surprise if he bugs Fae to the point of making the shit go live. His dried-up withered carcass would light up faster than the pine needles on an old

69

Christmas tree.

I turn my head and stare at Lowell. He's standing with the sun to his back and his profile is so like Zeke's, it takes my breath away for a moment. I feel the lump in my throat and swallow hard. I didn't think it was going to hurt this much. I sigh and shake my head, stuffing the can of worms into the back of my head. Twins or not, Lowell isn't his brother, and it won't do me any good to wish it different. Part of me wonders if I had the opportunity to save Zeke, if it might mean I could forgive myself for my own sins. It would be setting down that burden I've been carrying around. I think about his question for a minute before answering.

"Sacred ground is irrelevant. There are no rules I know of saying we can't go on it."

"We?" He looks puzzled.

"Demons." I sit up and look him dead in the face, letting the fire in my eyes flicker for a moment. I watch as his whole body goes rigid and his muscles tense like he is going to run. I might as well air out my dirty little secrets now. At least it will give me the mental check I need not to confuse him with his brother when he looks at me in horror.

"You're...you're..."

"We've already established demons are as dead as Dante. You're just going to have to get over it quick if we want to make it out of here without being captured." I glance over my shoulder at the open road, expecting to see storm clouds rolling in on the horizon, but the blistering heat of Arizona's sun continues to beat down on my back.

"This can't be real." He puts his hands over his

head and I try to think what to say to him. I'd had a few weeks. He has only a few minutes, not fair on the Richter Scale of mind-boggling, world-altering news, but life's full of the tough stuff. He's just going to have to grow a thick skin.

"Well, it is sugar!" Tabby pops a bubble at him. She might not put so much glee into the proclamation. She's making us look bad.

"Knock it off, Tabby!" Everyone pauses, but ignores Fae when she snaps. Fae gets off her bike and walks near the waist-high rock wall. I consider having the big heart to heart with her, but she has to sort herself out the way she does.

Lowell looks between Tabby and me. "How though?"

"It's simple. We all died, went to Purgatory, were given a second chance to make it into Heaven, and the perks of the position come with a shapeshifting corporeal body in this realm and down below as long as we gather the marks. Now here we are." I don't give the run-down on the religious rhetoric. I've had my days of people hollering they don't believe in Hell. I wouldn't say I'm a Christian or I connect with any other major religions, but it doesn't mean they aren't real. Or the Underworlds are associated with them. Raised by Christian foster parents, I still relate as an Omnist. I find truth in all religions now I'm dead.

"Heaven and Hell are real?" It's not the first time the question has been posed and it won't be the last. It's one thing to have devout faith as a human. It's a whole new ballgame to have solid proof sitting here in front of him. I feel for his shock since I was just as mind blown when I died and found out it was all true. I give him and Marty a chance to digest the demons are real data.

Marty walks over to Lowell and leans in to whisper something to him I pretend not to hear. Leo ruins whatever plan they're cooking up to make a break for it when she rolls her eyes.

"Please, Papi. If you thought you stood a chance of running, you would have done it back at the bar." Not that he would have gotten far with a titanium hip, but I say nothing on account of it would be considered rude in polite circles. We aren't very polite most of the time though.

Marty jumps and Lowell takes a step toward Leo. "You do anything to him and I'll- "

"Alright, enough." Leo looks like she's ready to pounce so I get back off my bike and walk to the center, putting space between the two. "We've only got a few minutes to decide. Holy ground is out. Even if we do make it there and a rule is in place, like some weird Dracula mojo, we wouldn't be able to get on the premises either." I look at my girls, hoping one of them is batting a thousand in the what-do-we-do-from-here department.

"I know someone who studies theology at the University of Utah. He's a good friend. He might know how we could get the mark off."

I turn back around to Lowell. He looks confused, like he can't believe he has just offered up one of his friends to help battle the supernatural, but he's on to something and it will be good to have him focus.

"Not a bad idea," I nod. I smile at him, loathing

the fact I already have a tentative end-game strategy in the works.

"Theology?" Tabby crinkles her nose.

I close my eyes and rub my temples. I should have known a gang of demons wouldn't be up to snuff on religious rhetoric. I received my limited knowledge courtesy of the foster home I'd been in most of my teenage years when Mum was hitting the bottle. The Anderson's were ok people, but sticklers for calling me out on my collective sins.

"It's the study of religious beliefs."

She shrugs again and goes back to watching Marty like he's her new favorite play toy and he just doesn't know it yet. She always did have a thing for older Sugar Daddies in her human days as a prostitute.

"I think that might be our best shot." I look at Lowell. "You and I will head there and--"

"I'm coming with," Leo speaks up as I start shaking my head. Lowell is already knee-deep, no sense dragging everyone down with me. "We're with you." She glares at Fae and Tabby. Tora leans forward.

"I'm coming too!" She really needs to stop raising her hand.

"No. You're the newbie and don't know the full extent of the consequences. Fae, if you still want to go back, it won't be held against you."

Tora slowly lowers her hand.

"Speak for yourself--" Leo starts to get off her bike, but I take a step near her.

"Leo, would you stow it for a sec?" I glare at her.

"Fae, I get it. If you want to go back, take Tora. I just ask you find Auntie J and tell her to call, OK?"

Faline looks at her handlebars and then traces her finger along the Harley Davidson logo on the gas tank. "Eternity is going to suck, but you chose me and I owe you. You gave me freedom. At least for a little while." She looks back at her handlebars and twists them, looking miserable but resigned. She'll pull through this. As a trial pharmaceutical test clinician in her human days, she developed a thick skin with the patients who weren't happy with the results. It has been a chore since she joined us a few months ago, keeping her from bumping into some of her patients who were terminal, but this isn't her first rodeo into the realm of questionable choices.

I open my mouth to say something and find the words won't come out. "Fae, that's--"

"It's decided, alright?" She looks around to the others who all nod.

I'm grateful they have my back and I'm not alone in this. "Fae, drop Marty off--"

"I'm going with the kid." It's the first time Marty addresses all of us and he points to Lowell. Leo rolls her eyes. "It's the way it's gonna be, girlie." I think Leo might kill him when he looks at her.

"Fine, but you slow us down, Old Man--" I point my finger at him. He climbs back in the sidecar and Leo throws her hands up.

"I'm staying too." Tora leans around Leo again, who smirks.

"When did this become a friggin' Democracy?" I say. "Fine. We ride out and meet at the University in the morning. Hole up somewhere for the night if you

can shake the Hounds. Lowell and I will head there
and try to get the mark off with his friend and then
we ride from there." Before any of them can further
argue with me, I kick Sugar back on and rev up. I wait
for Lowell to come back to the bike before taking off.
Since my girls are so good at sorting through all of
our troubles without my word being law, I leave
them to it, to figure out who's riding down which
highway in different directions.

I circle back and head southwest before hitting
the road north and directing my bike to the
University. The ride gives me all kinds of time to get
messed up in the head. The landscape bleeds together
in my periphery, like a smeared painting. The colors
are there, but so is the chaos of browns, golds, greens,
and reds all swirled together. It resembles my
thoughts, swirls of questions in the maelstrom of my
mind.

What the heck am I thinking? Taking on Hell
must be the stupidest thing anyone in Heaven or
humanity, has ever done. I'd like to say I can blame
Damien for the biggest blunder of all time. The only
one worse was when the Cosmos permitted Damien
to be born at all. Did the years of denial with Zeke
really made me think I can ignore what is right here
in front of me, right now? Am I that much of a screw
up I can't see this decision is the one sure to land me
in an eternity of hurt and suffering?

Lucifer offered me a deal. Atone for my sins
and bring in souls, day after day, knowing what is in
store for them. In some ways, it feels like a worse
punishment than if I'd just taken the pain. If I'd gone
that route, then I would just be facing an eternity with

my own suffering, not shouldering the weight of everyone else's by having to bring them in.

I sigh, resigned to my choice. I justify it as I'm choosing not to stand by and do nothing again. There are some things a girl can't go back from. Like spray on tans. That orange shit stains everything and sticks around forever and in places one shouldn't be able to tan to begin with. The decision to go against Lucifer and Hell itself is just another orange shit stain on all the decisions I've made in my life and afterlife. This mess is definitely the stickiest though.

After a few hours of inner war between doing the right thing and lamenting my decision, I pull into the parking lot of the University and park the bike next to a beat-up blue pickup truck. If the professor friend is as unkempt as his truck is when Lowell tells me, "He's here," I wonder if the man's theological ideology has as many rusty holes in it as this junker.

"Which building?"

Colleges aren't the most comfortable places for me. I get a few marks on them from time to time. I never told the girls when I turned eighteen and left my Mum to drown in the alcohol and the Anderson's from their oppressive micro-managing, I took out some student loans and given the solid life a go. That was before I met Zeke.

We walk across the campus green without saying a word. Rather than wasting my undead breath, I figure I can shock the Hell out of the professor for kicks and giggles, since it will be the last bit of joking around I ever do. But, for practical purposes, I figure it's probably best to cement a plan in place since I don't know how long it will take

Damien to catch up to us. There's so much to go over it's hard to know where to start.

I look around, taking in the campus. I have only seen this one in pictures when I was trying to decide where best to spend the government's money with my student loans. Brick buildings with faceless windows spurt up, forming a semi-circle around the courtyard. Perfectly symmetrical bushes line the walkways and walls of the buildings. A well-manicured lawn adorns the campus between each building and a centerpiece in the courtyard with a cherub stone fountain trickles serenely. If I had the capability it would make me have to pee rather than focus on studying. A bizarre modern art piece looks like someone bent metal scrap pieces around to look like a car accident, but purposefully done in the name of art, sits next to the fountain. Most likely the work of a student, it all looks like just another postcard-perfect picture of Americana. I am as out of place here as I would be at a glitzy and glamorous bachelorette party with drunk giggling women and a thong-clad stripper named Raphael. I make sure to keep my demon features under wraps until we're alone with the professor though. As much fun as it would be to rock their sheltered little worlds, there's no use dropping that bombshell on humanity. They aren't ready for proof it's real, even if it is a theology class we are headed to.

When Lowell opens the door of the red brick building in the center of the ring, the fluorescent lights glare down from above. Students and faculty stop and stare at us as we walk past. Lowell must have been here before because he walks to the far end of the hall with purpose as I quietly follow his lead. We must make quite the duo. Him looking all Boy Scout and me looking like a degenerate.

Lowell touches my elbow and it makes me jump. I'm not keen on being this close to this much humanity. My boots echo in the hall and I can't help but glance through the glass windowpanes in the classroom doors on either side of us. Faces peer back at me and about halfway down the hall, the feeling like I'm the freak kids used to call me in high school forces me to look down and count the tiles as we walk over them. I thought colleges were supposed to be different. Where every kid was accepted and being different was celebrated.

When we get to the end of the hall, Lowell pushes another doorway open and I groan. Inside there are about fifty students sitting in the raised seats of the lecture hall. All of them turn to look at us, as well as the middle-aged man in the sweater and tie on the dais at the center of the class.

I lean in to whisper, "What's with the professor and Marty? Don't you have any friends who aren't older than mummy dust?"

Lowell nudges me in the ribs with his elbow harder than necessary. I rub the spot where he landed a hit on my side and we begin the long walk down the steps as I feel the incredulous stares coming from the lecture participants. This just might be more intense than the wrath of Hell.

When we reach the dais, Lowell smiles apologetically to the teacher who looks between us. He blinks behind his glasses, confused, like he's trying to sweep away the cobwebs in his mind and see the situation clearly.

"Lowell, is everything alright?" The middle-aged man scratches his head. It might not be the best act because he doesn't have much chestnut hair left up on top of his head to be inadvertently pulling out.

Lowell shakes his head and the professor's bright blue eyes bug out. He has such handsome yet advanced features, but the shock creates an unseemly owl-like effect. "Turn the microphone off."

"As you can see, I'm in the middle of class."

"I would never interrupt if it weren't a matter of life and death."

The professor looks long and hard at Lowell. "Please, James."

After a moment, James clears his throat, leans over the microphone and offers an apologetic, "Class dismissed."

Students groan and begin filing out of the hall as James turns back to us. Who knew college kids could love this theology crap so much?

"What is going on? You look like you've seen a ghost. What do you mean a matter of life and death?" James keeps his voice down so it doesn't carry over the microphone. The last few stragglers siphon out the door before Lowell finally responds.

"Ah, well you see, it is a death. My death to be precise." Professor Dudard looks even more perplexed.

"You aren't making any sense. Do you need me to call a doctor? Who is this woman?"

Lowell holds up his hands and drops them like he's trying to offer up a reasonable explanation, but has none to give. "Well, there's no easy way to introduce her." He glances at me nervously and I get the "please behave" look.

I shrug and grin at him. I can't help having a little fun every now and then, and at the expense of the professor? This is going to be epic.

"She's the demon who was sent from Hell to collect my soul which was mistaken for my brother, Zeke's."

CHAPTER 6

Professor Dudard's eyebrows disappear into his thin hairline. It's a neat trick and with all of the disbelief planted on his puss, at least his eyebrows are on fleek for the occasion. So I do Lowell a favor and give the professor my sweetest smile featuring fangs, whiskers, and fire in my eyes.

I think I might be doing Heaven a solid when James stumbles away from me to one of the vacated seats at the front of the lecture hall, clutching his heart. Turns out he is just one of those guys who preaches a lot about the word, but his faith, like everyone else's, walks a fine line between the unwavering confusion of a tie-dyed t-shirt with some sick shades of doubt mixed in it.

I sit on the edge of the stage while Lowell coaxes the professor into breathing better by pushing his head between his knees, but when Lowell gives me the look, the one telling me I'd screwed the pooch on this one, I kicked my legs back and forth and look around while they get their Kum Ba yah yah's out. There are a lot of, "Sweet Jesus and Oh Lord's" coming from the professor. It does make him sound a bit prophetic, to be fair, but I figure there'll be Holy Water and maybe a cross shoved in my face if I try to get with the up close and friendly personals too soon.

It takes Lowell all of five minutes to fill him in on what he knows, which is a big fat not-a-whole-lot coming from his piehole, and then another ten minutes of the shady glances in my direction as they "theorize" about what might possibly be going on.

"Is she real?" James asks him.

I pinch myself. Yep, still here.

"She dated my brother back when she was, well, before she..." Lowell waves his hands like the answer will drop out of the sky. "It's complicated."

"But she's a demon?"

"You saw what I saw." They both look me up and down like they think I'm about to bust it wide open, but I don't play that way. It's more Tabby's style.

I sit here and they're talking about me like I blend with the podium. I glance behind me. Burgundy, the color of the staged backdrop, is so not my color. Besides, I'm dead, not deaf. In this day and age, a girl has got to take initiative or she'll be waiting 'til she's old and gray before she's invited to the party.

I jump down and hold my hands up when James looks like he's going to pull a runner.

"Chill. I'm not here to screw with the Almighty's plan. I just want to fix the mess my co-worker made." I think about it a minute and then grin. "Ok, so maybe I'm down to toy with the boy here for a bit. Heaven and Hell knows things need to get stirred up sometimes, right?"

James doesn't look amused, but I manage a smirk from Lowell so I figure I'm in the clear to add my two cents.

"Damien marked Lowell, not his brother, Zeke. When I showed up, I called him out on it, and being the smart-assed son of a-" Lowell jerks his head and I stumble over my words as I redirect the name calling. "Son of Satan, he thinks he's riding high and mighty on the decisions board and told me to bring him in. I didn't and now here we are, waiting for you to tell us how to get rid of the mark." I point to Lowell's chest and James looks.

"I don't see a mark."

I knew there was a reason I don't get chummy with the humanity types. Dealing with them is so tedious sometimes.

I turn to Lowell. "I thought you said this guy is smart?"

"I'm sitting right here!" Professor Dudard stands and walks over.

I'm curious to see if he'll back himself up a bit. I find men come in two categories. At least, all the ones I've ever dated. Either they talk a good game, but can't walk to back it up or they really are true to their word and can handle their business. Professor types have always seemed to live upstairs in their heads, but I've been wrong before.

"Says the man who thinks demons can't hear when he is openly talking and ogling them." I love issuing a challenge.

"Give me a break, lady. It's not like I learn every day demons are real." He crosses his arms and I shrug.

"Then what are you doing teaching theology if you don't believe in it?" Lowell pinches his nose and James does a thing where I can practically see the little mo-fo hamster in his head trip over the wheel. I guess he's the headspace with a big mouth type. "Whatever man, can you help us or not?"

"What kind of mark does Lowell have on him?"

"I wasn't aware there were different kinds of marks." What an interesting seg-way. It makes my little hamster summersault. Poor little guy. I shake my head, rattling the rodent of reason and try to make sense of the assumption there is more than one kind of mark. I'm the demon, how did I not know this? Auntie J has been holding out on me. Again.

"You're a demon. How can you not know?" He looks at Lowell who's making big with the not helping.

"Theology is your and Auntie J's bag of tricks, not mine." I cross my arms. I might as well stand my ground, but own my ignorance.

James looks confused like there is some fundamental belief humanity has about Christianity and the afterlife they all missed.

I suddenly have a thought and ask Lowell, "You studied theology in college?"

"Beer and bartending are a religion of their own." Scout crosses his arms and I cede him his point when those ears turn as red as the home fires in indignation or possibly slight embarrassment. Hey, not judging still, to each their own God, but if Dionysus is kicking around at the Sloshed Sloth with his acolyte Lowell, I'll have to raise a glass to him if I can ever return Lowell to his home.

Speaking of shootouts from higher beings, I take my cell phone out of my pocket. Still no message. Damn, woman, where are you? Auntie J is making female prep time for date-night look like a New York minute compared to how long she is taking to return my call.

"Who is Auntie J?" Lowell sits up, taking an interest in the little tidbit I just dropped a minute ago.

There's my boy. His mama must have taught him right. No sitting back and watching a lady take on all the hard and heavy hitter questions from his teacher friend.

"She's our handler in Purgatory. I suspect she can fix Damien's screw up, but she's not calling me back."

"By Damien, do you mean?" He can't bring himself to say it out loud.

"Son of Satan, the very one." I knew it was all a lot for this guy to take in, but it's like I'm waiting in the grocery store for his cart of disbelief to empty the Hell out and he's taking his sweet time about it, giving me a serious case of the road rage.

"Well, that might be something." Lowell rubs his chin.

"Well, if Damien is marking on behalf of Satan, we could potentially mask the mark because it isn't Satan's."

My turn needing the roadmap. "I don't follow."

"Lucifer is a fallen angel. Damien is a Nephilim. Two different species with two sets of rules regarding theology."

Light bulb moment and then it fades. "Yeah, but we are still no closer to removing the mark."

"But we have a place to start. Let's go to my office." Professor Dudard gathers some papers from the podium and drops them into a case and snaps it shut. He walks to the stairs leading off the stage as Lowell and I trail behind him. I start thinking about his theory regarding Damien and the Devil having two separate marks. Professor Dudard might be on to something after all.

We make our way up the aisle of the lecture hall and down a long corridor with pictures of people of note who have contributed to the school. It's interesting because I've seen some of them around Downtown, but here on these walls they are proclaimed as being invaluable to the school's resources and reputation.

The pale glow of the sun is filtering in through the ceiling high windows and I catch a glimpse of the horizon for an instant. There are no ominous thunderclouds looming in the distance, which is a good thing for us because it means my plan did buy us some time at least. I cringe. It does mean when Damien finally catches up to us--I turn away from the window, not wanting to think about it anymore. Well that, and my face is covered in a film of dust making me desperate for a bath in the blood of my enemies, or a shower, whichever comes first. Who am I kidding though? I haven't been able to look at myself in the mirror long and hard in quite a while.

Professor Dudard opens a door at the end of a hall I thought was going to go on forever. I get so preoccupied in my thoughts I run into the back of Lowell when he stops and waits for James. He jumps like I've scalded him with my touch when I put my palms out to steady myself and I check to make sure all my whiskers and claws aren't out. No need for wardrobe malfunctions today, thank you very much.

"Easy, Trina." He looks down at me. His face is coated in a thin film of red dust just like mine and an idea forms in my head. I love it when the light bulb flickers back on.

"If we can't remove the mark, can we mask it?" I study Professor Dudard's profile as we walk in the room. It's so what I expected I almost want to cry. I walk around the desk as he begins pulling books from shelves and I kick my feet up on a teetering tower of files. I pop open the bottom drawer, figuring he has something in stock, and pull out the bottle of Scotch I find hidden there. I'd prefer whiskey, but sometimes a girl has to roll with the punches.

"I just suggested that in the lecture hall." I watch James mutter to himself as he pulls books from the shelf.

I feel the lick of shame, like I broke the cardinal rule of college by copying off someone else's paper. Plagiarism is taken very seriously at this level. James is different though. He doesn't get in my face about it. It takes me a minute to figure out what grates my grill about this guy. I came in here thinking he was going to have a snobbish attitude like the college types get sometimes. I should be giving him credit where it is due, but it bothers me he has answers that might help us figure out how to fix Lowell and I don't.

"Trina, would you stop being an ass and help us out?" Lowell tosses me a book.

I catch it and flip open the front cover. I could never get through all the begets in the second chapter or the third. I can never remember. Genesis is mildly entertaining, like reality TV I think Eve should have baked a pie with the shit. They say a way to a man's heart is through his stomach, so in this day and age when everyone is offended by everything, I give the girl kudos because she was trying to keep it real and share with her man but, no. Himself the Lord Almighty got offended he was being ignored by Adam and Eve and then there was no more yummy apples, just a big stinky pile of rotten fruit and someone got offended. It's interesting to see humanity emulate discontent on social media now, but I skip my favorite drama duo and the begets to head right for Revelations.

I nod off a few times and a few versions later. I can't help it. There isn't anything revealing about Satan being cast from Heaven in this version then there was in the previous version, and the one before that. Lowell and James don't seem to be having much luck either, and about half the bottle of Scotch later, we're still no closer to an answer, but at least we're feeling good about it.

I toss the Bible back on the desk with the rest of them where the thud makes Lowell and James glare at me. Ignoring them, I get up to do a walk around the office. James has started delving into some of the deeper theology books. It's been so long since I've touched a standard bible, I hate playing catch up to James and Lowell. I glance at some of the titles on the shelf and my eyes seem to be swimming, or maybe I'm swimming in the alcohol when I reach the far corner in the office. It's the darkest part of the room. These books haven't been dusted off in a while and I run my finger through the film on the cherry bookcase as it reminds me of something I once read about the Devil's mark when Mrs. Anderson was hounding me about consorting with the "wrong types." Modern day witch trials would have been right up her alley.

I turn back around and ask, "What does lore say about the Devil's mark? If the one on Lowell isn't the real thing, then what does it look like?"

Lowell looks up from the Bible he has been pouring over. "You don't know?"

"Nope. I tried to get tight with the Devil but...you know how it is when you're a solid five on the scale and he's pulling nines and tens. He's completely out of my league so I don't see him much, or well, ever."

"The way you view the world is astounding, Catriona." Lowell shakes his head and continues reading.

"Yeah, well, you're about as dry and dusty as some of these old books here." I point to the shelf behind me. "Life can't always be viewed through rose-colored glasses. For real though, what does the mark look like?" I change the subject. I don't want to end up skipping down that road with Lowell, especially since it leads to his brother, the "wrong type."

"Well, the Devil's mark was a sign of the compact with the Devil. It was associated with witchcraft. Inquisitors often used it as a means to interrogate women and make them confess to a compact with the Devil. It has many forms, more commonly thought to be a blue or red claw mark from the Devil, and it was hidden on the body, orifices, armpits, under the eyelids. The accused was shaved of all body hair, so the Inquisitors could identify it and, woe be it to the accused who had a birthmark. Those were said to have been caused by the Devil licking the person and marking them thusly. Even scars or blemishes were considered and accepted as evidence."

"Not gonna lie, I would have Double, Double Toiled and Troubled as a teen to get rid of some of my acne. But it still doesn't tell us what his mark actually looks like." I'm refusing to entertain judgement because the prof just used the word thusly. He seriously needs to crawl out of this turn of the century style office and into this century. His explanation does nag at me though.

I turn away. I hate feeling like there's a major step I am about to miss and fall flat on my face. This is that moment. Why is this so important to me? We're trying to figure out how to ditch Damien's digits, not Lucifer's. I stare at the place where I swiped at the dust. It reminds me of some of those patchy birthmarks. I have one myself on my lower back where my spine meets the shanks of my ass. I'm just glad it's back there where I don't have to see it because knowing I have a tramp stamp au naturelle annoys me to no end. Tats are permanent and to each there own, but I choose mine wisely and only have two. The date Gigi died and then the date I died. I wanted someone to remember me. I watched my own funeral. It was as bad as I could have imagined. Only one person came and I can't think of her without tearing up. Of all the friends Zeke and I supposedly had, none of them came, not even him.

In the next instant, I feel the anger flare up.

Why am I so keen to draw this out then? Why bother saving his brother? Zeke didn't care one bit about me and here I am trying to save his one and only family member left living. Is it because I think I can somehow save him in the end too? Is it really a mark for my redemption and will get me to Heaven even quicker? What bugs me about this business is I'm usually tight with my motivations. Conflicted is so not my color. Not knowing why, I feel the need to stick my neck out for this one soul, it's what has my panties in a twist about it all.

To try and take my mind off it, I read the spine of the book just above where I made the mark in the dust. What a weird name. Codas Gigas. It's a black book with gold calligraphy letters, which I chuckle at the irony. Maybe this is the little placard I bemoaned not having been handed after walking through death's door. I misread the spine of the book, thinking Gigi dropped a line at some point. I pull it off the shelf and flip it open, frowning deeper and deeper the more I read.

"Hey, James, what's this book? Gigas reminds me of Lowell and Zeke's Gigi, but I gotta say, these pics aren't the epitome of a sweet old lady's musings." Apparently not my personal invite. There are folios, primitive looking, making me think of what would be in Grimm's fairytales.

"The Codex Gigas? The Devil's Bible."

I drop the replica of the 13th century manuscript on the floor like it's lit with the fire and brimstone of Hell itself.

CHAPTER 7

"The Devil's Bible? Why is it called that?" I bend and pick the book up with trembling fingers. It feels hot in my hands, which is strange given it didn't a moment ago. Is it like the marks? Can it sense I am a mercenary for Lucifer and the second the beacon is lit up like Time's Square on New Year's Eve, the object itself responds to the presence of a demon? I want to put it back down and never touch it again, but it feels relevant to all this madness, so I slowly walk back to my chair and place it on the desk in front of me. I hairy eyeball the thing, waiting for it to burst into flames or front with some other ominous portent. I think it's more foreboding when it sits there all ordinary and boring. I rub my hands together, feeling the energy of the heat as it spreads up my fingertips. It isn't unpleasant, just different, like I dipped my hands in icy-hot and I'm getting all the perks of the hot and not any of the uncomfortable cold.

"It's an illuminated manuscript. Said to have been written by the Devil himself. The original is anyway." James stands up and flips the front cover open. I lean forward, wondering if it's like a portal to the Underworld. This feels like one of those moments in a Horror movie that pisses me off and I'm always screaming, "Don't do it! Don't open the door of doom, you dumbass!" Obviously, I'm not one to take my own advice.

"If this isn't the original, where is it?" How can a replica have such a hold over me? If I ever come across the original, I'm running, far, far away and I'm not coming back. I don't even want to know what that kind of power feels like. There are some people who answer those questions like, if you could have one super power what would it be? Most people say mindreading, the ability to fly, extreme strength. My answer? I would have the power to nap like a boss.

"It was seized as a spoil of war after the Thirty Year's war and is now housed in the National Library of Sweden in Stockholm."

"Sweden?" Good. I never wanted to travel there anyway. Egypt has always been more my game. All the old stuff kind of looks cool in the movie with the cute actor. Sweden makes me think of the story with the boy who saved the town by sticking his finger in the dyke. Or maybe it's Finland. Either way, I've never been a save the town kind of girl so they can have their boy-hero.

"The original is the largest known illuminated manuscript in existence. Its cover is wood and leather and there are 310 leaves of vellum from over 160 donkeys or calves. Now, there is speculation, when Lucifer possessed the monks who created it, donkeys and calves weren't used. It has been theorized the vellum was made from the skin of Satyrs from Hell."

I sit back in the chair and stare at the book, chewing on one of the prof's pen caps. It would explain why the satyrs are bent on delivering the most torture and evil. All that rage pent up at serving the Master of Hell and what do they get? Satan skinning Uncle Billy for his skin to make a lousy book. Anger issues are easy to work out in the Underworld.

"I've seen the Satyrs. Depending on the level of Hell they are assigned to run, they are the ones who dole out punishments to the occupants."

Lowell shudders and takes a sip of liquid courage. I one-up him once his glass is full and pour some for myself. Man, it's getting deep here.

"Why is this book relevant? Why do you have it?" I look over at James. I can't place the nagging feeling like the answer is staring me right in the face. I'm being face-palmed by a knock off second edition. Why am I always pulling second string line up? I look at Lowell and shake away the curiosity about what life would have looked like if I dated him. There is no use traveling down that road. It only has emotional thorn bushes and I'm only slightly masochistic, not the whole hog.

"You tell me why it's relevant. You're the one who picked it up off the shelf." James reaches for the bottle and pours himself the rest. "As for why I have it, with any field of study, there is the good and the bad. The dark and the light. I prefer to focus my academic pursuits in the lessons of light. I obtained the copy because it is interesting to my students to see how one influences the other."

I stand and begin pacing the space just to the right of the desk in the middle of the room. The carpet, once blue with golden fleur-de-lis on it, has been worn down. I half expect James to jump up and end up in a vortex with me playing follow the leader. "I don't know why it's relevant. I just saw it and the cover reminded me of Gigi because of the word Gigas."

"Codex Gigas literally means giant book. It's over three feet long and weighs 165 pounds."

Lowell stares at the liquid in his glass. "It certainly fits Gigi's personality. Larger than life and a wealth of knowledge. I always thought I would see her in the afterlife. It appears it's not the case."

"Don't say that. We'll figure this out." James reaches across the desk and pats Lowell's hand. I'd never asked Zeke about his parents. I always figured there was some unwritten rule for those of us who ended up screwed out of having parents. You didn't say mum about it to one another. You know, respect for the grief and life of hard knocks. Gigi meant the world to Lowell, just as much as she meant to Zeke.

"When you told me the book was the Devil's Bible, it grew hot in my hand."

"I suppose it would react to an agent of the Devil."

James' musings make me feel totally Double-O.

"So, if Lucifer possessed the monk who illuminated it--"

"I suspect it was the entire monastery. These books took years to complete and some of it is missing from the original." He swallows the rest of his Scotch.

I close my eyes, stowing the desire to stretch out on the rug and dig my claws in. I'm in desperate need to dig into something and the good professor is irritating me with the big revelations because it's only complicating everything already going on in my head. I have to figure out how to remove the mark and now worry about a demonic book? I feel like I'm wading in a Satan infused swamp and he knows the rules of the board game, but I'm demonic gator-bait. "It From the Pit." It was the name of the game. I'm well on my way to being sucked into a vortex for sure.

"He must have imprinted himself into the book somehow. If I can feel his power, even in a copy."

"It is interesting you say that. We were just discussing the Devil's Mark as it pertains to Witchcraft. There are illuminated letters throughout the Devil's Bible that are also blue and red. There are other signs Lucifer has influenced the text. Folio 290 recto is an entire page comprised of an illustration of the Devil. This one folio has stumped academics for centuries, as it is directly across from a full-page depiction of Heaven. There is no explanation as to why the two illustrations portray the dichotomy of the two realms, but perhaps it is explained in the missing pages." I flip to the Folio he is talking about and feel the heat of the Satan depicted there, staring back up at me. I quickly shut the book and snatch my hand away, afraid I just gave away our position by looking into the eyes of Hell's creator.

"Missing pages? What's missing?" Lowell's speech is slurred and I glance over.

Great. Three sheets to the wind for this guy, or rather, folios. Should have kept a better eye on him, although if I were in his shoes, yeah, I'd totally drink me under the table too. Might make the prospect of facing Hell not even a little less piss your pants terrifying.

"Alright, Lowell. Time to put the Scotch away." James grabs his glass quickly before Lowell's basic motor skills tell him it's time to function. "If we knew what was in those folios then they wouldn't be missing. But the best guess is it is the first half of the book of Genesis and pages displaying the monastic rules of the Benedictines."

"Well, good on them!" Lowell flails his arms and tries to stand. It's kind of like watching a fish flop around on land. You know you shouldn't stand there and watch it because of animal cruelty, but you can't deny you've done it just once. Just to see if the poor bastard makes it back into the water. Lowell is no different. He ass-plants himself on the floor, which is probably a good place for him to be until it's time to sober him up. The way I see it, less damage will be inflicted this way. "Who gives a damn what their rules are, unless one of them knows how to get this mark removed!" Lowell's voice echoes somewhere around the rear left side of the desk.

"Are you going to take care of this?" James looks uncomfortable, like seeing a grown man break is not something in his brilliant mind he is equipped to deal with.

Lowell peeks out from under the desk at me.

"Why?"

"He's drunk and sitting on my office floor."

"So?"

"We can't just leave him there! It wouldn't be right."

"He's a big boy. He'll find his way back up

when his brain tells him this is all for real and he can either man up, or wallow in his misery until the Hounds come for him. Besides, I'm no martyr. Right or wrong, he put the bottle to his own lips."

James opens his mouth to argue and sucks in a breath, but then closes it and shrugs instead.

"I suppose you're the one who I should be talking to about this anyway."

"True. If there are pages missing, and Lucifer has them or knows where they are, it might mean there is something in it he doesnt want anyone to find out about. Like how to get rid of the mark."

"I was thinking exactly the same thing."

"It's always got to be about a book."

James snorts and begins collecting bibles. I watch him and taunt the drunk man under the table because it makes me somewhat happy. I hold the bottle above him and wiggle it, letting the contents slosh around inside, kind of like his brain. He swipes for it and I pull it away, making him miss. I can't ride, so I figure I have to take my stress relief somehow.

When the game grows tired, or possibly after getting the stink-eye from James for taunting a drunk man, I put the bottle back on the desk and dig my phone out of my pocket. Still no Auntie J and still no check in from my girls. Did Damien get hold of them? I figured he would have called to taunt by now. Panic threatens the edges of my psyche and I shove my phone back into my pocket along with my fears and kick at Lowell who is trying to hug my leg.

"Get off!" He's worse than Fran touching my colors back in Limbo. The savior saga is not my tale, but there's no point trying to tell him. "What the Hell are we gonna do?"

I click the next pen I come across under the rubble of James's desk. The sound is deliciously annoying, so much to the point even Loaded Lowell crawls out from under the desk and pulls himself into his chair and glowers at the pen. He sways dangerously for a minute, but James has his back when he walks up and sits again. He places a steady, comforting hand on his shoulder and Lowell closes his eyes. I wonder if the room is spinning or his head or if his whole self has just gone Tilt-a-Whirl. I love that ride.

"You tell me."

He keeps tossing the ball back in my court. I suppose I can't blame him for the hot potato pass. This is a match I started.

"I'm trying to help him." I thumb in Happy go Lucky's direction and I think he drools at me a little. Very awkward. "Look, James, I know my deal and why I ended up where I did. I could have ripped your spine out and beat you with it in front of the acolytes in your classroom, but I didn't." James stiffens and I click the pen again, but it gets jammed. I toss it on the desk where it leeches ink onto some important looking files. Maybe beating him with his own spine is a bit of a strong assumption of my strength, but point made. "If I wanted you dead, you would be."

"What's in it for you then?" Maybe the man does have a spine.

"Nothing but a headache and an eternity of torment when I get caught." I might as well make with the being upfront about everything because chances are when Damien catches up with us, he's actually going to be able to do what I threatened.

"There's the optimism I assumed all of your kind has." Maybe spine isn't the right word. Sassy ass is more fitting.

"I have a job and I didn't do it." I point to Lowell.

"You could have. Why is he so special?"

"I was feeling nice."

"How do you expect anyone to help when you lie? Something in your life caused you to end up where you are, but it also caused you to pause today and instead of looking away and sticking your head in the sand, you chose to…Habakkuk 1:13."

I am so not looking for a sermon right now.

"Your eyes are too pure to look on evil and you cannot tolerate wrongdoing. Then why do you tolerate those who are treacherous? Why are you silent while one who is wicked swallows up one who is more righteous than himself?" James reads the passage then tosses a bible at me he hadn't put away. I toss the CSB back.

"I don't need a sermon, padre."

"What did you stand by and watch without interceding in your human life?"

I stand up and move away, not ready for this pow-wow yet. There must be some way we can get to those pages to get the mark off. But they are most likely in Hell, close to Lucifer. I can't imagine he would leave them in the human world unless there is some unwritten rule about artifacts touched by humanity not leaving this plain. Maybe it's why portals had to be created for me and the girls to pass through? I figure it goes down like this, I bust back into Hell. Search the circles and eventually convince myself they would be no other place than in records, which is a whole other dimension of the Underworld I have only seen once. It's the written word of anyone who has ever passed through. Mostly it's written on human flesh and apart from the stink factor, it creeps me out. I mean come on, who wouldn't it creep out? Maybe Himself is keeping them cataloged in there?

I shudder thinking of the nightmarish system of organization in Satan's library. The Dewey Decimal system was bad enough. If only there was someone who knew their way around the Underworld and would also relish breaking into records and getting into all kinds of trouble. Apart from almost every demon ever, except for myself, I guess, I don't see Auntie J doing it. I pull out my phone and dial. Taking this mother of all stupid plans out for a test ride.

"Twice in one day? You really do want the beat down coming to you," Damien's voice purrs on the other end. He would have been one Helluva Hellcat.

"Do you want to piss off your Dad with me?" I leave Lowell and James in the stuffy office and walk back down the hall to the parking lot.

There's radio silence on the other end, as I knew there would be. This is not the question Damien is anticipating I am going to ask. Threatening, definitely. Begging, maybe, but not asking for an alliance. There's no one in the hallway, which is just as good. When I step outside and breath in the fresh air, I feel like all the heavy from the study session lightens up a little and I can breathe again. I take a deep breath and drop my proposition on him.

"Call off the manhunt and I'll make a deal with you."

CHAPTER 8

I need the negotiations with Damien to go in our favor. I've got no doubt he's already cooking up a scheme to ruin me, but he's been crafting the conniving a lot longer than I have, so points for being seniority. What better way to get what I want, then by getting Damien to pardon my transgression of going against Hell's rules? Damien knows Hell. He also probably has a pretty good idea where I can get what I need. Ergo, project persuasion is formed. I also have the nagging suspicion he wants something from me. It's called leverage.

I leave Lowell under the care of James, despite his protests. The last thing I need is for the inevitable sound advice from an inebriated idiot. Let's face it, drunk people always have something to say.

I pull onto the highway and open up Sugar, letting her purr under me as I make time to the Devils Canyon. I'm stopping off my trek northwest to pick up my girls. The ride is serene with dusk about to settle over the horizon like a comfy blanket and the stars peek out in a whisper behind the night sky.

"What's the word?" Leo answers on the second ring when I call and I breathe a sigh of relief.

I'd been worried, not having heard from any of

them for most of the night. Giving a damn is not good for my blood pressure. I never let the Hellcats know just how much I care. It would go to their heads and then we'd be forced to have the God-awful girl-to-girl chats, and I'm just not one who's down for the chic-flick moments. I'm more the kind who wants my bitches to know I love 'em, and if necessary, I'll bust some heads if they ever step out of line.

"I made a deal with Damien." I sit in the pull off along Interstate 84. It took a while to get out of traffic in Salt Lake City, but once I was on the open road, I felt the little taste of freedom I constantly crave. I rode for a while, letting the last twenty-four hours sink in. I'd been going on full tilt, balls to the wall all day, and now I have time to think it all through, I'm straight up mad as a viper that's been stepped on. Where does Damien get off making my afterlife so miserable? Why hasn't Auntie J called me back? Since when in the history of Hell, has a colossal fudge-up this big ever happened? Has it happened? I honestly don't know. I'm sure with the sheer amount of souls passing through Purgatory, there must have been at least one who didn't deserve it. I can't help but wonder whatever happened to them and what will happen to Lowell if I fail at this snowball's chance. It isn't like there's a playbook where I can read the rules and cry major foul.

Why hasn't Lucifer stepped in? I mean, it's his job, isn't it? He's the dude when push comes to shove, word is law in his domain. Isn't he around to step in when someone pisses in his morning Cheerios and sets the tone all wrong for the day with crap like this? I know I'd be raging if I had one job and someone busted in, messed my workflow up, and then walked out again. So why hasn't he come for me? Or Damien. I figure, in all this big old grand scheme bull, there's got to be a master plan somewhere. Is he just another player in the game? What if he doesn't hold the schematics and by rescuing Lowell's soul, with or without the interference of Lucifer, I decimate and tumble that house of cards? Playing in the sandbox of the big man upstairs, and without his green light, has never been my intention.

I work myself into a case of the crazies with all the merry-go-round in my head. I eventually have to check out mentally and just drive, because otherwise, I'm just going to work myself into such a state of anxiety it will make Black Friday Door Buster fanatics look like they're rocking the Buddha vibes.

"Are you out of your friggin' mind?"

At least, my girl, Leo will call me on my crap when I'm emulating the emo side of my femininity. Mum always said the best way to get a dude was through his stomach. Since I don't plan to cook for Damien, it leaves the other way, which is, well, yeah.

"I am not having sex with Damien," I snap at my phone.

Mum had some strange ideas when it came to life's big lessons, but like the candor from someone who's sauced, there was a gritty but straight up code she lived by. To say men respond to food and sex might be mostly accurate. I suppose it isn't PC to say all men respond to those two things. Even in Hell, you must be careful not to offend anyone. Which I think is asinine, but I'm beginning to accept the fact someone has scribbled all over my rulebook in permanent marker.

I took one from Mum's playbook and appealed to Damien's basic needs. He's been bugging me since I got in the Chasm about falling in with him, so I put that very thing on the table tonight. There's some saying about not playing all your cards at once, but I'm a pragmatist. I only have the one ace in my hand to play. It's all or nothing and I'm on my way to find out if he accepts my offer or if I'm walking into the very trap I figure he is going to set up for me.

"How can you even consider him? Gross!"

I sigh. "Leo, I get you don't play his way, or with any male, for that matter. But Fae and Tabby's first thoughts were similar to yours and I explained to them too when I texted them to meet up. Tag teaming with him for whatever it is he's after is my offer. Nothing more, nothing less. We're riding to see if he even agrees in exchange for what I want."

"Don't sell out, Trina. He's been after your tail since you got in."

"You think I don't know that? What am I going to do, Leo? It's only a matter of time before Lucifer catches up to me or the Hounds do on his behalf. Why not crawl in?" I raise my hand and let it fall back on my leg.

"Because you're better than him. Didn't you learn from Zeke?" Her tone is soft, but the words hit like a freight train.

I look out to the overpass at Devil's Canyon. The hills are shadowed in the fading light of the sun. Kind of like my bravado. I'd never admit to her or my other Hellcats, but this is one of those rare times I'm afraid. I was afraid when I was murdered, afraid of what was coming when I looked up the barrel of the gun. The dying part was easy. It was what came after. The gray mist terrified me more than the blast of the revolver and then the darkness came.

When I opened my eyes again, the fog was like a blanket, weighing me down and I ran. I ran so hard my lungs burned and there was still just nothing. It changed when the shadow cut through the fog. I find it interesting looking back at it now, I was afraid of the shadows themselves, but not what was inside the dark places because more often than not, my own imagination concocts fears a lot less bad than what is actually there. Auntie J gave me a few clues about what was in those shadows. She herself was on the other side of the shadow and it wouldn't be until later I would learn I should have been pants pissing, heart pounding, terrified of her. But I wasn't. I was relieved I wasn't alone in the mist and fog. There was hope in the reprieve of having to face eternity alone. I had been afraid once when I was a child and the cruel lesson of what my Mum was and what I meant to her, or didn't, was something I came to understand. But now, facing Damien and my own inner demons, I feel the knot in my throat again.

"I guess I walked into that one, huh? Yeah, I learned from Zeke. It's because of him I never would have considered Damien otherwise, but what other options do I have?" I drum my fingers on the right handlebar. I need Leo to see why this is the only solid plan if we're going to make it through. "The info we need, he has access to, and we don't stand a hope and a prayer in getting it without his help."

I can hear Leo shuffling on the other end of the

line. She knows the risk I'm taking in putting this out on the table. If Damien does backstab me, I'll be suffering an eternity alongside Lowell. If he does help me and I save Lowell's soul, I'll accomplish my goal and still end up suffering for eternity at the hands of Satan. But what totally gets my goat is where is Zeke in all of this? He's about to kick it if the men at the Sloshed Sloth were after him to begin with. I can't help but wonder what rock he's hiding under because even I can't deny the most probable outcome of this is I'm going to need him to transfer the mark from Lowell's soul to his own where it belongs.

"I don't like it, Trina." I can hear Leo's kickstand click up on the other end of the line.

"Which is why I need you here to have my back when he tries to pull a fast one. Get here." I thumb my phone off, knowing she is on her way.

She's the closest one to me on the highway, but Tabby and Faline roll up first. They park on either side and kill their engines. Neither one says a word, mostly because I nod at them in greeting, but make no attempt to chitchat from then on. I watch as the sun sets behind the hills and the valley is thrown into a purple and blue haze. It's the perfect cloaking mechanism for Damien. He'll see us riding up, if he hasn't spotted us already, and we won't be able to see him ride down into the valley. He'll most likely jump from one hotspot to another and pull out right near Devil's Canyon. There's no sign of thunderclouds, but either way, he still has the element of surprise. I have no doubt he can pull the stealth maneuvers if he needs to.

Leo is the last to ride up and having my gang

eases some of the tension in my chest. There's been one thing I have been sure of in the last couple of years and it's their loyalty. I'd thought I had the support from Auntie J, but with her going ghost through this whole thing, I can't be sure of anything anymore Is she in trouble with Satan? Is she being called in for my disobedience? If Auntie J is in the hot seat because she put her trust in me and my ability to achieve atonement, I might never forgive myself, even if by some miracle Heaven and Hell do. She stuck her neck out, and took a risk throwing down for me and this opportunity, I can't help but feel guilty if she's now in some sort of trouble because of my decision to take a stand. I have no way of verifying any of this though, which is what is maddening because if she's in Hell's hot seat, it's a literal hot seat and isn't that just going to burn her ass? I can only imagine the look of disappointment on her face when I figure this all out and get back. It makes my stomach roll thinking about it, so I shake myself and put my worries to rest for now. Prioritizing what I can and can't control is what is going to see this all through to the best outcome that can come of it.

Leona doesn't even bother cutting her engine. Her headlight would have given us away, so I figure there's no point in stalling this shit-show any longer. I start up my Sugar one more time and let loose with the full effects of my demon demographics. My tail whips out behind me. My claws elongate and my eyes catch fire. I can feel the heat in my sockets because it is the same inferno encasing the remnants of my soul. My fangs protrude as I grin while my gang suits up.

I kick Sugar into gear and pull away from the

turnoff, back onto the highway, and ride down into the valley. About halfway down, I hear the crack and boom from thunder and lighting. About a football field length away, four motorcycles appear through the veil between the mortal realm and Hell.

Damien and the Hellhounds ride toward us at full speed, but I don't back down from this game of chicken. I split his crew with my own, and Damien and I pass each other on the centerline of the highway. The whoosh of air threatens to blow Sugar off the road, but I hold tight to her handlebars and keep her ass-end aligned with her front as the blowback shakes her frame.

The Hellcats flank me left, right, and behind in a diamond pattern, and his Hounds and the succubus have to veer out around. Damien pulls to the right at the last minute and I'm pleased to see the annoyance on his face when I pass by. Good. A woman has to set her expectations on a first date and most men I used to date didn't mind if I enjoyed being on top.

I circle back around when the highway splits into a crossroad. My gang follows suit but break from the diamond pattern to form a line. We ride up to Damien and company and fall into a circling pattern for a few turns before he and I break free and face off in the center. The Hounds and the Hellcats close ranks around us as I flick out my kickstand with the toe of my boot and let my Sugar rest, leaning to the side, but I don't get off. This is a first date full of intrigue and seduction, as dangerous as it is, but he can at least get off his bike first and present front and center like a gentleman.

Damien leans back, taking his sweet time, and I

get the tactic. He gets off of his bike and looks back at Phil, as if he's looking for an answer to something. It's unusual because normally he turns to Doug and Dick for silent communications. Phil shakes his head and Damien turns back to me.

"Where's the mark?"

I shrug. "Zeke? I have no idea."

Damien's eyes flash red. It isn't red like flames, but a mix of crimson and scarlet, like blood. I think they might be creepier than my own.

"You are in no position to play games, Catriona."

My spine tingles when he uses my full name and I can feel my tail twitch. I've really stepped in it this time. "Did you think I would be stupid enough to bring Lowell tonight?" I lean forward on the handlebars of my bike.

Damien grins, flashing me some teeth. "I think you would have been smarter to--"

"Enough, Damien. Are you going to make a deal or not?" My temper sometimes gets the best of me and being put on the spot in front of his crew and mine isn't doing a whole lot for my patience level.

"Touchy, touchy." The smile he gives me is all teeth and no mercy this time. He's going to make this process as painful as possible. The bastard. "If I grant you the time to get in and search for what you're looking for, what do I get in return?"

I grit my teeth until my jaw hurts. His boys are snickering and I can feel the tension rolling off my girls in waves. Take one for the team, Trina. Yay. I think my inner cheerleader might be drunk or broken because I don't feel the slightest bit encouraged. "I told you on the phone what I'd give you."

"Yeah, but I want it spelled out. What exactly you are willing to do?" He folds his arms across his chest.

He's waiting for me to take sex off the table and I'm having a hard time swallowing the pride pill. It's like one of those horse-pill vitamins the Andersons used to make Fiona and I take. They knew damn well they couldn't be good for us if our bodies were having a hard time gulping them down, but no. With Damien though, it's all in or not at all.

"I will help you take over Hell. To deal with your Daddy issues, I'll help you defeat Satan so you can rule. In exchange, Lowell walks away, mark free. Saving him is the only thing that matters." I feel like I can retain some of my pride in knowing I'm trying to put someone else first, even if it means my dignity takes a hit if I must crawl into bed with Damien.

I see his boys snicker and I clench my fists in my lap, digging my claws into my palms. I wait for him to respond and he rubs his jaw as he thinks how to rope me in further.

He doesn't look back when his boys start to whoop and cheer, and I thank whatever God or deity is listening to this madness because I manage not to blush when I nod my head. It's not good enough for him though.

"You'll rule by my side. You'll be the queen of Hell and I'll be the king and as long as you agree to all the benefits that go along with the arrangement, Lowell walks free. Do you agree to those terms, Catriona?"

Man, he's just going for the home run with all

the sluggers he's aiming at my dignity and pride. Oh, for two. If he makes me say in front of everyone I will hop in the sack with him, he might as well slam it out of the ballpark on a home run.

"The Hellcats." His stakes are higher than I ever expected and I need to secure as much ground as I can. "You free the Hellcats too. Let them move on from Purgatory."

"That's a lot of pardons you're asking for." He looks around at each of my girls.

"Those are my terms. I'm giving up my shot at eternal salvation. In exchange, when you become ruler, you'll have the power to set them and Lowell, free."

He rubs his wrists where a black leather band is covering most of his arm and then looks back at my gang. After considering them for a moment, like he's weighing whether or not he can find uses for them and they would be worth more to keep than to set free, he nods. "Lowell and the Hellcats in exchange for your help overthrowing my father and his regime, then ruling Hell with me."

"Then I agree to your terms, Damien." I sigh, letting the tension built up in my chest, escape. There's no going back from it now. I figure I survived being murdered in a sense. I came back as a demon, mercenary biker-babe with my own gang, I'm a tough cookie. I'll survive this. "Now, how do I get into Hell for the info I need?"

Damien smiles, but I frown. It looks sad, like he was expecting something else from me, but I can't put a finger on what. I wonder how this deal will be sealed and the pit in my stomach is not loosening, even if the weight on my shoulders regarding the responsibility to see my girls pardon has lessened. I expected a blood oath. Something gruesome. Yet he hasn't procured a shady looking knife to slice open his palm and mine, and there's no paperwork materializing in an official looking folder. So, what's his game?

"What information is it you're looking for?" He unfolds his arms and his hands drop to his sides.

I study him for a moment. I know what he looks like, but I spend so much time avoiding him and trying not to make eye contact, I realize as much as his personality begs for people to notice the alluring perfection of him, there are flaws. His eyes are blue, but with flecks of silver in them. Apparently, he can change the color at will. I didn't given it much thought until now. I don't know why because we are all shapeshifters in our own right. But what I really observe about him, beyond the appeal, is the crow's feet around his eyes. The laugh lines. It's a peculiar thing to take note of, and yet, it's so telling. Of all the things Damien could be in terms of appearance, one would think absolute perfection would be at the top of the list, but it isn't. I find myself mesmerized by the tiny imperfections, in their own way, they are perfect.

"I want to see if there are any records on how to remove your mark. I figure Hell is a busy place. It must be kind of like prison. Everyone claims they didn't do it, boy cried wolf and all, but there's got to be a case in all of its history when there was actually an innocent wrongly interned."

Damien's laugh is like a shotgun sounding through the valley. "It's Hell. No one really cares."

"True, but not my point. Is there such a place? Like records or something? Would it be housed in the library? I know it's there. I've seen it once. How do I get in? I figure Lucifer has influenced written works before so there must be some written records of how to remove the mark. Can you remove it?" I shift my weight on my bike. I'm having serious doubts about the loyalty of his crew. Phil will probably keep his mouth shut about this plan. Maybe Charles. But Doug and Dick are essentially loyal to Lucifer and borrowed guns for Damien. I eye them up and down while Damien mulls it all over. Their silver collars of obedience remain dormant, but it doesn't mean Lucifer's beck and call won't happen at any moment.

"No, I can't remove it. I'm sure there is some way to do it, but I haven't paid much attention to the stuff. I guess it's a question for Auntie J."

"Yeah, cause we know how forthcoming she is with the info all the time. Where is she anyway? I've been calling her all day." I take my phone from my pocket. It's not like this place has any better reception than Downstairs does, but I still have to try.

Damien's posture shifts and he leans forward ever so slightly, his torso tilted closer at me. "She told us to work it out ourselves."

I blink. "Bullshit. She would have called me on something like this." I cram my phone back in my pocket and swing my leg over my bike to begin pacing in front of him.

"On my honor!" He holds up his hands. He screws up his face like he's aiming for innocent imp, but I know better.

"You don't have honor!"

115

He has the audacity to look offended, but I know better. How could Auntie J do this to me? How could she just leave me stumbling around in the dark, making deals with Damien I am sure to regret?

"It's true."

Everyone looks around at the voice calling quietly from behind Charles. I stop pacing. Even Charles gets a good case of the whiplash. Phil's voice is in a stage of deep and masculine and then rises on a crescendo and cracks with his case of the nerves. I feel for him. Thirteen sucks and to have to spend eternity going through puberty is probably the worst punishment anyone could inflict on any being. He clears his throat. "We--" He gestures to Charles, Doug, and Dick, "were in the dog pound when Auntie J said to take the shenanigans outside. I guess she meant outside as in a different realm outside. She's kind of--"

"Bottom line it, buddy." Charles is the one to speak up. His voice is as smooth as his butternut hair and skin.

"Ah, right. So, um, she said Damien should take it outside and the two of you should figure it out." Phil tries to duck back behind Charles' back, but he leans to the side so we can all see the kid.

I stare at him like I'm trying to look through his soul. "Alright. Auntie J is out. I'm sure she has her reasons." Probably cosmic ones, which are the worst kind. "It still leaves the questions, how do we get in and how do we find what we are looking for?" I turn my attention back to Damien.

None of his other boys look ready to play ball with me, but I do have to wonder what sort of gag order Damien has over them so they don't just scamper off to Lucifer and spill the beans. There must be a whole lot of doggy treats in store for this muzzle mission. When I get back and confront Auntie J though...

"Simple. We ask for the directions from the only person who has been given the extensive tour of the Underworld and Purgatory." Damien looks at me like he expects me to know who the shit he's talking about. I hate it when people call me out on my ignorance.

"Besides your Dad, who?" I wrack my brain trying to think back through the biblical stories to figure out who he's talking about, but I come up goose egg on the subject.

"Durante degli Alighieri, the poet who wrote about his travels."

"Dante Alighieri? The author of *The Divine Comedy*? *Dante's Inferno*?"

I bug eye Damien. He's talking about calling in the big guns on this one. I never for a moment figured one little soul could cause this much discord. I don't know why though. It isn't like I haven't been thinking about how incurring the wrath of Lucifer has been an epic decision in stupidity since I made it. For that matter, why hasn't He sent another volley of demons my way to sort this out? If Damien thinks bringing in the most notorious tourist of Hell is a good way to bust in and take care of business, then it's on for real.

"Who's that?" Tabby's fingers click over her phone and the pink jewels flash in the moonlight.

"Dante from *Dante's Inferno*? You don't know who he is?" Faline asks her.

Tabby glances up and shrugs.

Sometimes I wonder if it would be a blessing or a boon to be her kind of ignorant. I at least know who he is and know Damien has outed him as the plan.

Leo walks up beside me and takes a drag on her smoke. "Bloody brilliant. Just what we need to add to this mess. A celebrity with a fame-induced superiority complex."

I get the feeling Leo's beef isn't with his Dante himself and it has more to do with the rivalry between European nationalities, but we so don't have time to front.

"I know, I know. You already have a celebrity, me, and it's all the fame you need. Trust me, Dad was on a bender when he found out Dante spilled all his secret hidey-holes. But, if you want a smooth ride Downtown without meeting any of our coworkers, Dante is our man." Leave it to Damien to add to all of the drama.

"Small problem, how do we find him?" We need to focus, get back on task and the mission. It's time to ride and I'm getting antsy with all this hash it out and bond over our mutual issues.

"Oh, that's easy. We have a friend who has access to go and ask the poet to come and meet us to give us a tour."

"We do?" I look around like this friend will pop through the veil between Hell and earth at any moment.

"Sure. Phil might be fallen from Heaven, but it doesn't mean he can't go back for visits and talk to the souls who are there. Isn't that right, Phil?"

All eyes are on the kid again.

"Oh man!" Phil climbs off the back of Charles' bike and whips his t-shirt up over his head.

What the heck is this? Why is this kid stripping? I look back at my crew, who look as perplexed as I feel. I look down the road, waiting for child services to come and bust us all. I might be a demon, but even I have lines which are a no-cross. Ever. I refuse to look at them suffering in their torture chamber in Hell because I don't ever want to connect on that level of evil.

"Make like the wind and fly. Beat it, kid. Work those wings. You have to work out the divinity muscle if you want to get back upstairs to Heaven." Damien taunts and Phil's attitude is clear as day on his face as he rolls his eyes and snorts. Damien might be in charge, but the kid seems to be holding his own. He's still riding with them after all.

Phil disappears on a sliver of white light. It's kind of like the static on an old box TVs with the rabbit ear antennas. I always felt like the light on those TVs was like a space and time continuum and if I touched the screen, I would be sucked into another dimension. Turns out, I wasn't so far off.

Phil is back in another minute and he shakes himself off like a wet dog. Wilting feathers fly off him before he tucks them back into himself. I always wondered how angels do it; hide their wings. When he turns away from me, I see they are like a tattoo on his back. To humans, he would look like a kid who was badly influenced at a young age and inducted into the gang just to prove himself. Stereotype 101, he would have gotten the ink to look older and tougher. Now I know it's just his wings folded into his skin.

The molting? Not sure if it's a puberty thing or a fallen angel thing, but either way, it's kind of gross like a shedding dog. I feel bad for the guy, leaving his bits and pieces out all over the ground for everyone to see.

"Dante says to meet him in two days on Coney Island in New York." He pulls his black t-shirt back on over his head.

"Why does he want to meet at the park?" Damien barely spares him a glance.

"Because it used to be the site of the abandoned amusement park, Astroland."

"So?" Damien looks up with impatience.

"Umm, well, he said he'd help us if we help him bust out an old amusement ride. It's been locked up in storage since the old park closed." Phil twists the bottom of his t-shirt, like the prospect of breaking and entering and theft is not on his list of, want-to-do-today.

"He wants us to bust out an amusement park ride? What the heck is he planning to do with it once we get it?" This plan is getting weirder and weirder. I look at my girls. It's not like we can fit an amusement park ride in our saddlebags or the sidecar on Fae's bike.

"No idea." Phil shrugs.

"Well, did he say which ride?" I can't believe I'm even considering this. Maybe if we ride into New York, we can rent a truck. One of those moving trucks and all the company needs is the down payment and then we can return it anywhere in the U.S. Afterwards, the breaking and entering part on an island inundated with tourists should be easy, right?

Sure, about as easy as all of us riding up to Coney Island incognito in all of our biker gear. We'll blend right in with the fanny packs and cameras.

Phil clears his throat, so his voice won't crack. "It's the Dante's Inferno ride." He says the last bit like no one will believe him and he isn't far off. Not a single person says anything for a moment until Damien settles himself back on his bike and turns the key on his HD Fatboy.

I turn to my girls. "My afterlife is more bizarre than my living one was."

"We should bring the mark." I look over at Damien whose face is impassive. "It's more likely my father will send other demons or grim reapers after him while we're gone. With us, Lowell might have a slight chance of not dying soon."

I glance between the Hellcats. This could just be a ruse to find out where I've hidden Lowell, but I'm getting the feeling Damien doesn't need a road map to figure out where I hid him. Especially with his own mark on him. I think the only reason we got away from him before was because we had a head start.

"What about Zeke? The actual mark. You can't tell me he isn't going to be brought into this mess at some point."

"I like the way you think, Catriona! Kidnapping, breaking and entering, grand larceny!" Damien claps his hands together.

"Hey, it isn't my idea to break into an amusement park and steal a ride!" I flip my kickstand up wishing it was my middle finger.

"Aww, come on, Trina. Could be fun, yeah?"

"Not the point, Tabby." She goes back to filing her nails. Friggin' Hell, next thing I know I'm gonna turn around and her damn bike will be all dolled up. I draw the line at hot pink flames. Any of my girls get the idea to custom paint the crap on and they'll get the ax.

"We're going to need your homeboy, either way, Trina." Damien draws my attention back to himself.

"Fine, but he rides with me. Then we find Zeke and he can roll with you." I don't see any way out of this and he has a point, even as much as I don't want to see Zeke.

Damien holds up his hands. "It's not a problem." He glances at Charles who flashes some fang and it creeps me out. Incubi are typically known for being male demons who have a go at sleeping women and it's straight up nasty in my book, no matter how good they look. What isn't commonly known is they fall under the list of bloodsuckers; vampires. Before I got to Hell, I was like any other woman who fantasized about the bad boy type with a set of pearly whites. Then I died and learned the list of demons on the red stuff is a lot more depraved than humans realize and can be in no way classified as erotic or alluring. With Damien glancing at his boy Charles to help solve our troubles, well, it worries.

"If you want to trade one boy toy for the twin, that's your deal. Maybe you should think about loosening up a little though, Trina. Why choose one over the other when you can get two for the price of one?"

"Is that what you call the son of Satan and a

122

Nephilim, Damien? Two for the price of one?"

"I call it more like an epic phenomenon."

"Funny, I call it more like pain in the ass."

"Come on now, you know I'm a solid ten."

Damien spreads his arms wide.

"6.66."

"What? Why?" He pulls a face, jerking his head back and clenching his jaw.

"Because your personality is a Hell no. And before you get any ideas, touch Lowell and I'll bury you in the Underworld so deep it'll take another phenomenon to bust your ass out."

I start Sugar, annoyed at his laugh. I wish he had one of those annoying laughs that goes viral on social media. But no such luck tallying it amongst his flaws, which just grates on my nerves even more. I put my bike into gear and pull streamline with Damien, anxious to hear nothing but the wind whipping around me on the road as we aim our bikes back to Salt Lake City. My girls fall in behind me to the right and Damien's Hounds on his left so they fan out like a flock of geese. I never thought I'd see the day I'd be riding beside the leader of the Hellhounds to bust out a cheesy amusement park ride; or have a tête-à-tête with Hell's first cartographer.

Over the cacophony of engines rumbling and purring, he shouts, "Gear up, Kitty's and Canines! We're all going on a road trip!"

CHAPTER 9

"**A**re you out of your damn mind?" Lowell backs away.

"Lowell--" I take a step closer to him and his eyes widen. He looks a little haggard, coming down off his buzz, but my plan wakes him right up. I guess I've grown immune to the looks of alarm on people's faces when they see me, but it feels different coming from the man I'm trying to save. I may have denied I was not a good person, at least when I first died. I made my bed, my bones are lying in it, but the sting of distrust on Lowell's face is a whole other ball of spit on my demonic grave. "If we are going to get the mark off, we need both you and Zeke."

James' apartment feels like a prison cell with all of us crammed into the living room. Even the walls are gray. It's like, my man James, get a little spunk in your life, know what I'm saying? A little Va Va Voom or something because this is depressing. I've seen the inside of a couple county jails in my days running with Zeke. I think this might be even bleaker because at least in county, there was an end date to the incarceration. But this is James, setting himself up for the long haul of monochromatic despair. Forget black

124

holes of despair, gray is the color of someone who knows they need to stick it out, but it doesn't mean they're happy about it.

"Catriona, you aren't getting it. I'm not going with you because I'm not selling out my own brother."

Well, there's the wrench in the plan I've been forming since this morning. I figured this was going to come up at some point. I was just banking on it not coming up until later. But with Damien and crew tag teaming with us on this rocking ship to crazy-town, we need all hands-on deck if the plan is going to work.

"Lowell, it's not supposed to be you. Zeke is--"

"Trust me, I am well aware of the kind of man my brother turned into." Lowell folds his arms across his chest and leans against the counter jutting out from the tiny galley kitchen. His face hardens and I feel a twinge of sadness. Scout has grown a pair and is walking the line of being a man. Maybe he is what real men should be like. Have convictions. Who cares what they look like? Who cares how much money they make? A man with a moral compass who might teeter on the path but not stray is the kind of man I wished I'd fallen in with.

"Do you have any popcorn, Professor Dudard? This just got interesting." Damien kicks back on the slate couch and crosses a leg over his knee.

Now there's another man with convictions. He deserves to rule Hell. I guess I finally figured out what it was he wants. I'm not sure if it's good or bad though. I guess it doesn't matter since I agreed to sign up for the campaign. So maybe there is fallacy in my logic about what makes a man good. Or maybe not. I might have to rethink this theory, but not right now.

"Damien, shut up." I turn back to Scout.

"Lowell, I get it. You want to protect Zeke. But you must be realistic here. This isn't some fairy tale where everyone gets to live happily ever after in the end. It's a nightmare and maybe, when you wake up on the other side of it, you can come out of the serious tailspin you've been thrown into, after a few decades of therapy. Death and delinquents. It's what we do. I can't offer you the luxury package, just an exchange. Maybe we can just get your mark off, but Zeke is still on limited time." I step toward him again and lower my voice. "As messed up as it is, I don't like it either." I search Lowell's face, trying to convey how Zeke meant something to me, at least for a little while. I understand his pain on some level.

He rubs the back of his head and groans. "Catriona, I promised Gigi I'd take care of him. I've done the best I can. At least, I've kept him alive, but that's as good as it gets with Zeke."

"Yeah, he's like a cockroach. He crawls into some dark hole and doesn't emerge until the heat is off. Maybe cockroach isn't the right word? How about coward?" I spin back around ready to rip Damien a new one. He's pilfered James' bag of chips from the coffee table.

I open my mouth, but someone growls out, "Will you shut up?" Everyone starts the Ping Pong routine between Marty and Damien. So far, he and James have kept their mouths shut, but he takes a step from the kitchen into the living room and addresses Damien before I can rip into him with what I have to say.

"Alright! The old man has a pair. Tell me, Martin O'Keefe, yeah, Hell has your number too. Do you think there is a difference between cockroach and coward because it seems to me like they are one and the same." Damien pops another chip in his mouth and the crunching sound makes me think it might as well be my last nerve.

Gruff but shaggy bear, Marty is destined for the big house with no light at the end of the tunnel? I don't know the man, but the way he has pulled the uncle routine with Lowell is protective enough, he reminds me of a faithful Saint Bernard. More bark than bite. Cap it with standing up for a lowlife like Zeke? I look at Marty in a new light.

Marty's knuckles crack and I'm not sure if it's from arthritis or a veiled threat. Either way, the tension in the room amps up to an oh crap. "The kid's been looking after Zeke for as long as I've known the boys. You can't blame him for having loyalty, no matter how low Zeke has sunk to." Marty's voice is low but fervent. He feels for Lowell and Zeke, like they are his own.

"True, but you know as well as anyone here there's a price to pay for the depths he's sunk to. Whether it is now or not too far down the road, Lowell needs to come to terms with the fact Zeke's reckoning has come. He can either help us find Zeke or continue to stall and then my father sends the rest of his minions after all of us." Damien sits back on the couch with the chip bag in his lap. He picks it up and shakes it, having eaten the last of it. He crumples it up and tosses it on the coffee table.

"I don't owe any of you, anything!" Lowell moves toward Damien, but I step between them when Lowell spouts off.

Doug and Dick are shimmering around the edges, and whether or not Lowell, Marty, and James can see the Hounds glamor is debatable. Leo and Fae step away from the walls they were respectively holding up by leaning against them. I look in the kitchen and see Tabby place a hand on Marty's shoulder, and even Tora turns to protect James, ready to jump in if necessary. I feel bad for James. His face is pale and if he's feeling anything like he did earlier when I flashed my demon goods, he's in for one Hell of a surprise if Doug and Dick pop their inner pooch.

It's trippy to watch. Their eyes are hard to look into to begin with. They are devoid of emotion like they have been trained to emulate gargoyles. But when they begin to shimmer around the edges, it's like looking at the pavement on the highway when it is super-heated. It's hazy.

Barbecued canines aside, I step in to avoid conflict if possible. "You're right, Lowell. You don't owe us anything. But Zeke does and this is much bigger than you or me. You can either help us and in exchange, you get to live, or you can do nothing and stand by and watch as the Underworld comes for both of you. It's a crapshoot, but it's reality. I've been there and now I'm here. I feel--"

"You don't know anything about how I feel." His eyes are stony.

I say nothing. There is no arguing with those kinds of emotions. I know Fiona hasn't ended up like Zeke so she will never be in this mess. Maybe I am undervaluing the price of what one brother might do for another.

"I'm not telling you where he is." Lowell pleads with me after a moment and I wince. He might be standing his ground, but his tone is telling me to try and help. I wish Hell didn't owe him one because I might be inclined to toss him a bone if it were within my power. I begged and no one tossed me a bone until after I was dead. I bet it doesn't taste as good from my side of things as it would for Lowell if I help him out right now.

"Which leaves us right back where we started." Damien stands and walks to us with Charles on his heels.

He has a point. Even if I want to help, I already made my deal with the Devil. I stiffen and Tabby steps in front of Marty as he also makes a move, but Charles moves so fast, none of us see it until Lowell is clutching the side of his neck.

"He bit me!" Lowell staggers into the kitchen. Tora shoves James back and he stumbles into the kitchen, but she immediately dives for a dishtowel and presses it to Lowell's neck.

"Well, how else did you think we were going to get what we needed to track Zeke?" Damien looks genuinely confused and I blink a few times to douse the flames of fury in my eyes.

"Damn it, Damien!" I reach for Lowell who jerks his head away and grimaces. He pulls the towel down and looks at the bloodstain on it. I catch a glimpse of his neck and it's already starting to heal. Incubi must have other abilities than just the blood drinking.

"His twin shares his blood; therefore their souls are connected. I can track him now because we know where Lowell is, so the man in the south whom I can sense must be his brother."

The truth about Charles and how he's useful to Damien has finally come out.

"How far?" I grit.

"A few hours."

"Do you mind if I look, Lowell? I was a hospice nurse." Tora moves in front of Lowell and he slowly lowers the kitchen towel.

"And what did the newbie Hellcat prospect do to become such a naughty kitty cat?" Damien's constant instigating is going to end with my boot up his ass if he doesn't cut it out, but before I can tell him off, Tora looks over her shoulder and answers him.

"I was taking care of a ninety-three-year-old woman who was only being kept alive by her family because they wanted her continued social security checks. She was miserable and in pain so when I went to the hospital to gather weekly supplies, I stole some stuff from one of the pharmacy trays and gave her the option to go out the easy way if she wanted it. I felt so bad I did it and grabbed a cheap bottle of wine after the funeral. I was so drunk, I slipped and fell in the tub when I went to take a bath and the rest is history." She stopped talking and turned back to Lowell. "Whatever is in the incubus' venom is healing you already. You'll live."

Well eff-me, my girl's got some balls finally. "Alright, let's get this show on the road. Damien take your boys and pick up Zeke. Lowell and company will ride with me and we will meet you in New York in two days." I make a start for the door, trying to get this madness out on the open road where it can ooze some of its danger of imploding vibe. There's no use standing around here and waiting for the explosion between the gangs to happen.

"What, you don't want to go find your boy toy?" I don't answer him, but grasp Lowell's arm and turn him to the door. He shakes me off and walks out of the apartment, not having a choice in the fate of his brother. We outnumber him and his friends three to one, but I feel bad for him knowing he can't do anything for Zeke. If it were Fiona-- I push thoughts of my own sister from my mind and the rest of my crew follows grimly. Marty plunks down in the sidecar and Lowell swings his leg over my bike after I get on.

James looks around and Tabby pats her seat and giggles. "You can ride with me, professor! Maybe some of your smarts will seep in while we ride."

"Intelligence doesn't spread through osmosis, Tabby." Fae's annoyance with Tabby is just as apparent as ever.

Leo adjusts in her seat as Tora shifts her weight. We're all riding double and even if I had the desire to pick up Zeke, which I don't, we wouldn't have room to carry him anyway. The ride from the Devil's Canyon back to Salt Lake City was strained enough. Testosterone met bitchiness and the girls and Damien's crew took turns instigating one another on the road. Gangs don't ride together. It just doesn't happen and in the rare instance it does, it is never a pleasant ride. I tried to steer my girls separate, but

Damien was getting his digs in where he could.

The next two days with humans in tow is going to be interesting. My plan is to stop off at a couple of motels. It's strange, even demons need to sleep. Maybe it's recharging for the ruckus we cause.

We ride through the rest of the night and all day the next day. I take solace in the changing scenery. The rich browns and tans of Utah give way to winding roads through the mountain ranges in Colorado. Blue skies meet white-capped summits and basins of crystalline water. As we crest the pass through the Rockies, we ride low gear down into the grasslands on the other side and are met on the highway with green plains as far as the eye can see through Nebraska and Iowa. We stop just outside of Illinois when Fae feels a vibration coming from her sidecar. Some of the bolts attaching it to her bike have come loose and as our crew mechanic, it takes her half an hour to fix it, but it gives Lowell, Marty, and James a chance to stretch.

Tabby gets a kick out of watching them strut around like stiff penguins as the feeling comes back into their extremities. She's snapping pics on her phone. I wonder if Satan's social media pages are about to get lit up. Tora is a little worse for wear herself, not being accustomed to riding so much. But I sneak a peek of she and Leo cuddling near Leo's bike. Looks like Leo might be giving her a booty massage. Lucky bitch. Who doesn't like having their booty rubbed by their main squeeze? I'm not sure when Leo hit her with the loving, maybe during the day when Lowell and I were with the prof, but Tora seems receptive of the attention because I politely look away when they start kissing.

Besides, the rest of us give our bodies a good workout, popping tails and talons in a full body stretch that has us all groaning in ecstasy, and then we hang out next to our bikes. I spot Lowell's profile cast in a silhouette against the sun and make sure Sugar is secure on her kickstand. Poor girl needs a rest herself.

I walk over to where Lowell is standing off to the side of the road. "I wish it could be different Lowell." I try to talk to him reasonably now he's had a chance to process.

"Do you?"

His words are harsh, but they are the truth. Less than two days ago, I wouldn't have given a damn what happened to Zeke. As far as I am concerned, he was the one who murdered me by his actions, not the man who actually pulled the trigger. But hindsight is twenty-twenty. I knew rolling with Zeke was wrong.

" I care because I know how it would be if it were Fiona."

"At least she doesn't have to witness this..." He waves at me and I feel the heat rise in my cheeks.

Since when did he get off being my judge and jury? I turn and walk away. There's no point arguing with him. It's all going down whether he wants it to or not. If he wants to play the hero, fine. I didn't ask for this, but lesson learned. I'm not standing by and letting bad things happen to good people again, even if I'm one of the bad eggs like his brother.

"Fae, you get those bolts tightened down yet? God forbid we lose another one." I eye Marty. Can the old man really be destined for the land of despair? I guess we can never see a snake no matter what camouflage its skin comes in.

"Yeah, boss. One more, geez," she mutters.

I consider doling out the smackdown they are due for bailing on me in the Dog Pound, but instead, I walk it off. We don't have time. Two days to cross country is a long-ass haul and I have a feeling we won't be staying over for a full night when we come across the next motel. It will be doze, dash, and on the way again.

While Fae puts her tools away, I listen to her chatting softly with the professor. He didn't have to come, but like Marty, he fell in line because he was needed and it's what friends do. Even my girls have accepted my decision to make a stand.

I feel a stab of guilt for snapping. None of this mess is any of their problem. They're here out of loyalty to Lowell and me. It's my own doing. Fae laughs at something the professor says and I can't help but wonder in another time or place if she and the professor would have hit it off. She places a premium on intelligence and despite the age difference, he would be exactly her type.

I lean back against my bike and look up at the stars. The sky is a mix of purple fading to midnight blue and I wonder how the Cosmos determines who gets the short straw in life and who gets to stop and make wishes to the Heavens that end up being granted. It sucks when you die and you still don't get answers to some of life's big questions. What's my purpose? How do I fit into it all? People don't consider what happens after the corporeal body stops working. For some of us, it's work as usual. I just can't help but feel here and now, there's something bigger I am supposed to be part of.

I sit back down in my hot seat when I hear Leo start up her bike and I watch as everyone mounts up. I pull back onto the highway once Lowell reluctantly sits back down. I feel like maybe he could loosen up a little on my ribs, but in a standard pissing contest of all time, I say nothing when the pressure starts to hurt a little. I'm not going to get any deader and he needs an outlet for his anger. How many people get the ticking clock of doom for a loved one? It's not like it will be a sweet goodbye either.

We pull into the Stayside Motel in Illinois and take turns crashing out. I don't trust Lowell won't make a run for it; so we sleep in shifts. When I make the announcement, instead of arguing with me, which has gotten him nowhere, Lowell starts to give me the silent treatment. He stares sulkily at the paisley wallpaper and doesn't engage with Leo when she sits at the 1950's orange top and metal legged diner table shoved in the corner. The bathroom is a joke. I don't bother to try the rusted knobs in the yellow stained shower. There are some places too Hellish even for a demon to be in and this is one of them. It's just as well Lowell doesn't talk to me. I've been going steady for almost two days and Leo takes the first shift of watching over him. I roll up my colors and use my jacket as a pillow. I inhale the scent of the leather and close my eyes.

***

I can't distinguish my nightmares from reality. Every waking day is a torture without my freedom.

Slogging away for Satan, I can almost feel the shackles on my wrists and ankles, even as I'm given the liberty to ride free. This nightmare is different though. Have the Drudes caught up with us? I never thought we'd really get away with this without some sort of reprimand. I'm surprised Lucifer hasn't sent more demons before now, but as I stare down at the woman below me from the top of the ledge, I see tracks leading down to her, but a bar is banded across my chest and I can't get loose.

"Fiona!" I struggle, but the more I do, the more the box I am contained within shrinks. Her hair, the same color as mine, is splayed across the tracks. Her face is full of terror. She has similar freckles to my own, but her face is more elfish, where mine is more hardened. I'd recognize her anywhere though. Not by her physical appearance but by the energy that passes between two sisters. I can feel it now. Just as I can feel the box and the smaller it gets, the more my vision narrows, so the only thing I can see is Fiona, bound and gagged at the bottom of the tracks.

"Fiona you have to get out of the way!" I try to wave to indicate she should roll to the side of the tracks because as I scream it, I start to race toward her, closer and closer. I'm going to run right over her. There's no stopping the momentum. I'm going to plow right into her as I fall off the ledge I'm on.

My heart races faster and faster as the speed of the container increases. Wait, I am the container, I think. I think I'm suffering a heart attack as my chest constricts and the bar gets tighter. I can see the green in Fiona's eyes as they widen and I make out the freckles matching my own on her nose and cheeks.

Her red hair is caught in the tracks and just as the container, me, is about to slam into her, I scream again. "Fiona!"

"Trina, wake up. Catriona, you have to wake up." Damien's dark face is above me. He looks so earnest with faint lines of worry on his forehead and around his eyes as he continues to urge me to wake up. "Trina, love, don't let him capture you in a nightmare with his Drudes. Wake up."

Why is Damien being so nice? How did he get here? I look around and there is nothing but a void. Black mist hangs in the air like sheets drying out on a line. I put my hands in front of me, swiping at the mist like I used to when I would get lost in the laundry Mrs. Anderson used to hang out on the line. It's similar to the mist I encountered when I died, but it is denser. The mist is incorporeal and my arms slice through it, sending tendrils of smoke and fog spiraling away from my body. There's no more container barring me and keeping me from Fiona, but she is gone now. Where did she go?

"Damien?" I turn, searching the blackness. He was here. I know he was. I feel eyes watching me as I continue to wade through the veil.

"Wake up, Trina!"

There. He is there, not fifty feet from me. I race to him, calling his name. The bane of my existence is my savior. I reach my hand through the void and he stands there, staring at me. His eyes are so distant like he's here with me, but only in thought. My mind doesn't comprehend this until I reach out and try to touch him and he disappears again. I whirl around gazing into the abyss again. A figure stands about one hundred feet away this time. It isn't Damien though. Is it...

"Fiona?" I race to her, shouting. Is no one in this place real? Am I real? I look down at myself and hug my stomach. I still feel like I'm real. In terms of levels of torture, this one is the surest way to drive someone crazy. I look back up and see Fiona staring at me the same way Damien was.

"Fiona!" I continue to run to her. Somehow she survived the collision or there never was a collision, or what if, I was the never was?

The same thing happens when I reach Fiona and I stop running, staring wildly around, finally understanding what this place is. The Abyss, the place where nothing exists and no one is real. This is the place people go when they have no one to think about them after they die. As if the very thought gives power to the souls who are here, I stop and start seeing shapes in the fog. Profiles appear like shadows around me as I look at the forgotten. They are nameless, faceless souls, but the mere fact someone has remembered they once existed at all is enough to give them cause to rise.

I see Damien now. He's standing next to Fiona, which is peculiar because she should be running from him, terrified. But then I realize why they are here. They think of me. Fiona I can understand. Although with the falling out we once had, I assume she thinks of me with loathing and disgust, but Damien? It is strange the son of Satan would think of me when I'm gone. Why? For that matter, I turn and look at the shapes again, searching. I see them now, the Hellcats. Tabitha, Leona, and Faline. A fourth figure hangs back in the distance, Tora, even the new girl thinks of me when I am carried to this place. It brings me some hope, knowing I won't be forgotten like the rest of the souls here and I understand now why Lucifer hasn't succeeded in completely miring me in this nightmare. He underestimated the power of the people who do remember me.

I run for Fiona again. This time I know when I reach her, touching her isn't the way to rouse myself from this dream. Provoking her memories is. The more I talk to her, make her remember, the stronger I get.

"Fiona! Look at me! Fiona!"

***

"Trina, wake up! Trina!" Someone is shaking me. As I open my eyes and claw at her chest, trying to grab ahold, I realize I am contorted on a bed somewhere. I feel the sheen of sweat on my forehead and I see the rapid rise and fall of my chest as I claw at myself making sure I'm actually here.

"Fiona!"

"I know. You were dreaming." Leo lets go of my wrists as my hands curl in on themselves and I struggle to catch my breath.

"Drudes. The Drudes have caught up with us," I pant. My breath is coming in short bursts.

"What?" Lowell is standing beside the bed and looking down at me. He's trying to hide the concern in his face, but he needs work on his passive face.

"Drudes are demons of nightmares. Satan is sending us a message. He's aware we've flown the coop and he is going to start coming after us," Leo fills him in. "What I want to know is, why were you dreaming about Fiona?" Her eyes flash when she looks at me.

"It's nothing. It was just a dream," I mutter and sit up. My head is splitting and I stumble into the bathroom, slamming the door as I hear Lowell answer her. Seeing my sister again, up close and so personal, is perhaps the hardest part of this waking memory. I usually forget my dreams. There are things in Hell I really don't want to dwell on. But Fiona and Damien? Why was Damien there? Does he think about me that much? I splash water on my face. *Probably only to think of ways he can trap me forever.* I hear Lowell answer Leo's questions and I know I'll have some fire to face later.

"Catriona's sister. What do you think it means?"

When I stand up, I wince and gasp. Then I lift my shirt. My chest felt tight and sore when I got off the bed. I figured it was the memory and residual aspects of the dream, but there is a red line like a bar having been pressed to my chest. It's going to leave a nasty bruise, but message received Lucifer. I yank my shirt back down and push open the door to the bedroom.

"We can't stay here much longer. I think Satan knows about the deal. How rested are Tabby and Fae?"

"Good to go. Tora said James and Marty didn't give them any grief. Trina…your sister?"

"Not now, Leo. Later. What about you though? You good to ride?" I look at the dark circles under her eyes and wonder how much longer she'll be able to push on.

"I'll be alright. The coffee pot over there brews sludge so I'm caffeinated up and good to go."

I pull my colors back on and we leave the motel. The attendant at the front desk is relieved to see us leave. When I'd checked in for two rooms, he looked like he wanted to turn us away, but something on my face must have told him not to push his luck.

He sends an assistant, a young kid, out to check the rooms and when the teen comes back and tells him there has been no damage, he looks mildly surprised.

"We don't get a lot of your type who don't trash the place." He runs the credit card, Satan stamped and issued, and his fingers fumble with the buttons. I lean forward, reading his nametag.

"Aaron, this place is trashy enough. Why waste my energy on something that can't get any worse?" My unrestful sleep has left me in a bad mood and he's pushing the line into my sandbox of rude and detached.

Aaron, being the middle-aged meddler he is, doesn't say anything. He pushes his glasses up on his face and swipes his curly brown hair back from his eyes and hands my card back to me. The little sound on the card machine pings and indicates the charge has been accepted. I wonder how long it will take Lucifer to cancel my card? What bank does the Underworld use? I look at the thin black plastic card with a symbol of some horns on it, the chip and the horns are both stamped in gold. I shove it in my pocket. I decide not to question my luck.

Just as we are pulling out of the Stayside Motel's parking lot, I glance back and see Aaron silhouetted in the doorway. His profile shimmers and then bursts open, revealing a hooded figure with a black abyss of a face. I almost run Sugar off the road, but Aaron, the Drude makes no move to follow us. I kick Sugar into high gear anyway and it takes a good fifty miles and a lot of craning my neck around to make sure he isn't following us. So he's the Drude who sucked me into the nightmare. My girls squint at me and then behind us as we continue to ride. I'll have to fill them in later, but Aaron probably returned to the Underworld to inform Satan he met us on our journey heading east.

Feeling better with each mile I put behind us and with dawn approaching on the second day, we make time as we drive into the northeast of America. It always takes my breath away as we watch the flatlands become spotted with trees and shrubs and develop into thick forests teeming with woodland wildlife. Deer are always my favorite and they are everywhere as we drive through Pennsylvania and make our way east to the coast through southern New York. The one positive in this gig is getting to see how vast this country really is. Normally we would have portal hopped from the Midwest, saving a bit of a drive, but with the travel ban in effect for us wayward types, the drive has been as refreshing as it has been chaotic.

As we enter the outskirts of the city by midafternoon, the stop and go traffic begins to agitate me as all we can do is sit with the rest of the influx of vehicles. It gives me time to start worrying about the big fat set up this feels like with Damien. No doubt this is the perfect opportunity for Damien to rat me out and tell Daddy-O exactly where I'll be and at what time, so he can come get me. And yet, he was there, in my dream. The thing bugging me is this is all his idea. Yakking it up with Dante, getting his errand boy Phil to call in the divine favor. How's this all going to play out? I honestly don't see him playing this one straight, but I just can't see his end game.

The heat of the day is on us as we finally ride up into the parking lot of the New York State Department of Motor Vehicles. It sits halfway between Neptune Ave and Surf Ave. We take the Shell Road Entrance and park at the far end of the lot.

I look around. Figures Damien and crew aren't here yet. My bet on finding wherever Zeke is laying low will be at his Gigi's old camp on the Ogden River in Eden, Utah. Gigi left the camp to Lowell and Zeke when she passed and the brothers took me up there to spread her ashes. The camp is breathtaking and as Heavenly a place as the town it resides in. She owned a modest log cabin on the river surrounded by mountain views and the lake below. The Pineview Reservoir is so vast; it's almost like staring at the ocean.

As Lowell, Marty, and James walk into the DMV for a bathroom break, I'm given the opportunity to catch up with my girls.

"A Drude? You don't think it followed us?" Fae looks back down the street from where we came.

"That's the thing. Drudes can pop up anywhere. As long as there is a sleeping person." I hear the exhaustion in my own voice and see Leo's eyes drooping. She didn't rest at all. I have to think of something that will keep them all awake, just in case the Drude has latched on.

"So, Tora, a hospice nurse, huh?"

Leo's eyes snap open. It's been a long time since she has been interested in another soul. Occasionally, like the rest of us, she picks one up from Limbo, has her fun, and then brings them back upstairs when she's done messing around, no one the wiser the soul ever left Limbo. She turns on her seat to twist around and look at Tora, who shrugs and blushes.

"Yeah, but I wasn't a very good one. As you know."

I think about this. There are very few of us who get the chance at redemption. Sure, she screwed up big time, but it didn't make her a bad nurse.

"I don't know about that. We've all stepped in it, but if our intentions weren't at least lined up with a smidgen of good, we wouldn't be in this gig. Might as well tell you now; the man we are hunting down is my ex. He used to sell drugs while I stood by and watched him. I told myself he was just doing it to take care of us. But I made no move to stop him." I bite my lip, waiting to see if Tora will make a beeline for the exit. Or rather, away from us and back to Auntie J to renegotiate her terms.

"I was a pharmaceutical clinician. I ran tests with drugs that would have helped with cancer, but the results came back with more negative effects than positive ones. I kept on with my research, hoping it would yield better results. I ignored the fact the patients who signed up for the tests were terminal anyway, but even my efforts to save thousands didn't make it right." I gape at Faline, as do the rest of my girls. We never have the share your feelings circle. Tora plays with her t-shirt and nods, but I can see in her eyes the relief. We are our own worst judges. Even with judgement having passed on us already, we still have to live the afterlife for the things we did.

"I stole from my mob boss to pay for my sick brother's medical treatments. I was a hitwoman for a London syndicate and Higgins never respected me as a woman. It didn't make killing all those crooks ok, but he never paid me what he paid the others, and Gavin needed treatment outside Britain's medical capabilities, which means it had to be paid for. Higgins found out what I did and I kicked it on this bike when I was on the run from him." Leo pats her bike and Tora jumps, looking down at the machine under her. I suppress a grin as does Tabby and Fae. Leo pets her bike like I do Sugar. Besides our gang, they are our tickets to freedom from time to time.

All four of us turn and look at Tabby who is braiding the leather straps on her handlebars like she would if it was a prized horse about to enter a dressage show. She looks up.

"What?"

"It's share time, Tabby. We're bonding with the pledge." Fae's tone is as dry as the late afternoon heat.

"Oh. I was a prostitute." Tabby winks at Tora who looks uncomfortable. Everyone waits. Tabby continues to grin. She's like a puppy with no morals. Adorable and you want to scold her, but you know she doesn't know any better for humping the pillow.

"Tabby had it rough growing up. She turned tricks to survive."

Tabby doesn't seem to take offense to this. She once told me she felt no qualms about it because she did what she had to. I don't blame her. Survival makes people do what is necessary. I do have to wonder while she's working to atone for her sins if her heart is really in it. She's taking a different soul to her room most every night. It kind of feels like offsetting the books somehow, but it's between her and Auntie J, I suppose.

Thinking of Auntie J makes me angry. I can't believe she's just thrown the towel in and not stepped in to help fix this one. I don't bother looking at my phone again. As I look at my girls and see all their vulnerabilities shared in between the circle, I realize the ones who have my back when shit gets real are right here. Newbie or not, Tora's proving she can hold her own. Leo's as loyal as they come and Fae is the smarts of the group. Putting us in check with her practicality. Tabby? Well, I guess Tabby is my comic relief. Each of us is unique and brings something to the fold we all need. I can't have Fiona back in my life; that will never happen. But I have them and it's everything I need. I realize with a start, when Damien grants their pardons after all this is done and they go to Heaven while I stay behind, how much I am going to miss them. I don't see myself bonding with Charles. Or trusting Doug and Dick. Maybe I'll fall in tight with the kid though. Damien, well, I suppose there is a level of trust needing to be built to co-rule if we survive this, but it's going to take a long time. But my gang is going to be one of those places in my head where I stow the heartache and pain for a while until I can take the memory of each of them out, relish it, and remind myself someday, if I ever get out of my stint ruling Hell, I will be able to join them in Heaven. It's a nice thought. A hopeful thought and one I'm not sure why I am entertaining. Maybe ruling Hell will help me work through my atonement faster. Maybe it's like becoming a member of the frequent flyers club. The more hands on I am, rather than ride out, do the job and collect the mark and come home at the end of the day-then it means I rack up the points quicker. Maybe teaching all the other bad souls of Hell why they have been so naughty, will help me reach my goal faster. I've never been one of the PTA types, Parent/Teacher Association, but I guess someone has to step up and do it. Maybe my ticket has finally been called to take on the added responsibility. I'm down for it if it means the chance of time served comes a lot quicker. I'll have to ask Damien to hash out the details later.

We all fall into a stupor after Tabby tries to dish on some of the details of her Johns. No one is so desperate for bonding we need to know how size doesn't matter, or in her case, apparently it does. I let my head loll onto my chest, but don't want to fall asleep and keep jerking awake and looking up. Lowell, James, and Marty return and sit at the beat-up green picnic table reserved for DMV employees on their lunch. They must figure seeing all of us loitering here, eating in the breakroom is a good idea.

The parking lot of the DMV shimmers in the afternoon heat and my eyes begin to deceive me. I see the effect a lot on the highway and the open road out west in the desert, but here with the smell of ocean air blowing in over Staten Island, although it is warm, it is by no means an inferno of heat.

I should have known my eyes weren't playing tricks on me. In one instant I am staring at an empty parking lot, save for the poor schlub who has to lock up at five-fifteen on a Friday night, and in the next moment, five monstrous motorcycles are rolling into the parking lot just having appeared from the haze.

I hear Tora chuckle at the reaction of the DMV guy's face as he rubs his eyes. Must have been a long week, poor dude. He looks around and then spots me and the girls and all but trips over himself as he makes a beeline for his car.

For a man who is supposed to uphold the laws of the road, he peels out of the lot faster than a monkey on a banana.

I turn my attention back to the Hounds as they ride up. In the garage down under, their bikes are impressive for sure, but out on the open road, it has never occurred to me just how terrifying they really are. It's as if Satan picked their rides based on their personalities. The Ducati, the Italian bike screams arrogant, as is its rider Charles. The gothic style hearse attached to the back of a nondescript black Harley is being driven by Doug and an elaborate silver coffin can be seen through the glass panels on the side of the hearse as he circles around. The only reason I know it's Doug is because word got around about a year ago he attacked one of the Satyrs and used it as a chew toy. As a punishment when Charles came on board, Satan made him trick out his own ride so Charles' coffin could be towed around for the long hauls. Being the ass he is, Charles went Hella fancy, which is the exact opposite of Doug's plain and simple vibe. The only thing I haven't been able to figure out is, no matter how much I taunt him about it, no one will tell me what the Satyr did to piss him off so much to be provoked.

"That is beyond freaky." Lowell leans into my ear and I nod.

"So, talking to me now?" I turn my head slightly.

"I might as well. This is all going down whether I want it to or not. Just how do they not draw attention to themselves toting around a vampire coffin?"

"That's the point, Lowell. They do draw attention. They don't give a damn. Would you walk up to them and start something if you didn't know they were demons?"

"Oh, Hell no."

"Point made."

I watch as Dick, who can almost be Doug's twin, rides in on his BMW bike. The only reason he marred the side of his bike with the logo of a Hellhound skull is probably because he was ordered to by the higher-ups.

I find I am happy to see Phil on his own wheels. It doesn't have the Hounds' logo on it yet, but they must have picked up the spare bike on the way when they portal hopped through the garage. There'd been nothing stopping Damien from returning home. It took Lucifer a couple of days to figure out the coup de grace going on under his nose. So the cross-country trip would have been easy for Damien and his crew.

The small navy-blue Enduro is the perfect size

for Phil, and although I don't have a maternal bone in my demonic body, I'm glad Damien didn't try to force him on a ride he can't handle. I'm still trying to get past the idea of a teenager rolling with a biker gang, but there's nothing I can do about it. He'd resent me for stepping in and end up in a world of trouble and pain if I tried. Demons are the worst bullies.

Damien is the last to ride through on his Boss Hoss with the V8 motor mounted to the frame. It's loud and annoying like the demon himself, and I find it weird he is bringing up the rear. Gang leaders don't ride in the back. It should have been Phil's spot.

I catch the relief in his eyes, the tension lines slacken and his pinched lips loosen ever so slightly when he sees us sitting here. I think it's strange because I didn't know he cared so much. What's his game?

He pulls through the line and kills his motor, dousing the flames and not really caring about the gawkers around us and the tourists on the streets who just caught an eye-full of Hell. This is New York, baby. I love the people in this city who don't give a damn enough to care. As much as I hate driving here when we have to pick up marks, flaming motorcycles with sidecars and hearses aren't the strangest things any of the natives have seen. Human behavior is often a heck of a lot weirder.

"You good?" Damien's question is directed at me and I have a feeling he's asking about more than the trek cross-country. I don't fancy a trip down memory lane back into the abyss, but just looking into his eyes, which are their serene blue today, makes me feel better somehow, knowing he was there. Weird. I didn't know he could make me feel better. I don't want the other's picking up on my grateful emotes though.

"Where's Zeke?" I feel Lowell stiffen behind me and everyone looks around like they are expecting Zeke to magically appear on the back of someone's bike.

"The only place he would hold still." Doug tosses his head behind him. He can't be serious. I scramble off Sugar, almost knocking her and Lowell over.

"Damien! You weren't supposed to kill him already. We have to switch the marks!" I start toward him, but he holds up his hands.

"Easy, Catriona, he's not dead. Just contained. The little jackass didn't want to stay on the back of the bike. He tried to pull a tuck and roll. So I put him the only place he wouldn't escape."

I stare at him as my mouth drops. He put a living person in a coffin to transport him cross-country? He's crazier than I am. Although, it explains why he was able to get a living person through the portal without catching fire. Still, even as a demon, there has to be some part of this that's unethical. I run over to the hearse and slap my palms against the glass. How does he know Zeke hasn't suffocated yet? I look for a latch, a hinge, anything which will get me into the hearse and get the coffin open. When I don't see it, I turn back around.

"Open the coffin, Damien." I pinch the bridge of my nose, wondering if we are about to find Zeke suffocated to death lying beneath the lid. I never could figure how vampires in movies could punch a hole in them and then climb up through six feet of dirt. It just doesn't logically make sense. It would be an easy way for Zeke to go, but would make this whole fiasco an even bigger mess than it already is.

Damien walks over to the coffin and slides the glass panel open, apparently the hearse is spelled somehow. I squint and see silvery runes running through the panel. The cool air wafts out of the hearse and tells me at least Zeke won't be dead from heat stroke. It must act like the sidecar on Fae's bike, able to transition souls and acclimate the climate within to the needs of the person it contains. Damien then leans over as I feel his eyes on my face, but I watch as he releases a latch on the outside of the coffin. The silver latch clicks and a popping noise sounds as the seal on the lid releases.

Everyone waits, holding our breaths as Damien reaches over to push the lid up. Most coffins don't need a lock on the outside, the inhabitants aren't going anywhere, but when dealing with incubi, one can never have enough security keeping them under lock and key. I refuse to look at him, not ready to thank him for pulling me out of the Abyss. It's easier to be mad at him. He has broken every law of ethics this side of mankind. Even human prisoners have more rights than being locked away, alive in a coffin. He better hope Zeke's worst nightmare isn't being buried alive, because if a Drude hitched a ride on this one, I'll shove it so far up Damien's--

Damien doesn't get a chance to open the lid because Zeke comes busting out of the coffin.

The only thing I can think is he resembles a shrieking banshee. It isn't a pleasant sight. The banshees are the ones who inform Auntie J someone is about to die so she can tell Damien to go mark them,and then subsequently yours truly and company steps in to go and collect. Hell really is a well-oiled machine sometimes. The banshees are a spirit more than a demon. The pale complexion stands out about them the most. And the shriek. Zeke has both going on right now as he trips over the edge of the coffin and lands on the blacktop on his face.

I wince, seeing the road rash he gets as a result and when he rights himself, he pivots from side to side, cussing Damien and his crew out.

"Well, there's one I've never heard. I'm pretty sure doing those acts with my Mother is illegal, even by Hell's standards." Damien folds his arms over his chest.

I wait for it. The moment when Zeke spots Lowell and me standing there. He's so pissed off he's been kidnapped by demons, or terrified, or both, he hasn't noticed us yet. Seeing him is a punch in the soul I wasn't been ready for. I feel like if I open my mouth right now, I'll be shrieking just as loudly as he is hollering.

"Where are we? What do you want with me?" Zeke spins around like a mini tornado. His face is sweaty and even with the supernatural air conditioning, adrenaline would make him clam up pretty profusely, as is evident on his beet-red face.

It's at this moment he sees Lowell and I standing here, waiting for him to calm down when he really blows the lid off his top.

"Lowell? C...C...Catriona?"

Lowell mimics Damien's stance and I give

Zeke a cheeky wave. As he looks around at all of us, his eyes widen, and his face goes from beet-red to pale and his eyes roll back in disbelief right before he faints. It's like watching a bad 90's cartoon, when the character would swoon in slow-motion and fall to the floor. It seems like the thud of his body as it falls to the pavement takes forever, before it lands right next to the coffin.

CHAPTER 10

I send Tora for a bottle of cold water across the street from the DMV. She jogs back quickly, having grabbed two bottles from the man wheeling the trolley cart selling hot dogs and pretzels on the boardwalk. Carts like it are on every street corner in the city and when she gets back, I pop the cap on one and start pouring it over Zeke's face. It takes half a bottle before I get a reaction.

His face twitches and I give him an extra dousing when his eyes blink open. I've never been a sadist, but with the rapid blinking reflex going on, I figure it couldn't have been very pleasant getting a face full of icy water and it makes my twisted heart happy to get a jab in. My emotions rage in a battle between wishing I could crawl into the pavement and become one with the cement and wishing I could pulverize his already battered face into the black top some more.

I sit back on my heels and study his face. It never occurred to me, even as identical twins, how different he and Lowell are. Lowell's face has an aged innocence look to it. Like he's seen some shit, but he can still find the happy in life. Zeke's is twisted into an eternal sneer. Like he's caused the shit and he just doesn't care.

It's been a couple of years, but looking into his eyes, which are identical to Lowell's, the only difference is the light and hope in Lowell's. It is still a kick to the gut though.

"Zeke," I murmur. I don't bother showing him my true colors. No need to. I'm sure Damien and crew gave him a pants-crapping preview of the paranormal to come so seeing my dead face is shock enough. No need to add whiskers to the mix.

"You're dead," he whispers.

"You and your brother are so astute."

"But...how?"

"You telling me you don't remember your suppliers rolling up into our home looking for you and getting a face full of me? You know what, never mind. It's irrelevant now. No time to explain the boom-I'm-back-baby! Just roll with it. We have an appointment with another dead dude." I stand and turn my back, trying to hide the emotions on my face. Seeing him is double the kick to the psyche, as it was to see Lowell. The memories, the good, the bad, and what the eff all come rushing back, and if he thinks he just had a shock, it's nothing compared to the anxiety going on all up in my head. I'm offended, right? I mean, who wouldn't be if their ex got them killed then didn't even have the decency to show up to the funeral? The one emotion really digging its nasty little claws in is the hurt though. Even after everything he did, there is a small part of me still caring whether his end is pretty much nigh. I feel the sting in my eyes I swore when the day came of his reckoning, I wouldn't feel, and it pisses me off my emotions are like, "Nope! Tricked you!"

I avoid making eye contact with Damien as I pass him and I let his boys close in around Zeke so he doesn't make a break for it. I pocket the key to my bike and walk past Lowell. His face is chock full of compassion, which is going to be problematic when we pull the switcheroo out from under the mark of damnation rug. Of course, he feels for his brother, no matter how much of a scumbag he is. Thinking about siblings makes me think about Fiona. I wish...no. I can't do this to myself right now. I have my girls, each with their quirks to fill the void. Yet, there will never be a force on this plain or any other that can fully make up for the sibling bond. Leo pats me on the back as I walk past her to Sugar. Tabby has the decency to put her phone down for two seconds and Tora looks like she's about to pull another hugger, but Leo puts her arm out to s   top her. Fae's jaw tightens and I see the concern in her eyes, but the curt nod is all the reassurance I need she's there and she's got my back.

I shake my head, clearing my mental compass. There's no use heading down the path of emotional overload, so instead, I opt for heading to the boardwalk on Coney Island, which is just around the block on Shell Ave. I bang a left after the Aquarium and hear the thud of the boots from the rest of the party behind me. I don't stop to look back and see what's up. The looks on the faces of the tourists and the small family groups are enough to tell me we are as out of place here as a rabid pack of hyenas at a petting zoo.

Sounds and smells assault my senses. I smell the combination of greasy, fried food and my mouth waters when I see the cartons of French fries and plates of fried dough sprinkled with confectioners' sugar. I haven't been to a carnival in years. I could spend hours sampling the various things to eat. The neon lights from the rides flash brilliantly on the horizon in front of me and the faintest hint of ocean air blows in to mingle with the baked stench of body odor and rotting amusement park food in the many trashcans. Ah, Eau d'Brooklyn. There's a reason for the "I Love New York" signs everywhere. I hear the screams of delighted-yet-terrified ride goers on the Cyclone rollercoaster. The irony hits me. We are endeavoring to steal an amusement park ride to get back into Hell. A thought occurs to me and I turn around to confront Damien.

"Hey, how come you were able to ride through a portal at the DMV?" Everyone stops and stares at me like I've gone insane.

"Is this relevant in the middle of an amusement park?" James is the one to look around in alarm at the parents who are beginning to usher their kids away from our group as fast as they can.

"Yes. Why do we need to go steal an amusement park ride if there is a portal right back there?" I don't know why I am being so irrational, but it seems important. Either that, or I am needing to grasp onto something which makes sense to me because seeing my ex-boyfriend has sent me for a head spin.

"Apart from most of New York being on a hotspot, you must have endured the wait at a DMV when you were alive, Catriona?"

Damien has a point, those lines were sin and

evil wrapped up in forty-five minutes to an hour of my life lost, but I turn back around and keep walking. I feel the memories of Zeke creep in. I missed the look in his eyes, the detached one when he first met me on campus when I tried out the good life. The straight and narrow hadn't been my deal though. He was the first one to get me into the passion for motorcycle riding and one day when he was on campus, I couldn't resist when he offered me a ride. Just once, just to see how freeing it was.

By the time I'd tried to hop off the Zeke ride, it was too late in more ways than one. With an impish smile that didn't reach his eyes and the freedom from the Anderson's it meant I didn't have to adhere to the rigidity of their household if I left, Zeke caught me like a rabbit in a snare. Soft, fluffy, and innocent to start, but the few years we were together, his actions had skinned me and tanned my hide into the hardened shell of the woman I became. It was around that time I began enjoying the feel of leather. It would protect me against the road rash of regret every time I questioned Zeke about his actions or the validity of his "I-love-you's." I'd developed a love for having a thick skin and keeping the softness inside where it couldn't get hurt. Which was probably why when he began dealing right in front of me and not trying to hide it from me anymore, I kept the vulnerable parts that knew it was wrong wrapped in the cracked and toughened skin on the outside and never let them out where Zeke could see them.

I shake my head, letting my little hamster tuck the memories away again on the miniature wheel. They'd spun out of control and off track as I walked, but bringing myself back to the present, I focus on my surroundings.

My crew is flanking me left and right, with Doug and Dick grasping Zeke under the arms and guiding him along. Lowell, Marty, and James are in the middle of our group, with Phil and Charles flanking them and Damien, still bringing up the rear. I continue walking toward Coney Island. I look around at the various rides and food carts, wondering where in all this madness we are supposed to meet up with the renowned Dante, but I stop when I realize I have no idea where to head next.

Damien circumvents the group and I walk next to him in silence as he weaves in and out of the tourist groups. We walk through the park and exit at the rear, walking out on the boardwalk where I stop and stare at the bay. The blue water reminds me of the illusion cast on the open highway where I think if I just go a little farther, I'll be able to meet the place where the sky meets the earth, but the horizon always jumps when I get to the spot where I thought the two realms connected. It's why I love the open road and the ocean. I feel like I could go on forever and never stop. It was the one wish I had for my soul, but now I worry with my deal with Damien, I won't get the beauty of Heavenly eternity. Some souls in Hell are destined for eternal torture, and some eventually fade and blink out, their energy no longer able to sustain their existence. I wonder if in one hundred years, one thousand, I will completely lose my will.

"You won't. It's not who you are, Catriona." Damien whispers the words so softy, I should be the only one able to hear them, but it's debatable with

Hellhounds who have supernatural healing trailing us.

I jump in my skin. "Can you read minds?" No sugar coating it if he can.

"No, but it's the wistful way you look at the ocean. I've seen it on your face a couple of times now."

He has? When? Where? Has he been following me? "Why did you help me in the Abyss?" I figure we might as well have this out now. Trust between partners and all. But if he has been following me--

"Because you needed help."

"You aren't the helpful type. Can you see why I'm waiting for the other shoe to drop here? So, what gives?"

Damien doesn't answer me but stops at a hot dog stand. An old man with a long, wrinkled face looks up and grunts. His beard blows around the side of his chin and I want to reach out and pull it back into place because just looking at it makes me hot and itchy. Don't get me wrong, a man rocking some scruff or a well-trimmed goatee gets me going for sure, but his is wiry looking and reminds me of one of those scrub brushes for dishes in the sink.

"How many?" the old man asks. His Italian accent is so thick it takes me a moment to understand what he is saying. Then I notice the sign on the side of his cart. Dante's Dogs.

"Are you kidding me?" I look around at everyone else who looks just as shocked. James looks like he wants to cry. It's hard seeing a fellow scholar, a starving artist, when life has them so run down, they have to give up the dream. Except, Dante has been dead a long time so the hot dog stand is just a ruse.

"Alright, Dante, cut the crap. We came here for some info on how to get back into the big house." I cross my arms as the scent of overcooked, processed meat hits me in the face when he opens the lid to the steamer.

"Hey, lady, you gonna order a hot dog or not?" His hazel eyes twinkle when he asks and Damien accepts two from the old man. He moves slowly, his hands curled in on themselves from severe rheumatoid arthritis. No wonder he never went on to write another bestseller of his time. Judging by the state of those fingers, he probably lost the capacity to hold a quill. At least he isn't offended by our abruptness, but I figure it might do me some good to play nice.

"Sorry. Not hungry. You just weren't what I was expecting is all." I scuff my boot on the pier as two teenage girls walk up to the stand and order a dog each. Coconut and pineapple suntan oil wafts thick in the air and the bleach blond whispers something to her brunette friend and both giggle behind their sunglasses. They sashay back down the boardwalk as I whisper, "Down boy," to Damien.

"Eh, forget about it!" Dante raises his hand and then circles around the stand and begins walking down the pier toward the park's maintenance sheds.

"You aren't going to just leave your cart, are you?" Tora looks distraught at the thought of someone walking off with Dante's livelihood.

Dante looks back at it and shrugs. "It was never mine, Mia Cara."

She turns back and a man walks up to it, having come from the direction of the public bathrooms. He's wearing a red and white apron with a nametag, Dante with a picture of a flaming hot dog on the front of the apron. I chuckle and continue following the old Italian. The man stops outside the maintenance sheds on the boardwalk and points to one in the back and looks like it hasn't been unlocked in a few years. The navy-blue paint on the sides of the building is beginning to chip and the lock is lying rusted against the white slats of the vehicle bay.

"That one."

I turn around, noting the security who have been trailing us since we walked into the park. Whatever Doug and Dick said to Zeke when they escorted him between them was ensuring he keeps his mouth shut because Zeke hasn't tried to run or call for help. It may have helped he was trying to catch Lowell's eye the entire time, but whatever Lowell is feeling, he isn't making eye contact with Zeke. Emotions are running high everywhere.

"We can't do it in broad daylight." Damien nods at my assessment and Dante presses a key into my palm. His withered hands feel like paper on my skin, and the curled fingers feel like twigs, clawing at my palms.

"I'll wait at the Italian Ice place on the corner of West 15th Street and Surf Ave. It is too hot out here." With that, he turns and begins hobbling off.

I study the key in my palm. There's no use chasing after him, he won't be able to help us lift the pieces of the ride anyway. The key is just as rusted as the lock on the door and I wonder if it will break off in the lock when we try to open it. I'm also wondering how the heck we're going to get an entire amusement park ride out of storage, without anyone noticing. Before I get a chance to ask anyone if they have any light bulb moments about our problem, Officer Full-of-Himself and his partner Officer Awkward decide to buck up on some courage and question the sketchy looking biker gang about what we are doing.

"Problem here?" Officer F.O.H clears his throat. His question would have some more weight behind it if his voice hadn't cracked. His partner hikes up his pants, drawing our attention to his hip holster.

"Beat it, kid." Charles steps up and I elbow Damien. Now is not the time for the incubus to work his mojo.

"Charles, that's not how we treat the officers of the law." Damien starts laying the charm on thick and I'm still too preoccupied with how to commit grand theft to pay attention to how he handles getting us out of being criminally suspicious. I've spent time in the clink; anything they can nab us on would be a misdemeanor, if human prisons could actually hold us anymore. We'd still be out on bail within an hour. I do catch a snippet of the conversation though.

"Can't a motorcycle club enjoy a stroll on the boardwalk? We aren't harming anyone." Ok, so Damien's going the diplomatic route.

"You're scaring the tourists," the officer says.

"Yet I don't see how their discrimination and profiling is relevant to us being here."

Both the officers play the fish out of water routine, sucking on air like they think it will help them inhale some answers. "Just move it along,"

Officer Awkward finally commands.

What gets me is neither one of them thinks to ask Zeke if he is ok. This is clearly one of those situations where a man being manhandled by two ugly brutes is cause for concern, but the problem with society is, it is so focused on appearance, it doesn't pay attention to the problem right at hand. Not that I care.

I walk to where Leo and the girls are standing. If anyone can pull a heist, it's Leona. She ended up in the slammer for that very reason, although her Robin Hooding constituted paying her brother's medical treatments so even Hades took a hit to the sympathy bone on that one.

"You my girl on this?" I look into her eyes, hating seeing the confliction in the depths. Just like I'm trying not to turn the other cheek, she's working the, thou shalt not steal, debt off. I'm asking her to do the very thing I am; shun the sanctions of Satan.

"You need one of those moving trucks. Probably one you can rent by the day and return it anywhere in the U.S.," she muses. She was caught skimming the books, but with her cleverness, I'm sure Higgins, her former employer had her pull a heist or two. It seems rude to ask though. How is it, demons who are feared for their strengths are suddenly standing on a boardwalk in New York about to employ them for a cause for good? This whole thing seems like an exercise in hypocrisy somehow.

"My thoughts exactly." At least we agree to be hypocrites together.

"There's a rental company just up the street from the DMV."

It's a good thing Fae is more astute than I am. I didn't noticed it on the walk in. Those big orange and white trucks serve one purpose when I'm riding the road; to piss me off. Nearly half the time, the person who rented it doesn't know how to drive it and the other half are the paid drivers of the company and they don't give a rat's ass about their, "how's my driving" sticker on the bumper.

"Anyone know how to drive one?" I look at my crew and when I get blank stares, I resign myself to turn to Damien and company. No one here is willing to give up their bike's, which leaves James, Lowell, Zeke, and Marty. I don't think Zeke and Lowell are in the mood to help us help them get to Hell, so that leaves James and Marty.

"I hauled back in the day," Marty steps forward.

"Illegal immigrants don't count," Charles states.

"Damien, do you tell all your boys who is marked for damnation?" There's no use arguing with Charles so I turn on the one person who is responsible for his quip.

"It's our job, Catriona. Marty is an exceptional case, just like you and your girls. Who knows, maybe Daddy will grant him a pardon, as he did with you, or not. Not unless we overthrow him anyway. I have a feeling your invitation for atonement has been revoked."

I'm about to open my mouth and insert my foot when Marty says, "I don't regret giving those kids a ride to a new, better home. Legalities aside, it don't mean I don't have the skills to drive the truck."

He's got a point. I knew I didn't argue with Lowell about the ride along from the bar to begin with. Pats on the shoulder to me. It also makes me feel better. At least someone got some licks in. I'm tired of being beat on by the Hounds.

"Alright, cool." Marty's growl is resolute. He would make a badass TomHellcat if I can beat Damien to him first.

"Not cool! Marty, you can't--" Lowell pushes Charles aside who snarls at him.

Damien waves his hand and Charles' jaw snaps shut. At least he has a leash on the dude. Even if it is a short one.

"I told your Gigi I'd do right by you, Lowell. Your brother made his choices. I'm not going to let her down now. It ain't right. Zeke's gonna have to pay like we all do someday. But I'm not letting you take the fall for it." Marty's voice is low and earnest.

"Me either." James steps in and now don't we have a big old boardwalk bonding going on?

I begin walking back to the DMV. There's not a lot Zeke and Lowell can do to stop the plan to get back into Hell, but the further I walk away, the louder I hear Zeke's protests. His whining is a sure-fire way to get under my skin and I have so much to deal with right now, I just can't listen to it.

"Hey, boss. Once we get the truck, what's next in the plan?" Fae jogs up to my right.

"Tabby's going to play her part with those two officers we had the pleasure of meeting." My plan is coming into focus. It's a risky one, but at least I have one. Dress up like an officer then who is going to question law enforcement removing something? Not unless they want to get busted themselves.

"Really?" Tabby looks excited and I'm pretty sure the fact she doesn't have the look of regret, indecision, and self-loathing like the rest of us do, means she should have a one-way ticket to the circle of Lust. She's got her reasons for doing what she did as a prostitute, just like the rest of us who go to bed at night with our motivations; but damn, girl, lasso the libido.

"Yeah. We need their uniforms."

Tabby's eyes light up and she hikes up her already way too short shorts and cups her chest, fluffing her fun so when she skips down the boardwalk in front of us and approaches the officers, I bear witness to modern feminism at its finest. Can't judge her if she's having fun and accepting herself the way she is, right?

As I turn back onto the street and walk to the truck rental company store, I feel like this whole fleece is being committed in the name of farcical fun. It's also how I end up riding as the front escort of a rented moving truck on the highway to Maine. Once there, we will find one of the most secluded portals to the Underworld existing in the U.S. Our party consists of a stolen amusement park ride, two hostage twin brothers, a theology professor, a smuggling truck driver, a rheumatic prophetic poet, and two rival motorcycle gangs from Hell escorting the whole ensemble from the rear.

Life may be a highway, but riding it all night long with this much anxiety is starting to chafe.

CHAPTER 11

We have to pull Tabby out of a vortex of passion and lust. Not something I really want to be doing on such a nice night, but I should have predicted this might happen, given her proclivities. When midnight rolls around, the whole party is standing in the parking lot of the DMV waiting for Tabby to get back with a couple of capered cop costumes. I begin to get worried when she still hasn't turned up. I mean, I know the idea of a threesome is the new vanilla sex, but there's getting down and dirty with your job and then...yeah.

"Who wants to draw straws to go and pull her out?" I turn to everyone. Queue the awkward foot shuffling. It's been strange enough standing juxtapose between Lowell and Zeke, knowing I should be talking to Zeke and I should be apologizing to Lowell and also knowing they should be talking to each other. Communication is clearly not our forte. What the heck am I going to say to either one of them? "Hey, thanks for tagging along on our nefarious plan. Hopefully only one of you ends up dead, but it will most likely be both of you?" It's not exactly the most encouraging topic of conversation to bring up.

Fae spends her time making sure her bike is

secured. With the bolts loose on the ride over to the East Coast, the last thing we need is to lose Zeke out of the sidecar before we can get the mark switched from him to Lowell. I don't think we're going to get him back in the coffin without making a scene and we don't want to draw more attention to ourselves than we already have.

Twice now, police cruisers driving down the street have slowed and given us the stink eye for being in the parking lot. But since there's no sign declaring 'no loitering,' we haven't been doing anything wrong. Dick and Doug make sure Zeke is well aware if he indicates in any way there is something amiss, they'll make doggy treats out of him. There is some teeth-baring and low-key macho growling which, queue the eye rolls.

"I'll go and collect her," Damien says.

"You'd just end up joining them and the last thing we need is to be standing around here for another hour. Anyone else?"

"Catriona, please give me credit where it is due. Only an hour?" He winks at me and it's decided.

I toss my keys to Leona in case anyone needs to move Sugar and begin walking back to the Boardwalk.

I focus on the task at hand, not really wanting to see my girl in the buff in the middle of the element, but we really do need to get going. The last I'd seen Tabby as I walked away, she was talking with the officers just outside a small communications center. It's probably a small mobile unit, which works in tandem with the precinct down the road, but I am willing to bet the party started there and Tabby may or may not have taken it to one of the storage facilities. Ugh, why am I about to commit one of the worst sins known to mankind, coitus interruptus?

I hear footsteps behind me and turn around to find Damien walking up the sidewalk to join me.

"I've got this. Go make sure the troops don't tear each other apart." I turn away from him.

"I have no doubt you can make everyone fall in line, Catriona. The problem is I can sense my father's presence here."

It makes me take pause. More Drudes? "What are you talking about? We're all demons. Of course, you can sense us." I look around like I am about to see Satan himself slink out of the shadows, but when I look up and see Damien frowning in the direction of the police kiosk, I have to ask. "What is it?"

My stomach lurches when he begins running to the kiosk. I glance over my shoulder and see Charles running up to us too. I feel like it is never a good omen when an Incubus looks worried. His face is pinched and his eyes are fixated on the opening at the end of the street where it meets the boardwalk.

Sand lightly blows down the street at us. It makes me think of waves washing up at the far end of the beach when the tide comes in. It creeps closer and closer and I just know if we touch it, the effect of whatever is about to happen will sweep over us as vast as the ebb and flow of the ocean.

"Will someone tell me what is going on?" My words come in short clips as we sprint down the street. I knew smoking back in Limbo was bad for my health. Charles has caught up to me and we sprint to join Damien, but we slow to a jog now and I have this feeling like I really don't want to see what's at the end of this street, but I know whatever it is, Tabitha is in there and I have to get her out. She didn't ask to do this; I volunteered her for the job.

"Charles, I will handle him. Go back and tell the others to take the truck directly to the storage facility. There's no cause to worry about who sees you now." Damien's nose crinkles and he shakes his head like he's trying to get rid of a mental block.

"I can handle--" Charles starts to say.

I feel like Tora with the whole lot of clueless going on.

"I said go. He has power over you." Charles stops and stiffens then begins walking back to the waiting ensemble.

"And don't touch the sand!" Damien calls to his back.

"Why?" I ask, even despite my hesitancy to walk on it myself, I wonder what will happen. Then I think about Leona's part in all of this. If she gets caught stealing again, it will be on me both here in the realm of humanity and Hell. I advocated for Leo and my other girls to be pardoned; I need to keep my promise. With Damien changing the plan, I don't see how I can.

"Wait just a minute. If you're going to change the plan then--" I grab Damien's arm and spin him to me, stopping his progress to the pier. He looks at my hand on his bicep and I drop it. It's confusing because just for a moment, the briefest of seconds, I care about what he might be facing at the end of the street. Why though? Men are not high on my list of priorities, but Damien saved me. Is this why I am inclined to return the favor? His eyes are kind and I'm doubly confused as to what is going on when he smiles at me. His tone, however, is full of concern.

"My father has sent the one person who can control Tabby because of her vices. Your subtle plan has backfired. We should have taken the ride and left immediately instead of hatched an intricate scheme giving Hell time to catch up to us. When are you going to learn, Catriona? Satan doesn't need to follow the rules. He can be as blasé as he wishes."

"Who did he send Damien?" I can feel my cheeks get hot. I hate him calling me out on my one iota of decency in my demonic demeanor.

"Asmodeus."

I clench my fingers that were just gripping his arm. Asmodeus. One of the princes of Hell. One of Damien's uncles in a sense. The demon in charge of the circle of Lust.

"Damn it." I glance at the beach and bite my lip. I understand what's going to happen if we touch the sand. Like the sands of time, lust is a delicate and intricate caress of not just the physical senses, but more so the mental faculties. It makes sense it is creeping toward us, inching slowly along the pavement, like the crawl of a wanton lover begging for attention. It is ominous and resplendent at the same time, like the silence of a tsunami about to wash over us and carry us away in its beautiful, chaotic destruction.

"Tabby is damned. Asmodeus has wanted to get his hands on her since she stepped foot in Hell." He glances back up the street.

I notice for the first time the streets are eerily

quiet. It isn't what I would expect coming from Asmodeus' presence. I expect there to be more of a pornstar atmosphere banging out on the beach, but even with the late evenings diminishing tourist numbers, all I can hear is the bustle of trash blowing down the sidewalks and the scampering of little feet in alleyways to my left and right. With Asmodeus here, I wonder if the city will see an influx in the rodent population in about a month.

"Then what's the plan? How are we going to get out of this one?" Lust is a tricky sin. It's everywhere and it doesn't necessarily mean lusting after the flesh. Whatever is happening out on the boardwalk can be any number of things. I shudder at the thought, bloodlust being at the top of my worst fears of what we're going to find. On average, humans walk past a murderer eight times in their lifetimes.

"We're going to pull an old trick from my father's book." We begin walking again and I brace myself for the moment I step foot on the beach.

"Which is what?"

"We're going to offer him a deal. A better one than just a measly second-floor suite in Hell."

Why do I suddenly feel like teaming up with Damien is the "I'm in too deep" realization? Most likely because unleashing Asmodeus on humanity would put the human population in for a world of hurt.

"Do you really think this is a good idea?" I ask as we're about to make the first contact with the sands blowing up the street from the beach.

"It's the only plan." I consider this and pause

just before stepping onto the first grains. I don't know if it is me psyching myself up, thinking because I am a fellow demon nothing will happen, but when I step onto the sand about a block away from the beach, nothing happens. And then it all hits me at once, buckling my knees and making me sink to the pavement. The grains dig into my knees, causing pain to spike through my joints. But it is nothing compared to the wave of lust that hits me. The desire for...for freedom hits me so hard, it cripples me. I look up at Damien and feel the scalding tears pouring down my cheeks. He has to understand, he needs to understand. Trapped in an eternity in the Underworld as his co-ruler is my definition of torture. I crawl to him, not fully comprehending the revulsion I feel for myself as I clutch at the bottom of his t-shirt.

"Please!" I tilt my head back and my lips tremble. His face is a blur, but I can just make out the features of shock and horror as he cups my face between his hands. "Please." How do I express how much he has to understand what I need? Freedom. The very depths of what remains of my soul aches for it.

Before I can start to babble, plead some more, he bends over and scoops me into his arms. The instant feeling of relief overwhelms me and I feel my head loll back as I look up at the stars. I feel a buzz in my head, past the fog remaining from my lust for freedom, and somehow Damien is unaffected by walking on the sand. How is this possible? The question becomes lost in my will to battle myself as I try to cut through the haze. The ache has always been there, but the effect of Asmodeus has multiplied the feeling tenfold. I close my eyes against the stars, the yearning for the freedom to be as vast as the Heavens comes with gazing upon them, and my heart hurts too much right now knowing I can't have that.

I hear Damien's boots clunk along the boardwalk and in another few paces, I force myself to pick my head up and watch where we are going. We're around the area where Dante commandeered the hot dog stand and beside it next to the public restrooms is what appears to be a man. Except, he's not a man. He flickers like a hologram and I see three versions of him. Or maybe it's the lust I feel regarding my own life. Freedom from a past I can't change, freedom from the present conflicts I must overcome, and freedom in the future to be untethered to everything I have endured in my human life and my past life.

I catch glimpses of his demon form with a phallic-shaped tail and great sinewy wings. His eyes aren't cold like a demon, but full of the very sin with which he weaponizes. They're charged, molten pools of depravity and debauchery. It is the in-between form confusing my mind. It flickers in between the man and the demon, but it is the shape of the lust in which all of humanity craves and there is no solidity in the black cloud that like a Rorschach test, befuddles the mind.

Part of me wishes Damien would put me down. The other part knows if he does, I will crawl and beg again. It goes against the very fiber of my being to stand on my own to gain independence, but worse, I hate knowing I have to rely on him to protect me.

"Asmodeus, how are you, Uncle?" Damien's tone is casual, and I wonder if he is about to offer me up like a lamb for slaughter in his new deal with Asmodeus. It would be the perfect opportunity for him to backstab me, as I've suspected he might do. The only thing keeping me from not attempting to throw stones back in his direction is because if he does overthrow his father, then my girls and I might stand a chance to gain our freedom.

"Damien." Asmodeus turns and smiles.

"Please contain yourself for a moment so I can put Catriona down. We have a proposition to discuss with you and I feel she would be more amiable to negotiating terms were she to have equal footing."

He smiles again and I grit my teeth. Even without his effects, his particular sin is inherent in all of us. I wonder why Damien isn't crippled by its effect and I find it annoys me more than the irritating twinge I feel as a residual effect of my own inner shortcomings.

I don't feel a massive wave in the change of atmosphere so when Damien slowly lowers me to my feet on the boardwalk, I hold my breath, waiting for the debilitating feeling to assault me again. I let the breath out slowly when my feet touch the sea-worn planks and nothing happens. I feel like I'm walking on eggshells, knowing at any moment, if Asmodeus decides to Humpty Dumpty my kingdom of relief from my overwhelming desires, there will be nothing I can do to stop the wave of need like before.

Which is why I turn around and land a right hook into Damien's jaw for not preparing me for everything that has happened since going along with his little plan to make deals with his Daddy's demons.

Damien's head snaps back and his hand goes to his jaw. "What in the seven sins was that for?" He glares at me and there is a sheen of silver and mist clouding his eyes.

"Why aren't you affected by him?" I hook a thumb over my shoulder at Asmodeus, who is laughing.

"What makes you think I'm not?" Damien rubs at the spot.

"Because you're just standing there. You weren't affected at all! You watched me...you watched me crawl." I feel my tail and fangs snap out. It's painful because of how quickly it happens and I hiss. "Besides, you would never admit your shortcomings to anyone, least of all me." I jab him in the chest with my finger and one of my claws rakes down his shirt, ripping it and perforating the skin underneath. It's interesting to see Damien bleed. I don't know why I ever thought he was incapable of doing something so human-like. It calms me down a bit as I watch the trickle of blood run down his chest. But just as quickly as it came, the skin seals itself and he looks up.

"You might think I'm infallible, Catriona, but I assure you, I suffer from many of the same afflictions you and your Hellcats do." With those words, he strolls past me and walks up to Asmodeus.

Maybe he has a better grasp of his inner lust? What would someone like Damien lust after? I turn around, taking a few deep breaths, and walk to Asmodeus with him. There is no way I am going to apologize for hitting him. He watched me beg. Maybe he has made peace with his faults, but I will never accept mine.

"Well now, what kind of a deal would the rogues of Hell have for me?" Asmodeus clasps his hands in front of him. His grey t-shirt and jeans do nothing to glamorize the already plain visage he is wearing.

"What rumors have been going around the Underworld, Uncle Asmo?" Damien claps his palm in a handshake and it is strange to see him making friends with the enemy who could cripple us both if he wanted. I guess niceties are observed in negotiations for a reason. I keep my mouth shut. This is Damien's plan and since he holds the rules to whatever this game is and isn't reading them all off yet, I don't know how to play.

"Everyone's talking about the revolt. Exciting, isn't it? The commotion you two have stirred up."

"And so my father has sent you?" Damien looks around as if he is expecting the rest of his uncles to pop up.

"Satan has decreed you and your pet be brought in immediately."

I consider speaking up and telling him I am no one's pet. But the fact he didn't specify we should be brought in unharmed or not is what makes me bite my tongue hard.

"And what if I were to offer you freedom my father has never given any of his brothers?" Damien glances down at me and I am about to argue, but Asmodeus starts to laugh.

"What freedom could you give me my brother hasn't already granted?"

I look around at the comatose people on the beach. Whatever Hellish agony they are lusting after, it is within the confines of their own minds because they appear as if they are sleeping and nothing more. They're trapped within themselves, imprisoned forever until Asmodeus lets them go or they die from the elements or old age. Oh god! Coma victims are tragic enough, is this…is this what happens when Asmodeus is permitted the kind of freedom Damien is offering him? All of these people…

"No!" I can't contain my argument any longer. "Damien, you can't let him get to all of these people like this. You can't--"

"Trina--"

Before he can argue further, I act. I launch myself at Asmodeus, shredding my clothes as I do. I don't permit myself to lose full control often, but when I fully transition to a demon, it's not a fluffy housecat pouncing on the lap of an adoring middle-aged woman with a coffee addiction and the predilection to be eternally single, save her feline family. There's a reason saber tooth tigers no longer roam the earth. It's not, we ever went extinct, it's demons were put on house arrest so to speak, forbidden to roam freely in the mortal realm. I feel my teeth elongate like the fangs of a saber tooth. Fur erupts all over my body and I catch my reflection in the metal siding of the hot dog cart and see the fire erupt in my eyes. My fur itself is also live fire, not something scientists have ever been able to discover, even with the discovery of dead demons around the world, fossilized in ice and stone. There's a reason there are so few of those discovered as well. Demons are hard to kill.

I catch Asmodeus by surprise, which is my intent. It's not every day someone, even a demon, is tackled by a 300-pound prehistoric cat. I sink my claws into his chest and he begins shifting immediately. I feel the pain erupt in my skull as the niceties he'd temporarily put into place dissolve. Want and need consume me hotter than the flames of my fur and the only reason I don't succumb to them is at this moment, there is something I want more; to take Asmodeus down so he can't hurt anyone else here on the beach tonight.

I hear the screams of people who are coming back to themselves through a haze of confusion, but I can't lose focus. Asmodeus vanishes, deciding taking on one of the other Princes of Hell and a Hellcat is probably not in his best interests. The problem with the vanishing act is he leaves behind an agonizing wake of misery and fear. The few remaining people on the pier begin scrambling in panic. New York is full of some hot stuff at night, but a saber tooth Hellcat usually isn't one of them.

"Oh my God, do you see this?" is quickly followed by an "Aww man, oh shit!" from the guy who is clearly tripping. The pockmarks on his face combined with the chemical stench of narcotics makes my nose twitch. I growl at him and he takes off running down the boardwalk faster than a coyote with a hunting hound on his tail.

I claw at the pier in frustration, having needed to sink my claws into something, but then I am blindsided by a massive form tackling me, pulling me out of my enraged fugue. I slam into the side of the hot dog cart and crumple the tin siding. In a moment of blind pain, I look in time to see a huge form looming over me. It's Damien, but it's not Damien.

He is somehow more as his eyes glow silver in the night and gnarled black horns have sprung from his head. Large wings with black feathers and silver tips have sprouted from his back, a genetic gift from his father the fallen angel, and his mother rumored to be a Nephilim. In a catastrophic curse to the Cosmos, Damien was born of the forces of light and dark because the aura glowing around his enlarged form is silvery tendrils mixing with inky black vines of smoke and light. I see him now. I see the duality of all he is. I see the pain and the pleasure and the everlasting internal anguish of constantly warring within himself and my heart breaks for him. I thought I was so conflicted. Eternity felt like forever with such mixed emotions and feelings. He is the very definition of internal struggle.

I stand, shaking my body, but not attacking. I can already feel my spine start to arch as my tail and claws recede back into my body. The flames igniting my fur are tamped out and I can feel the heavy coat against my skin while I shake a cloud of ashes and singed fur off myself as it too rescinds into my body.

As the transformation back to my human form is complete, I am left kneeling on the pier with the grit of sand cutting into my knees. I slowly stand, feeling the ache of the full transformation as my bones and organs realign themselves. My skin and eyesight are extra sensitive and I squint as I look up at Damien. His true form is twice the size of his six-foot frame. I have the feeling he can be bigger, as he defines light and dark, he can also define space and time and manipulate it.

I hold my hand in front of my face as he starts walking toward me. My clothes have been reduced to ashes. If it wasn't for the massive cat's body forcing itself through and shredding them, the ignited flames of fur have reduced the rest to ashes. I press my back to the demolished hot dog cart, feeling the cold metal pressing into my back as he draws nearer. There is no escaping him. I wondered when he might turn on me, apparently me disobeying his order to heel like an obedient dog is his breaking point.

I refuse to cry, beg, or even cover myself up. Demons don't have the luxury of being modest. I continue to try to look at him through slatted fingers, but just as he stops right in front of me, the light and shadows swirling around him in a yin and yang miasma of color are too much to look directly at. I flinch as he reaches out and in his terrifyingly beautiful form, he grasps my upper arm and pulls me into his embrace. I struggle for a moment and then freeze. The heat from his light mixed with the cold from his shadows has an odd effect on my skin. It's the cloak of pain and pleasure from his aura and I am now aware of what he feels every minute of every day.

I try to open my mouth and say something, but it is raw from the heat of my true form. My singed vocal cords don't want to work properly and we have bigger issues than my discomfort and pain.

I try to express this, but as he hugs me to his chest, time seems to slow around us as he bears the mantle of his title, Master of Manipulation. I don't know how he does it, but his aura swirls faster and faster around us as if it is bending the rules of the universe. My clothes begin to slide back across my skin. Where they were once destroyed, they are now created. Perhaps it is the purpose of his existence. To create and destroy or to destroy and then create. He builds things up to tear them down, like a wayward child with blocks he develops into turrets and towers, but to create again, to form something new, he must destroy what is already crafted.

He smiles down at me as he finishes, giving me back what little bit of dignity I have left. I stare down at my body and see the same boots I'd pulled on this morning. I hear the creak of leather and hold out my arms to see my beloved colors are slung back over my arms and shoulders.

"That was a very stupid thing to do, Catriona." His voice is quiet as he fades into something less. If he is to be defined as more when he is in his true form, unencumbered by dimensions defined by humanity, then in this form he is diminished.

I try to stare around him and through him. I can't explain why, but I hate he has squashed himself into the profile of a man. It doesn't seem right somehow. Not now anyway. It's like a cockroach, manageable by the definition of its physical arrangement, but not by the fear it invokes upon sight.

"I'm not apologizing for attacking." I fold my arms across my chest, very aware since he gave me the clothes, he is quite capable of taking them back. It's twice now he's helped me out without an explanation. I don't trust it and even worse, I hate feeling indebted to him.

His lips twitch, "No, I didn't think you would. Always the champion for the people, Trina. The problem is he would have been a useful ally."

My throat is raw and I clear it, wishing I hadn't dumped the bottle of water on Zeke's face. "You saw what he did to me, to the people on this pier. If you gave him free rein..."

"Catriona." Damien sighs, rubbing his jaw, "You still don't get it. Lust is inherent in us all. He already has free reign. People who succumb to comas, most of them have such a strong desire not to be in pain anymore, it's the result of such fierce lust. Lust isn't entirely defined by sexual desires; it's what makes Asmodeus so powerful. He is not a prince of Hell you want to piss off."

Too late would be the understatement of the night. My actions might have just jeopardized the human race. I think about this a minute and then turn around and kick the hot dog stand. The metal screeches as it scrapes on the pier.

"Then what could you give to him he doesn't already have? I mean is this a battle we are just setting ourselves up to lose?" I want to punch him again, but it isn't going to do me any good.

"My willingness to offer him more was the deal, Trina. Now we'll be lucky if we make it off Coney Island without him coming back with a horde from Hell hot on our tails."

"Great. Just great. Maybe if you told me the plan..."

"Maybe if you stopped long enough to let someone into that thick head of yours to..."

"Stay out of my head!" I realize we are standing nose to nose shouting at one another and when I look around, I see the pier is completely empty. Pretty soon we'll hear the sirens from the 911 calls. "We'd better go find Tabby and see what's up. I don't like her being away so long. He might have...he might have gotten to her."

"Are you prepared to deal with the consequences if he did? It's a lot of responsibility to have put on Tabby. You know she's your wild card. As a leader, taking one for the team..."

I hold up my hand, cutting him off. I don't need the lecture right now. I get it. My leadership skills can arguably be deemed as sub-par, but my intention is even with the hits to myself and my girls, there's some big old purpose for the greater good or some bullshit. Damien falls into step beside me as I make my way to the police's kiosk and I don't answer him. Tabby hadn't crossed my mind since encountering Asmodeus and now I'm wondering what kind of mess she might have made with the effect of Uncle Asmo on the pier, the feeling of uneasy queasiness hitting my stomach, doubles when the rusty scent of blood assaults my nostrils.

"No, no, no..." I reach out with a shaking hand to open the door and then I feel Damien's warm fingers close over my own.

"Let me."

I'm already shaking my head. "I asked her to do this. She's my responsibility."

"There are things you are going to have to trust me with, Catriona. If you are going to rule by my side..."

"I trust myself. That alone will ensure I survive when I am forced to rule by your side."

"I'm not forcing..."

I shake my head, blocking him out. I don't need him to sugarcoat the reality. I close my fingers tighter around the cool metal handle and push the door open. The sight greeting me is worse than I thought. I expected to see Tabby sitting in a pool of blood and fleshy remains. But instead, I find Tabitha, huddled in the corner, naked, rocking back and forth with her tail and whiskers twitching in agitation as she stares at the remains of the two police officers, who judging by the scene, had succumbed to their inner lust and torn each other apart.

"Tabby?" I step into the small room and around some shredded remains of one of the officer's uniforms. "Tabby, sweetheart, can you hear me?"

She rocks back and forth some more. I hear Damien clear his throat behind me, but I ignore him. I skirt around the edge of the kiosk without disturbing the remains as best as I can. I watch as the pool of blood seeps toward Tabby's toes and some part of me, overwhelmed with the urge to protect her from the sight, steps in the path of the pool and I squat down. Tabby blinks and looks up at me.

"Tabby, come back, kitty cat. I've got you." I hold out my hand and she glances at it. I wait patiently, not wanting to spook her into shifting in the small space.

Tabitha reaches forward with trembling fingers and takes my outstretched hand. I close my hand, squeezing her palm and gently pull her to me. As she begins to stand, I rise with her and pull her into a hug, shielding her from the carnage behind me. I cradle her head to my shoulder and walk her out the exit, cringing when I hear the wet squelch underneath my boots.

"Give her some clothes, Damien." I don't bother to turn and try to find hers. I wouldn't be able to discern garments from guts at this point and I really need some fresh air myself. The smell is starting to get to me.

Damien holds out his arms to her, but Tabby refuses to let go and he pulls us into his embrace together. I close my eyes, not wanting to see his generosity even though I'm indebted to him on a scale of me zero, him, too many favors owed. It just makes ruling by his side for an eternity seem even longer when I have to face the invoice on my to-do list.

I feel the clothes begin to materialize on Tabby and I slowly ease my grip so when Damien lets us go, she is standing on her own. She sways a little bit, but I need her to get with it enough to get out of here. At least when we begin walking back to the storage shed, she follows in silence. I figure we have little time before the police show up and the last thing we need is to be standing over the remains of the slaughter. I round the corner onto the lane with the storage sheds and see the rental truck outside. As we approach, I see Leo and Fae standing guard while Doug, Dick, Phil, and Charles load parts of the ride onto the truck.

"Where are the others?" I ask Leo.

"We left her with the bikes. Marty and the Teach will help her look after Zeke, I'm not sure about the prophet guy, Dante. All he really talks about is food." She shrugs.

"Food?"

"Yeah, tonight he was going on about cheesecake."

"Looks like Tora's got her work cut out for her then. Even demons know you don't mess with a New Yorker's cheesecake."

"She's got to start proving herself sometimes. So I made a judgment call."

"I trust you, Leo. It's Lowell I don't trust to try to pull a runner." I nudge her shoulder as I walk up.

Leo nods at Tabby. "What's up with her?"

"Later. Just get her in the truck. She's in shock." I glance at Damien, but his face is expressionless. I peer in the back of the truck to find it's almost full of metal parts and boxes. Great, some assembly required.

"We almost done here? The heat's coming," he says to Dick.

"Yeah, we saw the mad rush off the boardwalk. Must have been one Hell of a throw down." Dick glances at Doug who hefts another box onto the back of the truck.

"Let's just say NYPD's finest isn't the worst thing coming for us."

"Damn." Leo glances around like she's expecting someone to jump out of the shadows. I feel the hair stand up on the back of my neck.

"Come on, let's get out of here."

Phil and Charles set the last of the boxes in the truck and as they hop down, Doug pulls the back hatch shut.

"All set," Dick says. Damien hops on the back

bumper, holding onto the sidebar. Leo joins Tabby in the cab to drive back to the DMV and I hop up on the other side of the truck. Damien's boys jog behind and it's a quick drive back with the streets being so empty.

When we get back to the DMV, I find Tora standing over Zeke and he's holding his bleeding nose.

"Tora?"

"He tried to run. Lowell tried to help him. So Marty stopped him. Then this one got lippy." She holds her fist up like she's going to hit him again and Zeke flinches. I see Leo's hand in front of her mouth out of the corner of my eye and I can tell by the full body shakes she's laughing. I try to keep my composure, but as I take in the scene, Tora looking some kind of fierce standing over Zeke, Marty holding Lowell back, and James and Dante comparing scholarly notes about the perfect cheesecake flavor, I can't help it and start laughing. I laugh so hard the tears roll down my cheeks as I walk over to Sugar. My sides start to hurt as I continue to chuckle. Marty crabwalks Lowell over to my bike and one look at his enraged face has me clutching my sides all over again.

Lowell doesn't argue when Marty gruffly shoves him toward the bike and tells him, "Get on, kid." He then turns and hops up into the cab and starts the rental truck up.

We're no doubt going to be on every street camera between here and the Bronx-Whitestone Bridge. We'll be on New York's most wanted by the break of dawn too, but by then, we'll have a few hours head start. Fae and Leo force Zeke into her

sidecar, and before he can try to escape, she threatens
to singe his ass into the car with her motorbike flames
and he clutches his knees looking all kinds of
pathetic, but he'll turn on us soon. I see the cold,
beetle-like look in his eyes, which suggests he's
planning something nefarious or at least sneaky.
James surprises me when he hops on Tabby's bike
and starts it up. I guess Lowell's geeky friend has a
little bit of game. Dante hops on the back with him
and I look up through the windshield to see if Tabby
is going to go crazy about anyone touching her bike,
but she still looks catatonic. I'm hoping Marty can
pull her out of her funk because Hell isn't going to
wait for the years of therapy we're all in desperate
need of. Damien and company all rev up.

We pull out of the DMV just as I see the blue
and whites flashing off the buildings a couple of
streets down. The memory of what is waiting for
them in the police kiosk is enough to sober me and
wipe the smile from my face. We go the long way off
Coney Island, taking side streets and heading in the
direction of JFK airport and then cutting back up
through Queens before catching interstate 678 so we
don't inadvertently run into on-coming law-
enforcement responding to the scene. The last thing
we need is for Leo to land herself with more grand
theft charges and any one of us to be hunted down
and questioned as cop killers. I'm beginning to think
there isn't any place on earth or in Hell that won't
have a full force hunting us down.

CHAPTER 12

After nine and a half hours, I decide it's time to make a pit stop. I know my ass is sore, I can only imagine what Lowell, James, and Zeke must be feeling. If they haven't been avid riders like the rest of us, then they are bound for the local drugstore for a heavy dose of the rhoid cream if they don't get up and stretch and move a bit.

I decide to pull into the far lot next to the trucking lanes. There are less tourists here and we are less likely to be caught kidnapping and being noticed for grand theft. As everyone else pulls in around and beside me, the loud roar of engines slowly begins to cut off, as one by one each rider kills their engine in appreciation for the short reprieve. I get off Sugar, and slowly stretch to my full height, arms above my head and doing the reach for the sky routine. I hear the crackling of spines and satisfied groans and moans from my fellow riders. The sharp spike of pain shooting up my back, is quickly followed by a dull ache flowing throughout my atrophied limbs, and then the sensation of pleasure quickly chases the ache away on a tingle. Lowell and James saunter off in the direction of the public bathrooms, and I crinkle my nose when Dante takes a sniff of the air, scenting out the food court in the rest stops inner sanctum. How he could smell bad café items over the stench of public urinals is beyond me, but he follows closely behind Lowell, and I consider having someone follow them to make sure they don't beeline it out the back door of the rest area, but figure my flight risk, Zeke, is still here and stretching out.

Stopping is a risky move, but one of necessity when the rental truck started running low on gas. Marty pulled alongside me on the Interstate and shouted out of the window, "The truck needs fuel!"

I nodded and made the decision to stop in here, and I watch as he pulls the truck up to the pump and begins the process of filling the tank. The best thing about our bikes is they are fueled from the fears of the damned, at least it's what I like to think Satan has set up for an endless repository of natural resources.

I look around, noticing everyone else moving around gingerly on sore limbs, and eventually loosening up and experiencing the same euphoria. Maybe it's the sensation dimming all our senses, because in the next instant, Zeke makes a jump for the nearest bike he can get his hands on. I watch for a split second, dazed and confused for a minute as Zeke makes a dash for Interstate-90 somewhere out here in the middle of Massachusetts. My confusion only lasts a second, as does everyone else's and it pulls Tabby out of her funk.

Damien and his boys are further back and in no position to stop Zeke once he gets going. They probably hung back further to call less attention to our presence but it doesn't help our situation now.

Chaos ensues as he starts the bike up and tears off onto the interstate. Thinking fast, I shout at Leo to round up the others as I tear after him. I clamber back on Sugar and start her up, the tires squeal and smoke billows up from the pavement as I see my afterlife flash before my eyes while I cut into the three-lane traffic. It isn't enough I've been glancing over my shoulder the entire trip for the NYPD, now we're going to have the Massachusetts Staties on our tail since one of their state police agency buildings is right up the highway in Framingham. I hear Damien's bike close to my own and on the left, but traffic is so heavy, it's going to take a break in the bumper to bumper to surround Zeke and muscle him to the side of the road or a rest area.

I glance over my shoulder and see him along with his crew pulling up fast and hard. They're taking no chances and weaving in and out of cars and trucks, despite the congestion. The look on Damien's face suggests he's ready to just run Zeke off the road and if he isn't careful of the way he's weaving in and out, he will force Zeke into the breakdown lane. Then he'll be crowned with the title of road kill instead of Road King. I downshift and let him take the lead as I cut in on the shoulder of the road, which is risky. The roads in New England are sketchy at best with potholes so large they can be named as craters. Riding the ridge is jarring and I let Zeke see how pissed off I am he's putting everyone in danger. I point to the next rest area, but I know he will try to split the lane and scoot out around Damien before he kisses the guardrail. I

shift again and drop back a few inches, giving
Damien the chance to pull up on the left of him and
begin muscling him toward the rest area exit.

I see Zeke punch the throttle one more time,
but he runs the risk of catching Damien's front tire. I
shout over the roar of the engines.

"Damn it, Zeke, pull over!" But the weasel isn't
going to go gently into the porter potty pitstop. He
downshifts, just like I figured he would try, and I
glance back quickly to see Dick and Doug already in
position, waiting for the move. He thinks he can slow
a split second and then weave out around Damien,
but they are flanking all of us. I'm happy to notice Leo
and Fae are hot on our tails, and a few car lengths
behind them is the rental truck.

I turn back and at the last second before Zeke
ends up kissing the guardrail, he veers off the exit
and the rest of us ride him into the parking spaces.
There aren't many people here, as the rest area is
closed for maintenance according to the sign on the
door. It's just as well because when he finally stops
and dumps Tabby's bike on the ground, I don't know
who pounces on him faster, me or her. She has every
right to kill him if he scratched her ride. I would too,
but I figure this smack down drag out has been a long
time coming and as I kill the engine on Sugar and
kickstand her out, I leap from my seat and tackle him
just as he tries to sprint around the front of my ride
and make a break for the woods.

"Get off me!" His fist connects with my jaw and
I taste blood. I spit and snarl just as Tabby joins in and
she clocks him a good one in the temple.

"You dumped my ride!" Her fists are going wild and I duck before she catches me in the side of the head too. I settle for pinning his legs, which he's trying to wrap around her. He may be smaller than Damien and friends, but he's spry and slippery, like an eel. I let Tabby lay into him for a few minutes, but it isn't without him getting his licks in. When he finally bucks her off, she's got a split lip and a shiny red cheek for her trouble, and I'm pretty sure the way she's gasping like a fish out of water he managed to ding up her ribs a bit.

I take her place, having let her get some of her frustrations out on him, not just for the bike, but for what went down on the pier. She needed the outlet, but now it's my turn to express a few frustrations.

I hear one of his ribs crack as the full force of my elbow slams into him. I can feel the anger and the hurt rising in my chest. Maybe my redemption will take a hit for these blows, but the man got me shot between the eyes. Talk about a migraine; there's no painkiller that can ebb the throb of such insult and agony.

My cheeks are wet as hot tears of rage and betrayal slide down my cheeks. I'd stuck with him, kept my mouth shut when the cops came calling. I'd played the dutiful girlfriend when his contacts came around asking questions about payment. I'd done the misdirect and then sent him the heads-up texts and look where it got me. I pick him up by the scruff of his shirt and head butt him, feeling the ache blossom between my eyes. Better than the one in my heart. It breaks his nose and blood spurts like a geyser as he hollers and clutches his face.

"Get off of me!" he screams again and I sit back on his lap. "You dumb bitch, you deserved to bite the bullet!"

I stare at him through the haze of pain in my head and wonder what I ever saw in him in the first place. Seeing everything I have as a demon, it really puts things into perspective. There are a lot scarier things in the world, this one and the next, than a chump like Zeke. As a demon, it's reasonable to argue I am one of them, but I consider as a scorned woman, in the worst possible way ever, it's more frightening than any supernatural aspect of my being.

"Remember this moment right now, Zeke. You're beneath me. You are nothing to me anymore." I look into his eyes and see the rage mixed with terror. It does nothing to tug at my heartstrings anymore. Life sometimes throws us the curveball but it answers some of the big questions. If you could do it all over then what would you do differently? That's the million-dollar Q&A right now. It's funny how now when I look at the past, the question was always answered, I just never had the guts to peek at the answer.

I stand and he instinctively cups his prone areas. He doubles over and protects his face with one arm, his stomach by curling into the fetal position, and his junk with his other arm. I snort and walk away. What I should have done years ago. It's a liberating experience in itself, being able to walk away. I never realized the power I was denying myself by sticking with him for so long.

As I walk back to scope the damage to Tabby's bike, I pass Dick and Doug who both stop and give me a high-five.

"Nice takedown, Trina." Dick is the one to speak first.

I raise my eyebrows. I'd never had cause to really speak with either one of them, but for whatever reason, this has resonated with them and they feel they need to say something.

"Yeah, yeah. She was so amazing. Like a Valkyrie. Can we get on with it? I want to go home," Charles speaks up.

"Get this piece of garbage in the sidecar." I turn back to Dick and Doug, ignoring Charles. I stop by Tabby's bike and she's checking it out.

Zeke's rabbit-routine seems to have pulled Tabby out of her shock, because she mutters, "Sorry, boss." I am the only one to hear her. I have a feeling she isn't just talking about being spaced-out to the point Zeke was able to get his hands on her ride. I'm pretty sure she is talking about the Police booth back on the Boardwalk, but I'm picking up what she's laying down. No need to get all extra about it.

"Not on you, Tabby. I asked you to do it, this one's on my shoulders." She doesn't say anything but continues checking her bike over. There will be some rearranging after we all grab a bite from the plaza and the truck finishes gasing up. I figure we can put either James or Dante in the truck with Marty because they aren't a flight risk, and then the other can ride behind Tabby.

Phil hopped off his own ride and is struggling to help Tabby pick her bike up. She checks over the custom paint job and Zeke ought to be counting his blessings because there are no scratches. If there had been, Tabby would have likely ripped a few scratches in his hide. I walk up to Lowell, who is standing next to Marty. Marty has a hand on his shoulder and Lowell is looking at his brother and I can see the rapid swallowing like he's choking on the unshed tears. He watches his brother being manhandled into the sidecar and there's the moment when he finally realizes exactly what his brother really is. He's nothing. He's not worth the time and energy Lowell has invested in ensuring he makes it through this life, in whatever capacity that may be.

"I'm sorry, Lowell," I speak softly so no one else can hear. I never worried about Fiona being the bad apple, since I was as sour as they come on our family tree. I can't imagine what it must feel like being the good seed and having to acknowledge the bad one. What do you do with that information? How do you cope with it? Is it somehow the family's responsibility to cut ties with the person? It seems like life keeps tossing me the big picture ball and I'm standing here holding the thing not knowing who to toss it to. The look on Lowell's face says the same thing. Sure, there's all the social media juju about cutting people out of your life who make you miserable, family included. But how many people actually practice what they post? Is there some inherent responsibility in all of us saying we have a duty to family no matter how much of a screw up they are? If that's the case, Fiona should be on the fast track for sainthood because she never gave up on me and Lowell is pulling a runner-up for title of the year.

Lowell nods and I drop my voice even lower. "I'm sorry, but I think you should know, if you help him pull another stunt like that again, I'll kill you both myself. There's something bigger here going on than the two of you. I don't want you falling through the cracks though."

"Sometimes you have to accept the casualties of war, Catriona." Dante has walked up behind me and I whirl on him. He hasn't said much and I'm thankful for James keeping him on board and occupied for the whole mess, but at the end of the day, Dante gets to go home to Heaven. His one-way ticket hasn't been revoked; he's just along for the kicks and giggles of the ride.

"I don't want to lose an innocent if I can help it," I tell him. The old man tugs on his earlobe and drops his hand. If anyone thinks it's weird two biker gangs are hanging out with a man in a plain blue robe who could pass as a monk if he wanted to, they aren't stupid enough to approach and say so.

"You know what I found most peculiar when I first toured the land of the dead?" His eyes twinkle like he's revisiting some fond memory and for a moment, I wonder if Heaven made a mistake. Is Dante actually some crafty psychopath who fooled everyone and derived pleasure from his sojourn into Hell? Or is he recalling the pathway to creativity when he began to pen the experiences of his voyage? The scholarly, creative types always get a glean in their eye when they think of something brilliant. It's literally the physical evidence of the light bulb switching on.

"What's that?"

"The Princes of Hell didn't care if the soul they were torturing or having tortured was innocent or not. They could see plain as day, just as you and I are standing here, the soul was white and pure. But they didn't care as long as they had something to rip into."

"What are you saying? One of the most corrupt places known to, well, man I guess, is corrupt on the inside?"

"It's exactly what he is saying." Damien has now joined the conversation.

I'm not sure whether to be confused or appalled. I mean, come on, this is Hell. It's supposed to be evil and now we're all standing around astonished it is?

"I feel like I missed the punch line." I hate it when I don't get the joke.

"It means either my father has lost control over his brothers and their respective acolytes or he knows and he just doesn't care. Either way, it's bad for business. Have you ever considered what will happen if Hell overflows?"

I stare between him and Dante, still waiting for the other shoe to hit the pavement.

"My dear, perhaps I can put it into perspective for you. Think of it like Yankee Stadium. Heaven has year-round tickets to some of the best seats in the house and access to some of the best nachos in the Universe I might add, but instead, the nosebleeds section is being crowded out. What happens when the seats get full up? Where are they going to go then?"

I'm shaking my head. Leave it to men to bring the conversation back around to sports. It must be an unwritten Universal truth somewhere, men will associate the big moments to competition somehow. But I get it. Life is a competition. The longer you live and survive, the more you win. So is the afterlife. Survival of the fittest. If the souls of the wicked consume the souls of the innocent in Hell, whether they are supposed to or not, then evil is going to start seeping out and getting a lead in the rat race to get to the empty spots in the big palace in the sky.

I look up to find the clouds are light and fluffy. The kind Fiona used to lie out on the lawn and watch. She never looked for animals like bunnies and puppies. She dreamed bigger. She found dragons and unicorns instead. If by the time she gets to punch her ticket, will her dreams and fantasies be destroyed by the filth that doesn't belong up there?

I catch Damien's eye and look away quickly. I imagine he feels the compulsion for both good and evil, and maybe it's his motivation in all of this. He recognizes the balance needing to be upheld.

"Maybe you're right. Maybe there are casualties, but it doesn't mean I have to give up on Lowell. If innocents have been overlooked, why not start with not doing it to Lowell?"

Dante shrugs. "Do you think there's a vending machine inside?"

I blink and it takes me a minute to realize what he is talking about. I've got his number now. Competition and food, easiest way to a man is his stomach and apparently a healthy dose of witnessing eternal torment for recreation. His next book is bound to be a bestseller. I can just imagine the drama.

"The plaza is closed, Dante. I'm not stopping again until we get to the Devil's Wall in Maine."

"What's so special about the Devil's Wall?" James asks, although the nervous sweat breaking out on his upper lip tells me he's not as naïve as he is letting on.

"It's one of the most secluded portals to the Underworld. I'm banking on Satan not having used it much because it is a mountain peak overlooking Mattawamkeag Lake."

"Never underestimate what my father is or isn't aware of, Trina," Damien warns.

I wave my hand at him. It's the best plan I've got and his good versus evil is starting to give me whiplash. He was easier to deal with when I believed he was just a constant pain in my ass.

"There's no vending machine? No food?"

I feel for Dante as I watch his face droop. I wonder if it's an angel thing to constantly need food. Wait a minute, I wonder if he's an angel at all or if Phil just went up to whatever variation of Heaven Dante was hanging out in and called the old man out on a mission. I'd get bored too after centuries of napping on puffy clouds, lyres, and especially all those cherubs flying around? Kudos to the mamas and the papas out there, but babies have never been my thing. It's no wonder he needed a vacation.

"Nope, just a whole lot of wilderness. You might get lucky and find some blueberries though. Except, we will be heading up the mountain so it's unlikely. Just a whole lot of foliage this time of year and maybe a moose. Probably a black bear or two." I pat the prophet on the shoulder. "You are the food, Dante."

CHAPTER 13

"How many demons does it take to screw in a light bulb?" I snort. It looks like Tabby is back to her usual punchy self. It must have been getting her licks in on Zeke that did it. He's looking on, bitter and angry, and I would be too if I were him. Charles has a firm grip on him so he can't rabbit, and he's being forced to stand there and watch the pot boil.

"Do we really have to screw in all of these tiny yellow bulbs on the ticket booth?" Fae wipes sweat from her forehead and glares at the box with the hundreds of yellow light bulbs. The white stand sits in front of the massive entrance to the ride itself, and I gaze up at the plastic and metal fake demonic Satan. I get the strangest sense like I'm not looking in the eyes of molded metal, but into the portal itself and seeing Lucifer staring back at me. I shake myself, willing away the heebie-jeebies. If Satan really does know what we're all up to, I'm sure he would have sent an entourage in the wake of the fiasco with Uncle Asmo. I still can't help but feel like as fake and cheesy as the ride is, because it is sitting on a portal to Purgatory, it seems to bring it to life in ways a normal amusement park wouldn't find so amusing.

The ride itself is enclosed behind the doors of the massive Satan figure. We set it up so it looks out over the lake, which offers a breathtaking view this time of year. In the rest of the continental U.S., it is scorching hot. But here, so far north of civilization and the decent cup of coffee I desperately need, the foliage is starting to turn for the season. Bright yellows and golds kiss the horizon, and there is a hint of orange with a touch of burnt red. Peak season will be in a couple of weeks for the good people of Maine, the Canadian Comrades. Tabby pointed out she wasn't aware Mainers were part of the U.S. when we arrived.

"Well, how many states do you think there are?"

Fae has been pissy ever since we pulled onto the dirt road. It leads to the access tote road to climb the mountain. We'd parked the bikes and the rental truck, and although the mountain itself isn't very tall, a sign we pass reads it is only 459', and just over half a mile. Someone has babysat Zeke while the rest of us lugged boxes up. Marty and Fae have been putting their mechanic skills to use and begun setting things up, and Dick, Doug, Damien, and Charles have been using brute strength to muscle the heavier boxes up the hill. The rest of us have been working in pairs or flying solo to get the job done. Fae used her big brain to calculate what went where and try to organize the situation, but since when have demons ever played well enough together to stay organized? Dick and Doug got into a dogfight when Doug dropped his end of a particularly hefty box, and Dick tackled him, causing the box to start sliding down the hill after them where they were rolling in a massive mess of arms, legs, teeth, and cuss words. Damien sorted them out as James, Lowell, and I tried to stop the downward momentum of the box, but it was so heavy, only two Hellhounds would be able to stop it. They were too busy being put in time out by Damien.

The end result was the box smashing into a boulder as the three of us jumped out of the way and the weight plus force of gravity sent it catapulting to its doom. Fae spent the better part of an hour bringing up each individual piece to the top of the mountain while Dick and Doug took a breather as they crammed intestines back into their stomachs and let the healing power of evil retain their insides. I can see the perks of being a Hellhound now. They aren't so far off from a Hellcat with the ability to heal quickly is one of them. But the setback put Fae in a bad mood, or I should say, a worse mood as she's always in a state of irritability, and the rest of us griped and moaned they were slacking on the job.

"Hey, remember who it was who loaded the damn thing on the truck in the first place!" Dick snapped as we all got off pot shots to his ankles on the way by. I couldn't look at the state of his clothes, which Damien pointedly not fixed for either one of them as he did for Tabby and me, or the ground around him. There was a quagmire of blood and bile and it stunk like acid on fried eggs and it made my stomach heave every time I climbed down the mountain and fetched another box. He and Doug weren't moving far as they rearranged their insides to heal and it's just as well. The last thing we needed was for them to be tripping over them like a couple of

kids with untied shoelaces. Better to give them the
hour than continue having to hear the squelchy noises
they were making.

Lowell and James took a breather from this one
too. To be fair, the rest of us were able to stomach the
scene because we'd seen similar back home
downtown, but being the freshies to the group, they
were dry heaving, which if Damien and I made them
continue to pass by the scene much longer, there
would have been more clean up on aisle 666 and my
boots can't handle that kind of grime.

It resulted in Fae's carefully laid out time
schedule in her head being thrown off by about an
hour. For me, it was still pretty good timing, but she's
always been the type to have a plan, stick to it and
execute it to produce the expected results. There's no
throwing the grey area wrench in her black and white
universe, which makes her a pain in the ass to work
with sometimes, but it's good she's along because
looking at the nuts and bolts of the situation, I never
would have known how to set this thing up.

After Dick and Doug get back on the job, Tora
calls me over and I can see her patience is at an all-
time low. I would have left Dante to babysit Zeke, but
he still seems kind of irritated we didn't make another
pit stop for the last five-hour leg of the journey. I
imagine he's sore after riding so long, but then I
wonder if dead people from Heaven can get sore? I
shake my head, refocusing on the task at hand.
Charles switched off with Tora who was on Zeke
duty, and she was all too happy to be rid of him once
the rest of the boxes were brought up. The rest of us
were busy helping ratchet metal pieces together and

supporting the load bearing walls at the direction of Marty and Fae. Since Zeke gave Tora the slip, and he'd clearly pegged her for the weakest link since he'd also tried it at the DMV, I can see the nerves etched on Tora's face. She's just waiting for him to try it again.

Which is why I told her, "Kick him in the jewels if he tries it again. And he will."

Tora nodded and Zeke spewed a mouthful of nonsense, stuff I'm sure would make Damien's uncles cringe, but I ignored him and went back to helping lug the freight. She's done with him now though, as he's purposefully trying to get on her nerves by chucking pebbles at her. She's been dodging them, but as the little ones were just irksome, of course, he's taken to throwing larger stones. I think it would be futile to point out he'd been living in a glass house for so long and shouldn't throw stones, but his day of reckoning has already come and gone, and it's up to me to fix the snafu in the proverbial paperwork. I beckon Tabby over, as I don't think it will be a good idea to put Lowell on him. Lowell has been pointedly avoiding eye contact with Zeke since yesterday afternoon at the rest area and I don't put it past Zeke to outrun James or Dante if he wanted to.

"What's up, boss?" Tabby snaps some gum and I almost ask her for a piece to give to Dante to get back on his good side, but I gesture to Zeke.

"Tora needs a break." Tabby stares at Zeke and I wonder what she thinks of him. He's not a bad looking guy, and Tabby is known to get a little pick-me-up sidepiece when she's feeling the vibe.

"Sure thing." Tabby takes out her cell phone and holds it up. This far north of humanity though, she's lucky to get even a single bar. We can't take the chance of Lucifer tracking us though.

"No cell phones. Sorry, Tabby. We can't run the risk of being traced."

She puts the phone back in her pocket and glances around. She stoops, picking up the last stone Zeke pelted at Tora, who is now making a hasty retreat for the manual labor, and she smiles sweetly at Zeke who promptly drops the stone he picked up a moment ago. It clacks against the bolder beneath his feet and he turns away.

It gives me the opportunity to ask, "Are you cool, Tabitha?"

She looks into my eyes and in the depths of hers, I see the visceral response to what she saw at the police kiosk. There are some scenes of reality that are etched worse into the minds than the person's worst nightmares.

"They just started ripping each other apart, Trina," she whispers.

I shake my head. "I know. Asmo-"

"Don't say his name," Damien's voice warns us from around the far corner of the amusement ride. He steps out from the shadow of the tall wall and shoves his hands in his pockets.

"Are you always lurking and eavesdropping on conversations you aren't part of?"

"Are you always going to meddle in the affairs of things you aren't supposed to be a part of? It seems to me if you hadn't, Tabitha never would have found herself in the position she was in the other night."

I wince and turn back to her as she watches the two of us. She squares her shoulders and turns away, keeping an eye on Zeke. Over her shoulder, she responds to him.

"I made my bed a long time ago, Damien. I've never had any issue lying in it until two nights ago and I don't blame Trina for asking me to help her step up and save Lowell. We all have vices to overcome."

I chuckle. I wasn't aware Tabby knew what the word vice meant. I'd assumed since she couldn't distinguish Maine from Canada, she probably didn't have the vocabulary to verbally spar with the big boys. Good for her. When I turn back to Damien, he's leaning against the wall staring at us. I ignore him for a moment and observe the ride itself. It has come together nicely. It's the original Dante's Inferno ride too. Not the remake in 2005 when it was converted to Dante's Dungeon. The park replaced all the internal stunts. Dante is keen to point this out too when we are toiling away to assemble it.

"I don't understand why you kids today seem to think it is considered creative to just remake something that was once a good thing. What's wrong with the old classics? Why mess with a good thing?"

"Then why did you write Purgatorio and Paradiso, old man?" Charles sets down one of the fake green and gray Satan wings next to a sheet of blood-red flame still needing to be attached to the outside façade of the ride.

"Purgatorio was a sequel and Paradiso part of the series. Not a remake. There is a difference."

With all of us working together, it has taken a lot less time than I thought it would to assemble it. I was worried about it being so open and exposed like this since the Devil's Wall is at the top of the summit, but the mountain itself is just a massive barren rock, we might as well send up a white flag of, "here we are, come and get us!" So far, so good though.

The tree line, mostly pine, spruce, and beech trees, ends about halfway up the mountain. Sitting exposed like this, the pre-dawn breeze whips around us and I pull my jacket tighter around me. Moving up and down the mountain with Phil turning the bright and shiny on his aura up so we can all see, I'd worked up a sweat with everyone else, but now we are settling down, I can feel the cold cut through my leather. It was interesting to see the kid light up like the star on top of a Christmas tree when Leo pointed out none of us were going to be able to see very well, but Damien gave Phil a nod and the kid's happy place on the inside lit up like a lighthouse. It makes me think of something else though.

"Did no one think of nabbing a generator? How are we going to juice this thing?" I look at the remaining boxes, which are just bits and bobs needing to be attached, but nothing of the fuel injected gas run machinery kind.

"I've got it taken care of," Damien says as he pushes away from the wall.

I snort and begin to walk away from him, but he stops me with a hand on my arm.

"Why are you running from me? Have I not proven again and again through this endeavor of yours, I'm on your side?" His face is earnest, but a lifetime of being stabbed in the back by people who should have been on my side makes me distrustful of just about everyone.

"You're the son of Satan. You can't possibly think I haven't considered this is all a ruse, Damien. Your reputation speaks for itself. You're like the ticket machine at the supermarket deli. Everyone takes a number and stands in line waiting for their carve up, only I'm not all about being filleted."

"That's a fair assessment, I suppose, but to be fair to me, none of the others in the cage are worth a grain of salt compared to someone like you who will take on Hell in order to do the right thing. You saw what I am. You saw both sides; the good and the evil. Yet you still compartmentalize me into the dark zone."

"No, you're wrong about that." I turn back around. I figure we need to have this out before we reach the others who are helping screw in the tiny yellow light bulbs on the ticket booth, much to Dante's delight.

"Am I?" He stops with me.

"Yes, you are too much of the grey area for me to be able to trust the fog. I got lost in it the other day, remember? When your Dad sent his goons, the Drudes, in after me in my own dreams. When I look at you, all I see is a haze; impossible to get out of once you get mixed up in it." I shove my hands in my pockets and kick a stone around, not looking at him.

There's silence for a long moment before he asks, "What have you learned since you've been in Hell?"

It's an odd question and I look up before answering. I consider the question and then choose my answer carefully. "Appreciation."

His eyebrows disappear on his forehead. "Huh? Not the answer I was expecting."

"Guess not. It just makes me think back on my life and how much I missed. It's not until we lose the things we take for granted, we realize just how important they were." I would give anything to see Fiona just one more time, but I would never tell him.

My heart flutters when he says, "Yes, but you didn't have anyone. No one except Zeke and..."

I stop him before he can give away my secret. My girls know about my sister, but it's not common knowledge amongst the rest of them and I'd prefer to keep it that way.

I cut him off, "Yeah, but it wasn't just about people either. It was life and everything this world has to offer. Until I got the gig for the devil, I never traveled outside of Utah. I never went anywhere except the Midwest. Our parameters are here in America and even now I discover something more beautiful than the day before. Can you imagine it extending even beyond that?"

"I never pegged you as the type to consider the bigger picture."

"Neither did I. It's a shame it wasn't until death when I developed the amount of appreciation I have for how magnificent this country is. I could ride for days and just get caught up in it all." I don't want to beg for freedom from him, after all is said and done, but I figure it's the closest thing I can get to expressing it when conversing with Damien. Still on the fence about him is tricky because he could turn at any minute, despite how adamant he is about being on my side.

Whether he's picking up on what I'm saying about not being keen on being the queen of Hell or not, he doesn't let on when he says, "It's too bad we don't have even that long."

I nod in agreement. I've gone about as cross-country as one can go in my situation, so I'll have to cherish the memories, even as rushed like a New York minute as they have been.

I watch as the sun makes its first appearance out over the lake and wish it were a sign the light at the end of the tunnel lay beyond them. I'd be telling myself a tall one if I didn't 'fess to wondering if somehow saving Lowell's soul, would be saving my own too. I guess it's not how it works though. Heaven and Hell don't measure on a tit for tat scale.

I pull myself out of my reverie and look him dead in the face. "If you double cross me down there, our deal is off. I will stop at nothing to take you down if you stand in my way. If Lowell..."

"I get it. If Lowell doesn't make it through, you'll offer my head up as a satanic ritual to appease my father and then spend eternity dancing on my grave and all."

I laugh. He knows me well.

"Yeah, something like that." I look away and at my crew. If we are going to pull off this half-cocked plan, I guess I need to let them in on the deets. I turn back to Damien, trying to think of what to say. He has come through so far. I have to give him credit where credit is due. He's been the damn knight in not-so-shiny armor but has saved my butt a couple of times now. Credit should be given where credit is due. I can't think of what to say though. Thank you just doesn't seem to cut it. I open my mouth, all fish out of water but he gives me the out.

"Thank me properly when we are ruling Hell and we don't have a portal to punch through." With these words, he turns and walks to his own boys to drop the plan, not giving me a chance to argue with him anymore. I walk up to my girls, figuring focusing on the plan is for the best right now. I can fight with him about boundaries and limits later. "There was a dwelling we passed and looks to be the only one for miles on the dirt road we drove in here on. We should hide the bikes." I tell them.

"Won't someone try and steal them?" Tora asks.

"Nah. The dwelling looks like a seasonal hunting camp and not a year-round camp. With the bikes well off the lane and hidden from view, I think it's safe to assume we can leave them parked."

"Maybe we should try to hide the rental truck though?" Fae asks.

"Yeah, maybe you're right. With the New York PD on our asses and starting the collaboration throughout New England for the little heist we pulled, the truck is a hot ride. Let's dump it so it can't be associated with us anymore."

"Yeah, probably for the best." Leo backs me up. We are just about to head down to the bikes and get down to business, when I turn and gaze down the mountain to where they are parked.

Serious trouble is what I see, as the eyes of the forests deceased predators, are glinting back up at us.

CHAPTER 14

It takes me a minute to process what I am seeing and I'm pretty sure the same goes for everyone else too. The horror of what is stalking us advances out of the dark. We didn't hear or see them approach because of the high winds, but since they are stepping out of the thicket on rotten hooves and bloody paws, we get a full view of what is advancing. All manner of creatures, large and small, predators and prey are making their way toward us. At the forefront of the advance is the larger of the vicious animals. The black bears and the charging moose and deer make up the generals of the assault. Smaller animals like raccoons, porcupines, and fishers make up the mid-ranks, followed by the smallest of animals; rats, squirrels, mice, and other rodents. Carnivores in the front, with the exception of the moose, and omnivores and herbivores in the back, but no less vicious.

To a Hellcat or a Hellhound, this might seem inconsequential, but the variant making them stand out apart from such a myriad of species banding together for the attack in an organized and unified front is the fact each and every creature is dead. They range in variations of decomposition from freshly wounded with blood still dripping to skeletal remains held together by sinew and rotten flesh. And they are coming at us, snarling and hissing. Their claws, the ones remaining attached to their carcasses, are bared, along with the remnants of their teeth and fangs. All are bared as the cold, dead eyes stare us down. They are lit from within with an eerie green and grey glow, like the gangrenous rot of their flesh has lit them on fire and it's what is glowing deep within the orbs. I press my hand to my nose. You'd think I would be used to the smell of rot, since it's Hell's version of scent of the month. I feel my stomach roll over as the putrid smell hits my nostrils, and I catch Tora out of the corner of my eye, the newbie not used to coping with the smell of decay, turn and toss her cookies all over the forest floor. Great, in addition to rot, we now have the acrid smell of vomit to add to the mix. It's a nasty-smelling cocktail of grossness all rolled up into a ball of not-fresh air.

A chill runs up my spine as I turn and see more of the entourage from Hell advance from the other side of the mountain, the zombie corpses advancing in waves as they step out of the forest. I feel the hair on the back of my arms and neck stand on end, and my spine aches as the visceral response to shift into the animal lying deep inside is called to defend myself and those around me. I hear James, Lowell, and Zeke suck in a breath and the low growls of my girls and the Hellhounds behind me. I can feel Damien behind me grow larger and when I look back, he's twice his size and the swirling miasma of light and dark. Dante is standing next to Marty by the entrance of the ride and smiles serenely from the ticket booth.

"I suggest if you have a ticket, now is the time to cash it in and climb aboard." He slaps the side of the ticket booth and all the yellow lights flare up, casting a glare on the approaching abominations of nature. They snarl and duck their heads, but it does nothing to slow the advance. The one advantage we have is they move slowly, some of them are calling their parts, as in body parts, up from the ground as they fall apart, and the energy it takes to keep reassembling, slows them down. Then there are others with bite marks taken out of their sides, or their heads missing, but this seems to do nothing to slow them down.

"What do you mean a ticket? No one ever said anything about tickets!" I shout over my shoulder. Apparently, Dante has been holding out on us with the juice too. I reconsider my theory. He's just on vacation from Heaven and not an angel. I wonder if he can make the ride go, or if it will be a joint effort between him and Damien because now is the time more than ever for them to work their magic.

"Oh, I'm afraid if you don't have a ticket, you don't get to ride." He looks around confused and I glare at Damien as I hear the first pop of bone and muscle and then the roar of Leo as she shifts to her Hellcat form. I hear Tabby and Fae follow and taking the lead from the others, Tora shifts for the first time too. I feel for her though. The first time is never pleasant. At least with shifting to full demonic form any time after is a cakewalk. If you've never heard a couple of tomcats in a back-alley fight scream, well then, you've been spared something slightly past eerie and just before terrifying, but Tora's screams are like a screeching baby inflicted with Scarlet Fever. It sets my teeth on edge and I only breathe once I hear the howling stop and the panting takes its place. She made it through, not that she could get any deader, but still, I feel for her.

"Well, I'll be damned," Marty breathes as he looks at the saber tooth demons.

"You are," Damien murmurs as he walks up and stands next to me. "How do you want to play this, Trina?"

I have to tip my head back to see his face and I find it is peculiar looking in the monocratic colors. His features are ebony and in contrast with the silvery metallic of his cheeks and skin.

"What tickets do we need? What is he talking about?" I squint at the hordes approaching, judging they'll be on us in under five minutes. At least, until a volley of corpses from the sky, owls, eagles, hawks, and crows begin dive-bombing our heads. My girls swat at the projectile carcasses and Phil has lit himself up again like when he brightened the trail. The birds are deterred by his light, and shrieking and squawking, they try to fly around the sheen, but end up crunching their half-rotten bodies into tree trunks and rocks. It's like hearing a trash compactor crunch the first layer of refuse in a garbage disposal in the sink. There's popping and crackling, followed by sickening, wet splatters. The few birds who do avoid his brilliance are able to continue to dive-bomb the rest of us. He swats at them furiously too, which results in his wings to molt grey feathers everywhere.

And no amount of Heavenly Hoovering is going to clean the mess up.

"No idea with Dante. Who knows what he's going to think up?"

"Which uncle do you think this little welcoming party is from?" I point to the oncoming as I swat a raven away from my head. I can feel my skin tighten on my bones and I know I'm pressed for time before I shift.

"With this much regenerative power? It looks like an all-inclusive package deal from all of them."

A silver tendril wisps past my ear from his aura and I can feel its warmth. I want to sink myself into it and be consumed, but letting myself be the protected and not the protector is a cop-out. My mess, my barrel of rabid monkeys approaching. Or rather mountain lions. Lots and lots of mountain lions and bobcats. Oh yay, a family reunion. I snort as in my state of panic, I realize we're the hors-d'oeuvres, no need to bring an appetizer to this party. Then I get the aha moment. I run to Marty and James, holding out my hand. "Give me your receipts."

"Huh?" James' face is white as he watches the approaching monsters.

"Give me your receipts from the rest area plaza. Now!" I hold out my hand as everyone looks at me strangely. James digs out his wallet and Marty takes a minute before he fishes his from his pocket. As James hands me over his receipts I start chucking the ones aside I don't need. "Come on, come on…" I scan them quickly until I find what I'm looking for. "Tickets! Coupon tickets for food. Dante doesn't eat in Heaven. He doesn't have to. It's always perfect there and hunger doesn't exist. Then, coming down here, technically, he hasn't eaten in centuries."

"It explains the hot dog cart," Damien mutters.

I turn to Dante and thrust the food court coupons through the ticket booth window. It's our only hope. Dante reads the coupons thoroughly as Marty hands his over. I shove those through the window at him.

"These will do." He tucks the buy one get one free meal tickets for the food court into his robe, and before James and Marty can get out their, WTF's, I explain.

"You can't just go to a store anymore without being handed back change, a receipt, and a few coupons to entice you to come again." Everyone, except the pouncing Hellcats, nod in agreement. No arguing with the truth.

Dante slaps a button on the machine and the doors beneath the massive Satan statue begin to light up. Cheesy carnival music supposed to invoke fear into the hearts and minds of the masses starts to play as the doors slowly begin to swing open, just as the first moose reaches the summit of the mountain. Damien is the first to intercept the creature, and it's like he engulfs the thing as he whips out his massive arms and grabs the charging moose by the antlers. It slams him into the side of the ride and the rusted metal creaks under the pressure of the two massive forms as they collide into it and each other. Time's up though. My clothes tear from my body as I feel my bones realign. I come out of the shift with fangs bared and claws sharp and ready. I pounce on the back of a half-masticated deer, probably one coyotes dug into, and I rake my claws down what remains of the spine.

It cripples the animal, but I realize it only takes a few moments for the thing to get back up and start moving again. Reality isn't as convenient as the theater. There is no beheading and then the baddies are down and out for the count. Regenerative means regenerative, no matter what state the creature is in. I feel mildly better when I look over and see Doug and Dick have got their dog on. They look like a cross between Maine's master of Horror writing's rabid rover and those massive black Cane Corso mastiffs, but they aren't ebony like the King's canine or the Cane Corso's. They're both a blend of scarlet and crimson, and although their fur isn't live fire like mine and my girls, I have no doubt they could burst into flames if they wanted to. Both have gone for the throat of a massive, half skeletal black bear, the whole lot of good it will do, and I wonder briefly if a Hellhound takes something out, if it stays taken out, but after they tear into the throat of the bear and it goes down, I see it twitch and start to get back up.

There is no winning this battle, no matter how much muscle and mojo we have. We don't have the numbers against a state, which is ninety percent wild forests. There's a lot of dead animals the princes of Hell are calling to arms against us. I guess I figured the attack would have come sooner, and in less subtle ways than it had, but there appears to be the massive smack down.

I turn my head to the side as a buck rakes its antlers along my side. It tears the flesh open, causing me to scream in rage and pain, and I can feel the blood gushing out, which causes a frenzy of bloodlust amongst the carnivores. I feel cool air hit my ribs, which means I've been gouged a lot deeper than I anticipated, and I limp a few paces back to the ride, trying to shield the vulnerable side. It won't kill me, but being shish kabobbed by an antler is one of the most painful experiences I have ever endured. My eyesight is hazy as I take in the battle going on around me.

Leo is helping cover Tora, who looks more terrified kitty cat than massive prehistoric predator. Tabby's gone classic pounce and play with her food before taking it down and out, and Fae is releasing all her pent-up rage simmering just below the surface on a daily basis. They're holding out, which is good, but it won't be enough. Damien seems to be the only one who has a lasting effect on his foes. When he destroys them, they stay down longer than anyone else's enemies. The humans amongst us have crowded in the doorway of the ride, which is for the best.

Lowell shoves Zeke into one of the cars of the ride while Marty and James cram into another card. They crouch down low, but after a few moments, Tabby takes a beak to the head from a rancid eagle and Marty hops out of the car and runs to her, shielding his face and head from above.

Before I can intercept him and push him back to the cars, the old man goes head to head with a shaggy old bear. I scream in panic, which comes out sounding like a garbled roar over the din of the fight. The sounds of the animals aren't any less noisy than they would be if they were alive, and before anyone can get to him, Marty goes under, caught in the worst of the best kind of hug, a bear hug. It's too bad for him it's a demonic bear hug. I scramble through the crowd in a panic, trying to get to him as Tabby realizes what has happened. I can't see Marty under the paws and claws of the bodies, and just as Tabby pounces on the bear's back, I go for the throat, which isn't really there and makes biting into the flesh awkward. It was eaten out by scavengers long ago, so when my elongated teeth make contact, I taste the rancid meat of what remains of the bear on my tongue, and I feel the scrape of Tabby's fangs as they crunch down through the spinal cord of the bear. It's an unusual experience, French kissing one of my crew through the neck of a bear, and I back off immediately, spitting and hissing as I swipe a large paw at its head.

The bear crumples and I search wildly around for any sign of Marty as I hear the enraged shrieks from Tabby. I can't find him anywhere and I have to abandon the search as much as my heart beginning breaking for the old man because a pack of foreboding looking squirrels begins charging the rollercoaster ride. I can see the look on Lowell's face as he searches the ground and the last thing I need is to lose another good one to this melee. I don't care what Damien says; Marty was a good one. I feel the hot angry tears, but they don't fall. I'm not sure I can cry as a cat. It doesn't matter regardless since crying isn't going to bring him back.

I begin pushing my crew at the ride and I'm happy to see Phil still holding his own. The vermin aren't letting him get close enough in all of his shiny glory, so he's stealth attacking what he can when it isn't paying attention. My girls, with the exception of Tabby, get the idea, and they begin working their way back to the ride. There's no other way off this mountain and out of this fight unless we let the animals shred every last bit of us.

Damien whistles to Charles, who has been carving out carcasses left and right. I haven't been entirely certain of the powers of an incubus, but he's proven himself useful because the dude can fly. It's making the attack from above a little less intense as he rips the skeletal wings from the birds in the sky. I feel my anger spike again as I consider the extent of what the princes of Hell have done. Seriously? Who does something like this? Isn't it bad enough there needs to be a pecking order when it comes to animals? I mean, I get their sense of humanity is a big fat nil, but there are some lines that shouldn't be crossed and using already dead animals to join the ranks of the demon army is a low blow.

Maybe it's just whenever I get cranky, I go kitty-cat out, but it still irritates the crap out of me as I pounce on probably one of my cousins. What did Bob the bobcat ever do to Uncle Asmo? Nothing, except lust after the little bunny hiding in the burrow. Now here we all are akin to relatives fighting after a holiday meal like we all sampled too much of grandma's special mulled cider. I may be the black sheep of my family, but there are other types of instigators within the family dynamic and the princes of Hell wear the mantle well.

Dick and Doug are the last to join us at the entrance of the ride. I hear the screeching of claws and beaks as they rake against the metal siding of the ride.

If we don't hurry, they are going to tear the thing down around us. I can just imagine how thrilled Fae will be if it happens and ruins her well-thought-out plans.

Dante exits the back of the ticket booth and calmly climbs into one of the cars. It must be nice to know the only place he is going if he ends up shredded for carnivorous mammal treats is straight back to Heaven. I gaze back into the mass of bodies on the top of the mountain, in hopes of seeing Marty, or even just an arm or leg of him. Something to help Tabby bury and ease the pain when this is all said and done, but there is nothing but piled up chaos.

Damien pulls the doors shut forcefully, but a few birds and some smaller animals have snuck through and are scurrying along the backs of the cars. We continue to snatch them up in our jowls and toss them from the ride or through the air when a tawny owl dive bombs Leo's head. I am beginning to wonder if we are going to get this show on the mountainside, when the whole makeshift building shudders as something charges and slams into the side of it. I grip the sides of my car and swat at another zombified rodent leaps for my throat. It crunches against the ground as bone and sinew are the only padding for its landing, and don't offer a cushioned impact. It happens again and again, as the animals come like gnats in the heat of a summer day, and I look back in my car to see Damien wrestling with a raccoon that snuck in. He flings it from the car and then I have to squint my eyes shut as he begins to pull energy from the destruction of the dead animals and recreate it into energy to power the ride.

He was right; he does have enough juice to power this bad boy up. The problem is the pests seem to have figured this out, although I doubt they are cognizant enough to know it is him who is the real threat. It must be whoever is controlling them and using them to specifically attack Damien.

I scramble over the back of the seat on my car and into his and begin swatting at the critters. My side aches and although I know it is healing, it isn't completely sealed up, and the movements I have been making on a purely adrenaline boosted effort are only delaying it from properly closing.

My efforts seem to help though because, in the next minute, I feel the jolt of the ride as it begins to move forward. I stagger in the seat and bump into Damien, who loses concentration momentarily and glares at me from his cloud of smoke as the car slows. I work my way through the pain of having hit the back of the car on my injured side by picturing him as being a poster child against anti-smoking campaigns.

The car slowly gains momentum again and the screech of the tires combined with the howls of the animals and the growls of the rest of the gang, drown out the carnival music, which is a small blessing in my opinion. Fake demons and pseudo-scary monsters pop out from the dark crevices of the ride as it rounds the bend on a track. I know once the ride comes full circle, the idea is to punch our way through the portal where normally, the ride would come to a stop, signaling the end of the attraction, but as slow as we are going, I don't know if we have enough momentum to make it through.

The movement of the ride has deterred some of the animals that can't fly, which is good for us, and as more stunts pop out from the shadows, the remaining attackers becomes easier to manage amongst all of us. The ride picks up speed as we round the last bend and I can feel the momentum carry us in a downward trajectory as it is aimed at the lake and the side of the mountain.

I'm just starting to think we all need to bail and jump out the side of the cars, but Damien gives his last ditch effort to punch through the rusty portal, which has us punching through the wall of the ride, and the cars tumbling out over the edge of the mountain and we start to plummet into the lake like some bad cartoon strip. Glass shatters and metal screeches as there is a hole in the side of the attraction and I figure we're all falling to our doom when reality rips and tears, simultaneously trying to suck us back out and pull us in at the same time. I duck into the bottom of the ride and in my terror, I close my eyes as my body shrinks in on itself and I'm left lying naked on the car's floor.

I wait for the crash and the pain, but apart from some heavy jolts, where I feel Damien's boots connect with my ribs from being jostled because he is so big, no tragic crash comes. The ride skids to a halt along a stone floor, and I figure with the entire racket it makes, it won't be long before someone comes to investigate. However, when I slowly raise my head to look out over the edge of the car, I see we're in a large cavernous space, with massive stalactites hanging from the ceiling. I figure we must have made it back, but where we are back home is the question. It isn't like we had a pair of red shoes to tap together, and there's going to be people singing to us as we head on our merry way, but as I sit up and feel the clothes start to materialize in Damien's last dose of energy, I see everyone else has made it through the portal relatively unscathed.

"That was one trippy ride." I sit up and quickly assess the gash on Lowell's forehead. Apart from the bleeding, he is upright, and James is pressing a piece of cloth he either ripped from his own shirt, or Damien conjured up for him, to the cut.

Damien's voice is hoarse when he responds, "As far as first dates go, a demonic portal jumping Hell-ride is on my list of top ten."

I glance over at him and his diminished human form. He looks drained and I am beginning to wonder if he can even walk. He'd given us all back our clothes with the exception of Dick and Doug. Charles didn't need to shed his skin when he began flying. My main concern apart from Tabby's vacant expression again and Tora's terrified sobs, Dick and Doug have been thrown from the cars. They're alright, but that's the problem. Their silver collars start to glow as their master calls to them now they are home. I hadn't considered the collars of obedience would be a hindrance, and now we are here, they remain loyal to Satan himself.

The realization comes too late when both sets of scarlet eyes turn on all of us and with teeth bared, they burst into the flames I expected them to do on the mountaintop as they begin advancing on the nearest car with Zeke and Phil in it. I scramble to get out as Dick and Doug start to charge and take a flying leap onto Zeke. I can't help but entertain the panicked thoughts, was this Satan's plan all along? Is it that easy for him, to take the intended target out using Dick and Doug? It's so simple it's brilliant. Which will mean I have no way of switching them even if I do find his library. I curse as I realize Dick and Doug's attack has been part of his arsenal all along.

CHAPTER 15

D ante is the one who faces off against Dick and Doug. He drops a pair of shiny wings like an awkward accessory at Fashion Week. They flutter, sounding like sheets rustling in the wind, hung out on a clothesline to dry in the sun. They look strange on his frail body, but the effect works, as the two Hellhounds Dick and Doug. I kick out a metal sheet which is trapping me in the wreckage of Dante's ride. I smell oil, metal, and rock and I stumble out of the car that crumbled like a tin can against the impact. I begin shifting refuse from the wreckage, looking for my girls. I find Tabby with a busted lip in the next car, and Leo and Tora in the car after her. It takes all four of us to each grab a side of the car Fae is trapped in because it is collapsed in on itself. As we each begin pulling in opposite directions, the car starts screeching an awful protest against the warped metal, and the sound is similar to the banshee reapers hired out to collect souls in Ireland. The wail of metal is as loud as the sound it made when the car first impacted against the wall, and it is now protesting its injuries for the second time.

Dante forces them back by the purity of the light being emitted from his wings. It's interesting to watch the forces of good pitched against the forces of evil. Although Dick and Doug the level of evil in the two is subjective to what one defines as evil, I guess it would be more appropriate to say the smackdown is a classic, light versus dark forces.

Fae is a little worse for wear, and we have to stand guard over her body as the fracture in her skull begins to knit itself together. Seeing her brain exposed is stomach rolling, because she's my brains of the operation and I prefer hers intact. As Dante continues to brandish his ethereal energy, Dick and Doug continue to snarl and growl, but have no way of getting through to attack any of us. In another ten minutes, Fae blinks her eyes and growls before sitting up. I move quickly once Tabby starts pulling her to her feet, and help Lowell, Phil, and James from the wreckage. Their scratched and bruised but I'm grateful to see they have remained intact from the crash.

Damien moves fast, or as quickly as he can, given his depleted state and Charles helps him. Together they grab some of the warped and twisted metal from the park ride and with their combined supernatural strength, they fashion a makeshift cage. Now its bait time, I guess.

I squat in front of the cage and wait. They can't stand Dante's light and they have the pressure from Damien, Charles, and Phil on the opposite side, a cave wall to their backs, and the only other way out is through me.

They aren't stupid though. They go for Damien and Charles first and the kid holds his own as he uses his own fading light to pressure them. Cue the fight or flight response and they are left with no other option than through me. I feel like I should be doing this for a snack like in the cartoons.

"That's right. Come on, puppies! I'm sitting right here like a good kitty-kitty." I whisper it more to myself, but the sound echoes and bounces off the massive stone walls. It's cold and damp, which suggests we might be somewhere near one of the rivers of Hell. Doug and Dick growl at me and I tense, snapping back to the task at hand.

They charge at once and just before they sink their teeth in, I lunge to the side. They twist and turn, trying to scramble away from the very cage Damien and Charles hastened to build while I wonder if it's going to hold.

Dante moves calmly forward, pressuring them with his light as Damien and Charles work together to bend the bars they left in the front so it creates a slatted, prison-like metal door.

Just as Damien is about to pull his hand away, Dick, the darker hue of crimson fur, lunges forward and bites the back of his hand.

"Ah!" He snatches his hand away, but the damage is done. I watch as blood drops to the floor and he clutches his palm to his chest. I tackle Charles who is standing too close and we go down in a heap on the cold stone floor as he snarls and snaps his jaws at me. I deck him in the jaw for good measure and his head snaps back and smacks the floor, jarring him from his bloodlust.

Dick and Doug are already rattling the bars of their temporary cage and I wonder if we should toss him in as a doggy treat for good measure. It would settle them down momentarily and it would at least keep him occupied for a bit if it doesn't kill him.

"Get off of me," he snarls on my face. Spit shoots up and hits my cheek and I grimace.

"Are you under his thrall?" This feels so bad-vampire movie moment.

"Whose thrall?"

Charles tries to buck me off, so I give him a quick right-hook to the nose and sigh. With the amount of decking unruly men in my life lately, I'm never getting into Heaven unless it's to be drafted into the boxing league. Does Heaven have a boxing league?

"Satan."

"Don't say his name. It could call him to us."

"You didn't answer my question."

"Seriously? I'm sitting here telling you how to avoid him."

"It could be a ruse. Look how fast he turned Dick and Doug on us." I sit back and glance quickly around. Damien is still clutching his palm and leaning against one of the cars. Zeke is sulking near Lowell. Maybe he's accepted his fate now we have him down the elevator, so to speak. Lowell and James are watching in stony silence, as are my girls. Tabby looks wrecked, but we don't have time to grieve properly. Thinking of Marty makes me wince. I turn my attention back to Charles.

"Dick and Doug wear the collars of loyalty. As soon as we set foot here, I suspected they would turn on us."

"Then why didn't you say so?"

"Because I'm not required to answer to you and Damien didn't ask. Although I expect he held the same suspicions as I."

I look at Damien and Charles manages to take me by surprise and kick me off. I land hard on my hip and curse when I hear the crack. Pain shoots through my side and I grit my teeth to keep from crying out. I lie there, looking at the ceiling a moment and wonder what would happen if I just wait for them to come find me. I close my eyes against the pain and the sight of Marty charging a bear, when he was all kinds of tall, dark, and grizzly himself, brings a fresh wave of emotional pain.

I sit up and carefully ease myself onto my feet, testing the hip. I doubt it was broken, cracked maybe, but it's already healing. I eye Charles suspiciously. If he holds no loyalty to anyone except himself, he could betray us at any time. Dick and Doug, I get. The evidence is worn around their necks. But Charles is walking a fine line.

If Damien suspects him of any kind of treachery, he doesn't let on though. "Enough," he says to both of us. He is still clutching his hand and I can see his form flicker in between the man and the massive version. When it lands on the bigger version of himself, the silver and black tendrils of his aura are off somehow. It takes me a minute to recognize it and when I do, I gasp. Tendrils of crimson red begin to place their way through his aura. It isn't a lot and he

seems to be melding it with the light and dark well
enough because his breathing has regulated a little
more, but does this mean he's part Hellhound now? I
always knew he led the Hounds and I assumed he
could shift into one if he wanted. Now he can.

"Damien?" I take a step closer to him and the
silver flooding his eyes is now rimmed with two
pools of scarlet. It's like looking at a lunar eclipse of a
blood moon.

"It will be fine, Catriona. I just need a minute to
fuse it within somehow."

I nod and turn to my girls. Leo and Fae are
consoling Tora and Tabby. I have to trust Tabby will
pull through. She bounces from attachment to
attachment, and as much as she was fond of Marty in
her own strange little way, she'll work it out. It's Tora
I'm worried about because she looks on the verge of a
breakdown. It isn't being the new kid on the block,
but if she goes catatonic, or worse, then it could be
potentially problematic.

I eye Charles and wonder again if he can be
trusted. My gut reaction is to say no and leave him
behind, but it isn't my call. It sucks having to play
nice with my peers and not be the sole person in
charge. I only hope whatever juice Damien got from
the Hounds is enough to give him power over
Charles if it comes down to it. Dante and Phil are
talking quietly, and I wonder what advice the old
man is imparting on the fallen angel teen. Hopefully,
something to motivate him to get up out of this place.
Whatever the kid did to warrant a trip downtown
that's so bad, well if the big man upstairs is listening, I

hope he'll reconsider the kid's case. This is no place for a teenager; I don't care how wrong he's gone.

I hear the metal on the cage start to creak and Damien doesn't look keen to get anywhere near it so I begin looking for a way out. The walls are vast and remind me of the portal wall in the garage, except there aren't any cars parked within sight and the floor is rock instead of flat concrete. Combined with the musty smell and the moisture in the air, I'd say my initial assessment we are somewhere around one of the rivers is pretty accurate, the question is, what level? The rivers don't run strictly on Limbo's floor. They run deep and wide.

Dante answers my question before I have time to ask it. "I'd say we are around the Acheron, the river of sorrow."

"What makes you think that?"

"Because the cavern is a desolate place. It reminds me of those afflicted with the woes of their sins and cast into the fourth circle of Hell, greed."

"Then where is everyone?" I look around, still not seeing or hearing anyone."

"They are here and yet they aren't. Some have been crushed under the weight of their sin, while others remain lonely, forever damned to walk alone with the burden of their sin, instead of the benefit of life's more precious treasures."

"You mean family and friends?" I look around, still expecting to see a figure wandering, lost and alone, but there is no one.

"Precisely. Those who know only this torment would have run and hidden at the first sound from us, as they are unaccustomed to coping with the presence of anyone or anything apart from their collective vices."

And I thought the abyss was bad. Imagine spending eternity with your only company being the gold or fortune you'd amassed for yourself and no one else. I shudder at the thought. As much as I love Sugar, I can't picture spending much time riding around with her. Humans aren't designed to be singular people. At least, it's my theory. We're supposed to have someone to care about us, even if it is just a friend or sole family member. I don't want to dwell on the wails of anguish I feel like are suddenly sounding in my head. They may not be bouncing off the walls in this place, but it doesn't make them any less real.

"Which way to the library?" I glance between Dante and Damien.

Dante points past where Dick and Doug are caged. "The Acheron is that way. We can follow the river, as it leads to the seventh circle, violence."

"How is anyone who is violent to another person woeful about it?" Leo's nose crinkles like she thinks Dante has gone crazy since stepping foot back in his old stomping ground.

"Because there is more than one kind of violence. There is violence against oneself, isn't there?"

Dante begins walking to the far end of the cavern. We all quickly follow, not wanting to be left in this place on our own. I keep an eye on Lowell, James, and Zeke. Being the only humans amongst us, it's a wonder they survived the jump through the portal, but I suspect it has something with Damien's ability to conjure up energy as a protection.

He falls into step beside me as we walk, but doesn't say anything for a while. I can hear the echo of Dick and Doug raging against their cage as they try to bust out and I figure it won't be long before they do.

"It bothers you, doesn't it?" Damien says after a while. We came to the place where I thought the cavern was a dead end and the wall rose up and up into the sky so far, I couldn't see the ceiling. It turned out it was just a bend in the passage. I can hear the faint rushing sound of water now and figure we must be close to the river. We still hadn't come across anyone, although we passed a mound near the wall of the cavern. It glints, gold encrusted, and hunched over looking like someone bent over at the waist, under the pressure of such a weighty burden. It made me shiver when my eyes tried to study the figure, and I blinked and looked away because I realized I just didn't want to know.

"What bothers me?"

"Marty. Phil. All the people you can't save. Maybe even Lowell."

I remain quiet, not sure how to respond. Of course it bothers me. But what is the darkness in Damien going to do with an affirmation like that? What is he fishing for?

"They don't deserve this place," I say softly so no one can hear.

"Who says you get to be the judge of their fate?"

"You did when you made the deal with me to rule. Are you rescinding the deal?"

"No, I just want to know where you stand when it comes time to implement new rules. What parameters consist of the hard-headed Catriona Clarke's moral standing."

"This isn't funny, Damien." I stop walking and whirl on him, only to notice he isn't laughing.

"I never said it was." He appears to be human now. His blue eyes are back in place and fixed on my face. It's unnerving because I know what lies underneath the serenity of the blue.

"Then why do you keep pushing? Do you think any of this has been easy? Putting my girls in danger, Marty, having to watch Lowell grieve for a brother who isn't even dead yet?" I wave my hand at the backs of Lowell and Zeke. If they hear me, they don't stop to listen. The one redeeming quality about Charles is he has a firm grip on Zeke's upper arm so he can't run.

"Are you sure compassion doesn't extend to Zeke too?"

Damien's question jars me and I have to consider it. I want to say no. I want to be so detached, marching him to his own certain death means nothing to me.

"That's not fair, Damien. And you know it. Why is this so important to you?"

"Answer me this. Did he never treat you right? Did he ever love you the way you deserved?"

I chew my bottom lip. I know the answer, but saying it out loud means accepting it and it's harder than I could have imagined. "No."

"Then he was a fool." Damien's words send me through the wringer. Damien, the son of the devil, is capable of tenderness and emotion with more depth than what he can sink his naughty bits into? Who would have thought? Until he opens his mouth again. "And so are you if you can't distinguish the ones who belong here and the ones who don't."

I throw my hands up, exasperated. He has more mood swings than I do when I'm craving chocolate with a dash of the open road. I miss Sugar. I wonder briefly if the bikes will be ok, then resign myself to the fact, even if the human authorities find it, it's unlikely the girls and I will be given a reprieve from this place for a good long while to go out joy riding.

I stomp past Damien and stand with Dante as we look up and down the Acheron river. I gaze into the black waters and squint, trying to decide if I've just seen a face of anguish swirling in the depths, and figure it's all in my head when another one pops up. I jump and point at the water.

"Did you see…"

"Of course, the river of woes." Dante shrugs and pulls a packet of cheese crackers from his robes and begins snacking away.

The girth of the river rapidly becomes an even bigger problem we have to address. There's nowhere to cross and I get the feeling if we try, the faces in the water will drag us under with their collective misery. There's something to be said for the old adages and if misery loves company then why does it leave me throwing caution to the wind and plunging my hand

into the icy river when I see the face of Marty swim
by?

CHAPTER 16

"No!" Damien grabs my wrist and yanks it back as the faces of misery swirling in the water begin biting at my fingers. I figured a skeletal hand would pop up and pull me under, but I guess misery goes full tilt when it expects its victims to participate and drag people under. It makes me think of giving a t-rex a crayon and asking it to draw a picture. The crayon is useless without the capability to reach to paper. The faces gnash their teeth and although the sharp edges are a little more effective than molded wax on paper, I feel the nipping at my skin and know like a school of fish, they could latch on enough to pull me under if they wanted to.

"We have to save him! Damien, it's Marty. He's in there. Why is he in there?"

Tabby runs over and begins scanning the water and I scramble over rocks, trying to catch a glimpse of Marty's face. I can hear the echo of footprints on the rocks as everyone chases after me. Charles glides overhead with Zeke in tow. He's carrying him with his hands hooked under his armpits, and the evil place in my head wishes he would drop him in the water so we could be done with this whole mess, but I also know the easy way isn't the right way.

"Do you see him?" Lowell shouts up to him and the sound is like cannon fire. If Hell wasn't aware of our presence, it probably is now. Although we did make quite a ruckus by crashing into the stone wall of Greed's domain.

Charles shakes his head and I continue to frantically search, although the swirling of faces gets faster and faster the further we run. Just as the river is about to skirt around a bend, I slip and fall, landing on my stomach. My hand splashes into the water and in an instant, the faces are on me. Their bites sting and I try to shake them off. I scramble to my feet and realize they aren't just faces. Long, tapered trails of what looks like wet goo trail down from the backs of their heads. It clings to my pants when I shake the head biting between my thumb and forefinger, and it even feels gooey to the point if I had to call it anything, I would equate it to being the snot of the Acheron river.

I pick at the face latched onto my hand like a leech and manage to peel it away, casting it back into the river, and that's when I see him again.

"There!" I shout. I see Marty looking back at all of us, and if he could shake his head, I would say he is trying to warn us off. I'm about to run further when something bumps the back of my legs and takes a leap, splashing down into the river. I squint into the gloom, barely able to see anything because the sconces lining the walls every few hundred feet flicker and cast deceptive, hallucinogenic shadows on the wall. The moisture in the air threatens to distinguish them, plunging us into darkness with our fellow uglies that go bump in the night. The fire burns but somehow feels diminished in both light and heat, and the walls of the level are grey stone with green lichen growing along them, so the effect is to cause the corridor along the river to be cast into a pale green light.

I can just barely make out the head of what looks like a massive dog in the river. It growls and shakes its head, and I can see the faces of misery latching onto its fur. They're like a swarm of ants crawling up over the particle of food they are devouring and in the next instant, the dog's head goes under. I hold my breath, fearing the worst and thinking my gut instinct is right and the Acheron has now claimed Damien, but a swirl of the water a few feet away has me stepping back as the massive dog begins to rise out of the water. In his jowls, he's carrying one of the faces, and it's squirming in his mouth like a writhing squid. It's not the one bothering me the most.

I run forward and begin grabbing the greasy wet blobs and ripping them from his fur and casting them back into the river. There are dozens of them and I scream, "help me!" over my shoulder.

Leo joins me in ripping the globs from the dog's back as he continues to pant and hold the one in his mouth. He's so massive, for a moment I thought maybe it might be Cerberus, but it can't be because this dog only has the one head and Cerberus has three. I steer clear of that dog. He looks bored sitting near one of the entrances to Limbo like he's ready to use any soul looking mildly tasty like a chew toy.

Damien's coat is a brindle color, with streaks of black, silver, and red. Having been bitten, Damien fuses the Hellhound shapeshifting ability into his powers, and the result is the tri-colored, vicious looking creature standing in front of me. I watch his powers in action as the colors meld together in a kaleidoscope of colors. It's like watching tie-dye in action only in fast forward. One second, the colors bleed up his hind legs in streaks, and then in the next the blend and meld in a whirlpool of the tricolors.

It takes another minute to wrench the last face from his fur. They aren't easy to grasp. I would think someone's soul would be more vaporous, but apparently, when they go for a dip in the Acheron, their misery molds them into something more vicious. I crinkle my nose. They smell like they've been bathing in the Underworld's sinus passages too. It smells like the jelly on the outsides of canned, processed meat paste.

When I'm all done, Damien sets Marty's gelatinous head on the ground and holds one paw as his form begins to shift. He grows bigger, although, in his Hound form, he is twice the size of Dick or Doug. He grows to the swirling mist I'd first seen on the Boardwalk and as he does, a misty hand reaches down and picks up Marty. I'm not sure if the jelly Marty clings to the smoky hand, or if the smoky hand solidifies when it makes contact with Marty, but it snatches back, and I have to back up a few steps to avoid being sucked into the cloud. I bump into Lowell who is looking on in amazement.

"Do you think he can--"

"I don't know." I squeeze his arm. Of all of Damien's abilities, I feel like I haven't even seen half of what he's capable of. But bringing someone back from the dead? It's a far stretch.

It takes another few minutes for the swirling to stop, and as it ceases, I hear Tabby suck in a breath as we all peer at what is lying at Damien's feet as he slowly begins to pour himself into the shape of a man.

A Hound, an old grizzled one, lays panting at his feet. It isn't corporeal, at least not all of it. It looks like the sticky plasma substance from the river, but the longer we stare, and the more it breathes in and out, the more solid it becomes. Damien's voice is raw when he speaks.

"It's the best I could do for him. He belongs down here, he always has. His smuggling was done for money, out of greed--"

"Yeah, but to try and save those families from a life of misery and starvation." My protest causes everyone to watch the two of us. I hear Charles groan like he is exasperated having to listen to another one of our arguments and conflict of interests.

"However noble his intentions were, Catriona, he's still a sinner and knew what he was doing was wrong. Do you want me to unbind him from the Hound link I now share with Dick and Doug? I can cast him back into the river if it's your wish." His hand twitches and I jerk my head.

"No, you know I don't want you to. My concern now we know both you and he are linked to the Hounds in the physical sense, will your father have a hold on you too?"

"Not in the way he does with the collars of loyalty. But you would be naïve to think he doesn't have some power over all of us in his domain."

It's not the answer or reassurance I was looking for. But this is not a place one goes to find reassurances either. I let the argument go, score another point for Damien and another hit to my pride, but there's no use arguing it for now.

"Can he walk?" Tabby is kneeling beside him and her fingers tremble as she reaches out to him.

I want to tell her to stop because I am afraid her fingers are going to move right through him. There is one thing the mind grasps onto for reassurance and it's being able to touch the ones we care about. I think it's what makes death so grievous. The reassurance is taken away. We have to convince ourselves the person who has passed is in a better place. But what happens to the ones who we know might not be in a better place? I think about Fiona and can't begrudge Tabby her opportunity to prove to herself Marty is still here, even if it is in a different capacity. Different doesn't necessarily mean bad, I suppose.

"He can walk. Well, more like he can float." Damien crouches down and puts his hand over Marty's shoulder. When his fingers make contact, there's a squelching sound, like Marty hasn't fully solidified into the mold Damien poured him into.

"Will he be able to come back?" Tabby has never had much going on for her upstairs, at least it's the front she likes to portray, but at least she has the courage to ask the question we are all thinking.

"You mean shift back to a man? Yes," Damien tells her. Tabby nods and stands.

Marty begins to stumble around on his hind legs, and his form jiggles until he has enough strength to stand. He tries to yip, but the sound is more like a garbled yodel.

"We need to keep moving since we've been on level four for too long." Damien walks back to Dante, and they move away down the corridor.

I make it a point to avoid getting anywhere near the water and Leo moves in next to me.

"Do we have a plan once we get to the library? I don't think Zeke is just going to go quietly, you know?"

"I'm waiting for him to make another move, but what's he going to do? Call attention to himself in Hell where the entire place is manhunting all of us?"

Leo's nose crinkles and she nods. One other thing, boss--"

"What's that?"

"You smell really bad."

I stop walking as she moves away. When she turns her head and looks over her shoulder, smirking at me, I raise my sleeve to my nose and cringe.

"Yeah? Well, it's what happens when rotten souls are thrown in together to decay even more for eternity."

I flap my arms, trying to air out the smell, but it's useless. I keep walking behind Damien and Dante. I hope they know where they're going because I've never really explored the other levels. How are we going to get to the center of Hell? Last time Dante was here, he had a guide, and now he is the guide. I consider the other pressing matter. What am I going to do about Zeke? He's been looking jumpy the entire time and I've been wondering when he's going to make a move. I don't see him just allowing the switch to take place.

As we round another corner, I see a simple door in the wall Dante is heading toward. Hell has a back entrance? I smile at the irony of my own joke. At least I can find some humor in all of this.

As Dante opens the door and peers into the darkness on the other side, Marty walks up and sits next to Tabby while Lowell stands on his other side. I watch as Lowell's fingers twitch like he wants to pet his head. I have a feeling if Lowell tries, Marty might bite him.

I push past Charles and Zeke and ask Damien, "What's going on?"

"We're just scoping the back stairwell."

"Are we in the clear? Will this lead us straight down?"

"It will lead to treachery, the ninth circle of Hell, and from there is a bridge we have to cross to get to the center."

"A bridge? What's the catch? Is it rigged to blow?"

Damien's face is solemn, but he says nothing.

As we begin to descend the narrow stairs, I move to the left and press myself against the railing and the wall. The steps are so narrow we can only fit two-abreast and Leo bumps along on my right. The silence is deafening save for the echo of our boots on the stone walls. It sounds like heels on tiles which have been muffled by felt like on the bottom of table legs, so they don't scratch the floor when it is moved. We walk in silence for a while and I count the steps, wondering how we haven't been caught yet by other demons, souls, or even the satyrs under the employ of the princes of Hell because of the dull thuds.

The steps seem to go on forever and the lower we go, the colder the atmosphere becomes until I can hear my teeth chatter. How is it the Dog Pound, being on the sublevel of the Underworld, is nice and cozy, but Treachery is like walking buck-naked into the arctic? I can see my breath in the blue flames, which don't really flicker in the sconces because they are frozen, and yet still emitting light. Like with the green flames, I never really notice when the flames go kaleidoscopic, it's even more bone chilling, hair-raising than normal flames.

We finally come to a landing with another simple door. I guess the employees of Satan have grown accustomed to the comfort and convenience of the elevator. It's no wonder no one has broken it yet.

Dante pushes through the door and the sight greeting us is glacial in every sense of the word. Souls are frozen into the mile-high ice walls, their screams of pain and terror are permanently etched on their faces, but what really gives me the creeps is their eyes move as we pass by them. I can see a massive black lake up ahead. It's frozen over with black ice, so instead of looking at the faces of the souls in the wall, I fixate on it instead. I figure Lowell is my one good deed. I start with him, one soul at a time. One soul at a time. I continue repeating my mantra in my head as the lake gets closer and closer, and I can see the bridge Dante was talking about. It leads to the far side of the cavern.

By the time we reach the edge of the lake, I'm hugging myself and pressed against Leo who has Tora on her other side. Fae and Tabby seem to be doing the same, and James and Lowell have at least attempted the macho endurance, but as we stand there, they too are pressed in close to one another for warmth. That leaves Zeke, who is still in the clutches of Charles, who doesn't seem bothered at all by the cold, even though Zeke is shaking so hard his teeth might rattle out of his skull. Phil and Dante are still lit up like Christmas bulbs, although the more the kid lights up, the dimmer his light gets every time and I'm worried about him. The only one who doesn't seem affected besides Charles and the angels is Damien. Marty doesn't seem to mind the cold because it is freezing his jelly-like substance into something more solid. Either that, or he's simply getting stronger by the minute as he becomes his new status as a Hellhound. It's difficult to say under the circumstances.

I peer around the edge of the lake and there is no way to get to the other side without crossing the bridge.

"What now? What happens when we step foot on it?" I ask Dante. I don't have to look at the black ice of the frozen water to know there are more faces.

"The bridge is a tool for reckoning. It determines judgment," Dante replies.

"Huh, I thought the lore was scales were used to determine the weight of one's soul." Fae hasn't said much lately, but leave it to her to know the lore. It's helpful though.

"That's Egyptian lore," James' teeth chatter.

"It's the belief of a whole other pantheon."

I eye the bridge and wonder what determines if someone's weight is judged as treacherous or not.

"Treachery, or here at the mouth of Cocytus, is designed for those who have betrayed their loved ones. It is also reserved for those who have forsaken the Almighty. Anyone who is guilty of this sin will be sucked into the lake and river, and frozen for eternity." Dante's lips twitch but I hardly find this amusing.

We are all guilty of this sin to some degree, which says what about our chances of redemption and saving Lowell's soul? We stand a big fat snowball's chance? Even just for being here we are technically betraying our employer, Satan, so by default, we are all doomed, except for maybe Dante and James, but I'm not banking on the professor being a saint. This just makes me more resolved than ever to see to the new regime of Damien and I. There needs to be a change in the system and what better way to do it than work on the inside?

"Then how do we get across without freezing to death or becoming even deader?" The ice looks like the kind that froze some of the original saber tooth cats back in the days when they were given free rein to roam the earth.

"We take the only other route available to us, of course." Dante smiles at Charles. It's strange to see because up until now, Dante has ignored Charles and he has seemed to not mind the personal insult. But

Charles glares at him, shakes himself, and then wraps his arms around Zeke. Dante unfurls his wings and I get it. If we can't cross the bridge, we might as well go over it because that he can fly us.

Damien also releases his wings, causing his body to shift. The form he presents seems to fit here like this gigantean domain was built for him. Damien opens his arms and cringing at the closeness, I force myself to walk to him and let myself be picked up before Damien launches himself into the air, followed by Charles who doesn't need wings, but rides the energy currents, and Dante, who is carrying Phil because Phil's wings have molted too much to be able to support his weight.

It takes about five minutes to cross the lake and when they set us down, I step back from Damien and turn away, but he catches my arm, forcing me to look at him.

"We're so close. No matter what he says to you, don't give up on your convictions."

I frown, wondering what that was all about, and then I gaze up at the massive obsidian door, which leads into the center of Hell. Phil puts his palm on in and I wait, holding my breath to see if he's going to be sucked into it and join the many faces in the ice kingdom of treachery. There are only four in the door. I recognize one from his likeness in the Bible, Judas. The difference between these four faces and the ones in the lake and walls is they represent complete immobility. Not even their eyes move. They stare back at us, unblinking, but I get the feeling they can see us just fine.

"You don't have to do this." I feel the familiar voice caress my senses as Zeke moves in close. So this is what Damien was trying to warn me about. Even after all this time, Zeke hasn't lost his charisma. He might have lost his composure a few times on this trip, but he still knows how to dial up the charm when he wants to.

"It's not a question of whether or not I have to do this, Zeke. It's a matter of when we find the answer when I do this." I steal my feelings from him and resign myself to being as icy as those around me. He pauses for a moment and tries again.

"We had something, you and I, Catriona."

"*Had* being the key word, Zeke. Then you stood by while I got shot. You did nothing and I was killed."

"I am s--"

I whirl on him. "If you say you're sorry, I'll push you onto the bridge myself. You aren't sorry. You never have been. You didn't even go to my funeral, Zeke. You don't feel remorse. In fact, I don't think you feel anything at all. So, save me the pity party. I'm not buying into your schemes anymore. Go ahead and make your move. I know you will. But you need to know, I'll be ready for you when you do. You got me killed and I'm not standing by to let you betray Lowell either."

I walk away from him before he has time to make a rebuttal and stand next to Phil. The kid can't do much to comfort me when I have to face some of the biggest mistakes in my life, but at least he's someone to be around at all. I can't say the same for Zeke as he starts kicking the walls next to the door.

Let him rage. When the masses come for us, I'm
banking on being in the library with the answer to
switch Lowell's mark to him, so they take Zeke
instead. My last bargaining chip will be Lowell and
James don't belong here, and with Dante being an
innocent from Heaven, I'm not sure everyone will
challenge him making an escape. I can't say the rest of
us will be granted the same reprieve, but then I
remember my mantra. One soul at a time.

It takes another ten minutes or so to get
everyone across the lake. When we're all standing,
staring at the doors, I wonder if we should knock or if
we should try to just sneak right in. I reach out and
grab the handle, a massive ring made from the skulls
of demons judging by the horns protruding from the
heads and the fangs in the mouth. They are fused
together by some kind of leathery rope, and it doesn't
take a theologist with a minor in demonology like
James to tell me it is skin.

I tug hard on the door and it doesn't budge.
My girls are the first to step up and help me, and
we're all heaving against the massive frame, but it just
won't move.

Panting, I let go of the ring and raise an
eyebrow at Dante who has been here before. He
shrugs.

"Don't look at me. The door was open when I
was here last time."

"Great, now what?" I tilt my head back and see
the latch about thirty feet up the door. It's made of
talons linked together, and if unhooking those isn't
going to be difficult enough, the fact it's way up there
is problematic. "Can you fly up there and unlock the

door?" I ask Dante and Charles. Charles shakes his head.

"This isn't my mission. If you want it unlocked, figure it out."

"Do you have any control over him at all?" I ask Damien. Before he can answer, Dante grunts.

"I don't think I will be permitted to touch the lock."

I sigh and look around. I suppose I could try to climb the door, but with what? As I'm searching around for some miraculous ladder to appear out of nowhere, Damien launches himself off the floor and hovers near the latch. It's not as easy as prying the talons apart. It takes him a few minutes to figure out slicing his palm on one of the talons so blood trickles onto it, is what makes the talons spring apart.

When Damien lands in front of the door, the veins on the back of his hand begin to turn black, like the venom in the talons is webbing out into his system.

I watch, fascinated before asking, "Are you going to turn into some kind of comic book hero now?"

"Doubtful. I always root for the bad guys anyway."

"You'd be more fun if you were rocking the pleather and the tights. Now can you open this door?"

Damien's laugh sends a fissure through the ice on the door because the sound is so foreign in the desolation of this place where sound doesn't exist. I worry momentarily about a cave in, but then he reaches out and tugs the handle and the door to the center of Hell finally creaks open.

Before he walks inside, he whispers, "It's nice to see the spark is still in there, Trina. I was beginning to think it went out."

"My little joke was in the face of fear at having to potentially meet your dad. It was in no way an invitation for you to consider role-play in that perverse head of yours. Oh yeah, I'm getting you figured out, Damien. Energy. Whether light or dark, it's what makes you uniquely you. People are drawn to you because their souls are comprised of energy. And it doesn't matter one wit to you if they are good or bad. You feed from it and in turn, they feed from you. Well, I'm just here to tell you, queen of Hell or not, I'm not down for the freaky stuff. That's up Tabby's alley."

Damien's eyes bleed red and silver around the black pupils and I figure I've taunted the beast enough. I step through the door and run into the back of Dante.

"You're letting the cold air in. What's up, Dante?"

"I don't understand. Lucifer is supposed to be frozen here at the center of Hell from the waist down. It's his punishment."

"My dad figured his way out of the little time out torture my grandfather inflicted on him eons ago." Damien steps in the door and shuts it behind him. His eyes fade and are back to a normal blue. It's like watching clouds part, and clear skies revealing themselves from behind the storm. It's mesmerizing and I have to shake my mind back to clarity.

"He did?" I think it might be hard to shock an angel, but if it is, a pat on the back to Damien for accomplishing the task because Dante's jaw hits the floor.

"Oh yeah. He's around here somewhere. Find the book we need in the library over there and get out before there's a family reunion." Damien points to a room off to the side of the entrance chamber and what do you know? Books galore in view of the open doorway.

CHAPTER 17

I tip my chair back and let the legs fall back with a clunk. It annoys everyone around me after ten minutes and Damien threatens to knock me completely over the next time I do it. Satan's study isn't the most comfortable place to sit, but at least there are chairs. What I could really use is a shower. One with water and soap, and not just for my aching, stinky body; but one like a baptism for my mind and soul. Some of the stuff I have read in the last couple of hours is enough to make me cringe on the inside for an eternity.

We've been pouring over books, looking for any sign of the missing papers from the Devil's Bible for hours. Turning up empty, we changed tactics and just began looking through the rest of the tomes in the library. If it wasn't for the horrors depicted in the pages, I think James might have had a field day. But even Damien turns his head away in disgust a few times and he is the dichotomy of good and evil. He should be able to stomach all kinds of the big bad.

Whatever the human libraries and museums are holding are just powerful copies of some of the books. I don't care how much authenticating scientists and historians have done. Evil has seeped into the copies, making them appear to be authentic, but being in the presence of the real deal, books like the *Malleus Maleficarum*, the book that launched the witch hunts back in the day. *The Prince* by Machiavelli, which was a laundry list of tyrannies and subjugating the people. He could have given Uncle Asmo and brothers a challenge for their princely crowns. Of course, the library wouldn't be complete without *Mein Kampf* written by Hitler, but I toss it aside and decide to save it for bathroom material when the Wi-Fi goes down in Hell and I can't play my favorite game on my phone.

I bang my head on the table after closing Kramer's *Malleus Maleficarum* and wish the headache would go away. James doesn't seem to be any closer to finding the answers we are looking for and I'm having some serious déjà vu about his office. The only thing missing in this library is the alcohol, which is a shame because I could use a drink. I get Kramer. I even get Hitler and Machiavelli. Scholars have provided insight around the world as to the meaning and motivations behind their works. What I don't get is the books of torture against demons. From all appearances, it seems like Satan has a serious hate-on for his creations. The most horrific books are the ones devoted to destroying the beings he helped to create in every horrific way possible. I figured there would be books about torture. I even assumed there would be books about torture on humans, but the ones disturbing me the most are the ones I just looked at. I didn't need to know how the lock on the door to the center of Hell was made and what device was used to rip the talons out of the griffin guarding the front entrance to greed. I get it, there are priceless treasures here in the center of Hell needing to be guarded, but now I have images of a talonless griffin hopping around in front of the elevator on level four.

I take my preferred position in the center of the room and begin pacing again. Fae is still reading a book with some sort of shroud covering the front of it and James is rubbing his eyes. No one else has cracked a book, not even Damien, but they are all seated around the library, lost in their collective thoughts.

I'm so rundown from the past week, it takes me a few turns around the room for the aha moment. The last time I had an epiphany, I'd been doing something innocuous like swiping my finger in some dust. I walk over to a random shelf and frown at the lack of dust. Either Satan is really picky and keeps his library squeaky clean, or dust mites are cognizant enough to leave well enough alone and not touch the baddy books.

"What are we missing?" I turn to everyone in the room. "If he were going to hide missing pages from the Devil's Bible, this would be the most logical place, right?"

Damien rubs his chin and sits back in his chair. "I would think so."

"Then apart from the prince of Hell himself to give us answers, what are we missing? Where are they?" I take in the tan walls.

There are hard wooden chairs around a couple of tables. I figure there probably aren't too many people who come in here for a study session, so why bother with the comfy furniture, but we scoured the library from top to bottom. While James, Fiona, and I got to work reading books, everyone else was checking the nooks and crannies, looking through old scrolls and parchment made of people, and come up empty-handed. With the exception of Zeke and Charles, no one found a thing, and I'd even sent them out into the center room and the antechambers beyond to explore, but the majority of those rooms were empty. I scuff my boot on the floor and stomp my foot in frustration. What? Did I think the answer would be right in front of my face when I walked through the door? Of course Satan moved the pages. If he knew the plan all along, he would have taken precautions, which just leaves us sitting in a big musty library all wrapped up in a pretty package.

I open the door and peer outside into the freezing cold before shutting the door quickly against the chill. I'm just about to suggest we all get out of dodge as I'm walking back into the library when I see it. Fissures run along the floor where I had been walking. Absentmindedly I was tracing the cracks with the path I took, but it didn't register.

The pentagram I had been walking the lines of is laid out in the stone floor and runs under the rug and a couple of the tables. I begin pushing furniture out of the way and as they see me doing it, my girls begin to help rearrange the room to expose the symbol.

"Pentagrams are often associated with Witchcraft, but the misconception is they are symbolic of evil," Fae recites the info like she's reading from an encyclopedia.

"Some say it can just be equated with a five-pointed star." I point out and we all stand back. I wonder what we're supposed to do now we've discovered it, and in my gut, I know it's the key to finding out the secret of what we came here for.

"It's also a symbol used in a Devil's Trap," Damien points out. He approaches the star but is careful not to step in it, like knowing the secret is out, the symbol will magically spring to life and trap him since the blood of his father runs through his veins.

"So, we can use it to call your dad here?"

"Yes, but why would we do that? We're hoping to avoid him," Leo says.

"Because if it's a trap, we have leverage. He doesn't get out until he tells us how to switch the marks. Or gives us the missing pages to do it ourselves." I bite my lip and look at the star. It seems logical enough. But even I am thinking there's a flaw to my brilliance somewhere. "I get it's risky, but what other option do we have? Dick and Doug will be hot on our trail, if they haven't gotten out yet anyway, and it's only a matter of time. I don't think any of us need some dreaded portent in the sky. Just look out the door at the lake to know we're in too deep. What have we got to lose we haven't lost already, and we're just waiting for the reaper to come and collect?" I stare at each of my girls. I've asked so much of them already and I know asking them this is asking them to risk it all. They could make a run for it now. Maybe they'd even last a few weeks, months, possibly years on the other side. But to last any longer than that roaming free would be an insult to the universe's biggest jailer and I don't think he'd take the slight very well.

My girls seem to come to a silent agreement as they each step back and near the apex of one of the five points. Even Tora takes a shaky breath and takes her place. I expect some massive explosion or sign to come from the pentagram, but nothing happens, leaving us all standing looking some kind of stupid.

Zeke starts laughing at us. Charles too, but I ignore them. There's got to be some way to call Lucifer and before Damien can say it out loud, I've already dropped my fangs from my jaw and raked my palm across the point. Tabby, Fae, and Leo follow suit, and Leo walks over and scours Tora's palm, as she's too new and out of control to just shift a fang out. We don't have time for her to go full feline, and so Leo walks back to her point of the star, and we all hold our palms out, letting the blood drip onto the floor. I'm just about to march over and open the door to Treachery again and start shouting for Lucifer to quit stalling and get his ass down here when everyone around me starts dropping to the floor.

I panic and my heart races as even Marty sinks down on his old wrinkled canine haunches and curls up for a snooze.

"What the--"

There's no loud bang and no blaze of fire and brimstone. One second, I'm whirling around looking at my comatose comrades, thinking Asmodeus has finally caught up to us, and the next, I turn back around and I'm staring into ice blue eyes set back into dark umber sockets.

"Good evening, Miss Clarke." Lucifer's voice is quiet and deep. So many misconceptions about him, so much shock absorption my brain is trying to process.

"Lucifer." I check out my gang, who are all sleeping, along with James, Lowell, and Zeke. Charles, Dante, Damien, and Phil seem to be frozen, and it is difficult to ascertain if they are awake or not. I keep my eyes on Lucifer as he clasps his hands behind his back. He looks like he belongs in the library. His jacket is navy blue with the elbow patches and his trousers are tailored with a button up pale blue shirt highlighting his eyes. I want to scope the pocket and see if a pair of glasses are tucked in the front, completing the scholarly look, but I don't dare take my eyes off him.

He steps out of the pentagram. So much for the trap. I turn, watching him as he approaches the table and begins looking at the books we have out.

"You're looking in the wrong place."

He turns back to me and I'm still pulling the fish out of water routine. My heart is pounding so loud in my chest, I'm sure he can hear it. He made it beat again, I bet he can make it stop at any time he wants to.

"Ah--"

"The content I hid in those pages wasn't anything evil. Contrary to what my father believes. It wasn't my influence over the Benedictines that produced the illuminated manuscript."

"Umm--" Why am I not dead? Or deader? Or in severe amounts of pain. "Why am I not on fire?" I didn't mean to blurt the question out, but there it is, lying between us, out in the open for everyone to see.

Lucifer chuckles. "Because I am saving energy to practice a modicum of patience with you for taking so long to get here."

"Huh?"

"You haven't figured it out yet, Catriona?"

"Figured out what?" I think he might be drunk, crazy, or both because he sure as Hell isn't making any sense.

"Use your head. Damien has been trying to tell you all along. Dante too." Lucifer circles Dante who is frozen in place, and I worry with one flick of a finger, he'll make ashes out of the angel. "You are going to take over the rule of Hell."

There's no use for it. I walk over to the table I was reading at and I sit. I'm too tired for this crap. Either he is going to really lay into me and kill me or he's going to continue the mind games. Either way, I don't have the energy anymore to stand there with my mouth hanging open, catching flies. This feels like one of those moments the Anderson's were preparing me for a lecture on the dangers of being young and naïve, which always turned into a tirade about the sins and behavior against the Lord. I can't do it again though. He won. He caught up to us and we walked right into his trap.

"Oh no. That won't do. You can't give up yet, Catriona. There is too much to do." He wags a finger at me and my eyes bug out further.

"What in the seven sins are you going on about? You knew Damien and I were coming to overthrow you all along? You knew Dick and Doug would turn on us. You knew--"

"Everything, Trina. I knew everything. But what you don't know is such a long list it would take an eternity to talk it all through. So I am going to make it short and sweet and I hope you're as strong as she says you are and can handle it."

"She? Who is she?" I start to stand, but Lucifer walks over and touches my forehead and there is no long, titillating conversation. There is just knowledge. Knowledge I shouldn't be privy to, save for the fact I have reached some level or plateau of awareness reserved solely for the divine. I might not be consciously aware of what it is, at least I wasn't at first. But now, here I sit weeping for the knowledge I have. The cosmic questions we ask ourselves daily. Why am I here? What's my purpose? What happens after it's all over? The proverbial big picture flashes through my brain and I cry for it all. The good, the bad and the painfully mediocre. Even for the people blessed with the fabulous existence far surpassing the rest of the masses. They're all connected. All a part of "the plan" whether they believe it or not. It doesn't matter what they call "it" or who they believed scribed the initial blueprints, because the scribe is one and the same, with many names.

I sob the hardest because believers or not, I now know they are all in trouble. Someone didn't account for all the variables and there they all are in serious trouble. Stuck in an eternal cycle like recycled plastic for hundreds of thousands of years until someone throws a wrench in the plan. A crazy idea loosening the nuts and bolts to relieve the kinks in the system and has to figure out what to do with all of the excess. Lucifer has been privy to the plan the entire time. It's just none of us ever knew it.

"Why tell me?" I can't wrap my brain around the amount of info he has just given me. It isn't even the full scoop yet. But it is enough. I figure it's best to start simple.

"Because you know they are in trouble and you are one of the few people who can help. One soul at a time, remember? It's your mantra, is it not?"

I nod stupidly, trying to process everything he has just put into my head. Secrets I don't even think Damien knows about.

"Why me? A sinner? A demon? How can I possibly help? I'm still trying to save my own soul. Redemption and atonement? I was a nobody. I begged. I'm not a savior." It's like some twisted version of Ouija where I keep asking the questions, but my damn spirit keeps trying to answer because I'm technically already dead and it, me, tries to answer my own game with the nonsensical psycho-babble bullshit. "How do you expect me to save seven billion souls? Not counting the ones overcrowding Heaven and Hell?"

"One at a time, like you've been saying all along."

I get why he's called the prince of darkness because it's one tall order of bleak and next to impossible on the rocks. Hope feels like the useless little umbrella the bartender always serves up with it. It's pretty, but only serves a singular purpose, to stab the olive in the end, but you wonder if you've got enough brass to toss it all back in order to get to the delicious inebriated little nugget of happiness.

Because that's what happy is. Drunk on the love of life. No other substances needed. Lucifer senses my dilemma because he offers his best shot at encouragement, as twisted as it might be.

"Not everyone gets to be the savior, but that's ok; because if there weren't ever people who needed rescuing, who would the superhero types who sometimes loiter in the dark places have left to save?"

"I'm not a victim," I tell him. I made my bed. The thing is damn comfy when I go to lie down in it. I don't need saving, apart from what I am already doing for myself. I may be a beggar and a sinner, but if I've learned one thing in my afterlife, it's getting down on my knees and accepting the bullet, isn't in my genetic makeup anymore. The defining moment. It came to me after the worst happened.

"I never said you were. You're a survivor. It's why I chose you. It's why my son chose you. Saviors aren't always the ones with the false bravado, Catriona. Saviors are delightfully flawed. That's why it makes you so perfect. You can connect with those whom you are trying to save."

I think about Damien. He'd been so cryptic all along. Does he know Heaven and Hell are in serious trouble? Does he know the apocalypse is pretty much upon us? All it needs is a little kickstart to really jump off and get going. I think about the police officers and whoever the man was, Aaron, before the Drude took him over. His body is no doubt lying, rotting somewhere, waiting to be found if it hasn't already. But the thing is, had he not been in trouble emotionally and mentally, the Drude might not have possessed him to begin with. I feel for him. And I feel for the police officers. Maybe Lucifer has a point. Maybe I need to take charge and fight, whether I'm terrified of the battle to come or not. Leather or a cape, I guess no one really gives a shit what I'm wearing, just as long as the job gets done.

The effed-up thing about the apocalypse is everyone can see it coming, but no one ever knows what to do about it once it arrives. There're always the signs, natural disasters, babies born with inverted faces and all that gross stuff including the man on the corner of the street shouting his blessed head off about it. You would think someone would have grabbed a pen when history repeated itself, again and again, and written the blueprints down. I'm pretty sure the main man Noah tried to, but he got sidetracked counting and recounting all those animals. So, like any good supervisor, he delegated the task. Only he gave the job to someone who wasn't up to par with the seriousness of the situation. Probably a carpenter because the whole passage in the Bible was pretty much dedicated to the dimensions of the damn boat and yet historians still can't agree on how big it actually was.

I shake my head, trying to clear the cyclone of confusion and disbelief. Lucifer sits and with a wave of his hand, conjures two cups of coffee. I'm too shell-shocked to consider they might be a ruse to poison me. At this point, I'd welcome the reprieve from the splitting headache.

"You want me to save the world when all I'm trying to do is get the mark switched from Lowell to Zeke. All of my plans to see that liar, thief, and murderer put where he belongs has caused you all of this headache and yet you still trust me enough to do it?"

"It's interesting you clump murderers amongst the liars and thieves."

"Why? What are you getting at? It's what he is." I sip my coffee, the first real form of any sustenance I've had in days. I moan with delight.

"Murdering someone is perhaps one of the most honest acts of violence a person can ever commit. The intensity of the anger and the rage is so pure, there is no opportunity for their soul to deny it."

"It doesn't make it right!"

"I agree, which is why there is a special place in Hell for them, but it's not the point. Sure, they might lie about it in your courts of law later. And perhaps the moment of unadulterated hatred came before they sought out the intended victim to commit the act, making it premeditated; the point is it was there. The one defining moment categorizes their soul and sets it apart from their other sins."

"That's one Hell of a scary thought," I murmur looking sideways at him.

"Hell is a scary place if you really think about the different reasons why souls are here. It's why Cain from the Bible is charged with torturing the souls of the murderers. It was a special torment I thought up for him. He never committed such an infraction against the purity of his own soul before he killed Abel, but once he had his moment of clarity, he crossed a line. It slays him every time he has to rip into another soul, especially if they themselves were like him. Never having committed the worst of atrocities before they committed the act of murder.

The torture comes with the knowledge it was a
choice. He chose to act upon his anger and hatred,
just as they did."

"That's...that's so evil!" I look up at him in fear.
He smiles at me and what horrifies me the most is it is
kind.

"Is it? Is it evil to make his punishment his own
choice? Again and again, day after day, he has to
choose to act upon the evil burning hot within himself
in order to torment his peers. He made the decision,
Catriona. Remember that. You know all too well the
consequences of repudiation. He embraced the pit of
evil festering inside himself and he is now forced to
embrace it again and again. That isn't evil in itself. It
shows him it is there and he must utilize it to carry
out his duties. It teaches him honesty. It's the second
reason why I didn't interfere when you decided to
stand alongside Damien. You chose to do nothing in
life. You stood aside and watched. You are a rare gift
because you have learned in your afterlife to not
continue to turn the other cheek, even though it could
cost you the redemption of your soul."

I rub my forehead. "I take it the opportunity
has gone out the window. I did go against the rules."

"What rules? Do you still not understand?
Choices are what define us, Catriona. There isn't a
single soul here who is being held against their will."

"What?"

Lucifer doesn't answer me but takes a sip of his
coffee. He crosses one leg over the other and leans
back in the chair. I wait for him to answer before
continuing. When he doesn't, I press.

"What do you mean? There are souls who can't possibly leave. The goo in the Acheron River. The frozen faces in the walls outside. They're trapped."

"Trapped of their own volition. If I may say so, it is a special little torment I drummed up specifically for this place at the behest of my father. You've been looking for the sleight of hand, and as the master of deception, I do think I've overdone myself." Lucifer winks at me. "A little influence here, a touch of suggestion there, and humans will believe anything you want them to."

The significance of what he is telling me is not a single soul in this place must stay, but because they believe they are being forced to, here they are. They put so much stock in what they believe written by the hand of a few men, they don't look deep inside themselves and find an inner truth. One that tells them although there have been faults, and there is culpability to be had for the choices they made in life, they can choose to believe they are worthy of redemption. If the message about the cross and the death of one of the big man's own is true, why then do people still believe so much they deserve to be punished? I get it now. The mission he has for me about the apocalypse. My mission with Damien has never been to save the world from eternal damnation and take over ruling Hell. Hell itself is the biggest lie of them all. It has been to have the brass enough to stand up and tell people they deserve to be redeemed. The first person I am supposed to start with is myself. I snort in disbelief. The expectations just keep piling on, don't they?

"If you don't believe me, go outside. The first face on the right just before the bridge." I stare at him and he smiles again, encouragingly. "Go on. Your friends will still be here when you get back. Tell her it's time to go."

I get up from my chair and move woodenly to the door, unsure of what to believe in anymore. For so long we, as in people, have believed we are destined for punishment, only to find out the threat to the system is because of our own misconceptions. We are our own worst critiques. These words have never rung true more than when I step outside in the frozen atmosphere and find the face of the soul Satan guided me to.

I feel the hot tears run down my face as I reach up and the icy cheek I cup sends jolts of pain through my fingertips. The eighties hair woman with the bad life and the downtrodden disposition is frozen in the wall. The only reason she's here is she believed her treachery of forsaking the Lord is cause enough to see her be sent to the ninth circle of Hell. She was never given a choice. At least, not in her eyes. She never had anything in life worthy enough to prove to herself she deserved anything better, in life or in this.

I press my forehead to the ice and the pain far exceeds the headache I have been entertaining for the last three days. The cold cuts through and when I pull my forehead away, it's like being a little kid at recess who was dared to stick their tongue to the frozen flagpole. Eighties hair Fran watches me through frozen eyes.

I whisper to her, "You don't belong here. You never did. I'm sorry. I should have helped when I met you in Limbo. It's time to go. You need to go. Get out of here." I wait as her eyes begin to burn brighter as she hears my words. Just planting the kernel of hope into her is enough to give her the strength to believe she belongs someplace other than this one.

I watch as her face first cracks away from the wall and then the rest of her begins to slip away from the vacant area, which immediately freezes over. I wave to her as she begins to float upward, to the next floor. She doesn't need an elevator if she truly believes she doesn't belong here. She'll find her way out.

I stand there and watch her go until I can't see the shining orb anymore. I walk back inside, wondering how people who claim to see orbs in the human realm are actually seeing souls from the other side. Satan answers my question.

"They are the ones who believe they don't belong here, but haven't figured out they belong there instead. Or they don't believe it yet, so they are stuck in between."

I sit back down and pick up my coffee cup with shaking fingers.

"I trust you understand if this news gets out, it will completely unbalance the universe as we know it."

"Then what am I supposed to do about it?" I ask him.

"Continue saving the world, one soul at a time."

I never should have thought of the mantra, but I suppose it is a good one. I sip my coffee silently as I consider the magnitude of what he is requesting.

"Does Damien know?"

"He is on a different path, but he needs to know, and I am counting on you to bring him on board." Lucifer touches Damien's forehead, having appeared next to him in an instant. Does he fly? Teleport? The guy's ability to appear and disappear at will is freaking me out. Has he always been watching us? I shiver, thinking about the many hours spent in my bedroom air-guitaring to some of Joan Jett's, greatests. So awkward. I turn my attention back to what Lucifer is doing. The tenderness is not what I would expect from him.

"I'll try, but I mean, I don't know what I have to offer him to convince him to trust me."

"You'll figure it out. These might help." Satan pulls a few sheets of paper from his pockets and lays them on the table. They are the missing pages from the Devil's Bible.

I set my coffee aside, still not sure how I ended up grabbing a cup of Joe with Lucifer, but I unfold them. There are copies of the same pages I'd seen before. The calligraphy letters in red indicating the Devil's Mark and the same copy of the folio of the Devil as was in the copy of James' version.

When next I look up, Satan is gone, not leaving me any chance to ask if the hordes of Hell are going to get off our tails, or how we are going to get the mark off Lowell. It looks like my free pass on just visiting in this Hellish Hasbro game has just expired.

CHAPTER 18

"**O**f Ou Momi, Almi: Damien is Born." I squint at the words scrawled in ink under the folio I am reading. "What?"

My friends all came to slowly. I was left sitting there with my epic case of shock and dismay, and when questioned, I hated having to be so evasive about it all. I let them know the spell worked and when we summoned Lucifer, he gave us a free pass on account of the massive info dump he put me through. I didn't tell them about the major revelations he bestowed upon me, just, we chatted, and he left after giving me the pages.

"What do you mean he just handed them over?" Damien demanded.

I knew this was going to be hard. I didn't realize having to withhold most of the truth put me on a level with the liars and thieves I'd been so quick to condemn. I watch Zeke as he pulls himself into his chair and clutches his head. Am I so far off? Is withholding information about the truth in a way lying about it? According to Lucifer, it's all subjective, which is what the issue is.

"We had coffee, he gave me some reading material, and here we are." I tap the papers on the table sitting in between the two coffee cups.

"It's not that simple. It's never that simple with my father." He begins pacing.

"Of course it isn't, but just trust me on this one. I have a feeling we still have to answer to the rest of your uncles for evading, so we better hurry. But why is your name written on the bottom of the page here?" I point to it again and he, James, and Dante crowd in.

"I don't know." He tosses his hands up. His eyes are a murky brown like he's conveying the message, "This is total bullshit."

"Look at the letters written there." Fae also looks at the papers from the far side of the table.

I squint, not seeing what she is pointing at. They are listed just above the strange saying. I flip to the second page and try to read it, but it's in a language I don't understand. I hold it out to Damien and Dante, but they both shake their heads, so I turn back to the first page. The material is delicate and I'm afraid if we handle it too much, they will begin to break down. Satyrs are tough, having to torture people day after day, but never being contained under the strap themselves, they haven't developed very tough hides when they're used for the mundane tasks, like being filleted and having their skin stretched out to make manuscript pages out of.

"It's an anagram," Fae says after a minute. I look at the list of letters, but I still don't see it.

"Fae, care to share with the class?"

Fae gives me the "why am I trying to reason with stupid" look and I give it right back to her. We don't have time to waste here. We still need to figure out how to switch the marks and get out of dodge until the vengeance from Damien's uncles calms down a bit. From what I can gather, it hasn't been Satan coming after us directly, and I express this to Damien, although I hate not telling everyone why. I wish I could just have five minutes alone with him. Ok, maybe ten to explain it all, but the likelihood of that happening is a whole lot of none.

"It's all the letters all jumbled up. The anagram makes the saying and the letters all come from the calligraphy Devil's marked letters in the Devil's Bible."

I read the letters again out loud. "ORAMMUBEONOLMAMAONDIFIIS." We all move the letters around on the page, matching and accounting for each one as we go through the list. Sure enough, it's all the red letters from the illuminated manuscript, and they all fit the anagram written on the bottom of the page.

"Ok, but what does it mean?" James asks. "I haven't seen some of these names before, in any language."

"It's a demonic language," Damien says quietly.

I can see now where he gets his features from. In a sense. Lucifer presented the black face to me today, and although Damien is white, neither one of them are comprised of something so simple as a singular form.

"What does it mean?" I ask again.

"Everyone out." Damien nods his head to the door. No one moves. "I said out. Get out." Damien picks up the papers, folding them and putting them in his pocket.

"Damien--" I reach for his hand, which has disappeared into his pocket, but he shakes my hand away.

"Everyone except you, Catriona." No one moves a muscle and then Damien turns on them, snarling.

"Get out now!"

Tora is the first to jump, followed by Phil. I figure she needs an out, and the kid has seen and heard so much crap lately, disobeying Damien's orders isn't high on his list of priorities. The others filter out slowly. Charles leads Zeke by the arm. My girls are less anxious to leave me alone with Damien, but I give them a nod and they reluctantly leave. Even Marty slinks out of the room. Lowell is the last to hesitate and he looks like he is about to argue. I can't blame the guy, it's his life on the line, but James nudges his shoulder.

"Come on."

When the door closes, Damien sighs and sits down, tapping the rim of his father's coffee cup.

"Are you going to tell me what it means?"

"You haven't figured it out?"

I sit, too exhausted for more mind games. "Damien, please. The English is pretty straightforward, what does Ou Momi and Almi mean?"

"Ou means a South African chap and Momi means the God of Ridicule."

I get the origins of his heritage now. "And Almi?"

"Almi means a woman who feeds one's soul or lifts the spirit."

I think about this. "Ok, everyone knows the rumor your mother was a fallen angel. I don't understand the significance of everything? Why the big secret?"

Before Damien can answer, a voice speaks from the shadows in the corner of the room. "It's significant, child, because when my son was listening to the conversation between you and his father, he figured out he's been sent to help his father save the world, not destroy him in the process."

I whip around and Auntie J walks out of the shadows.

"Auntie J?" I jump out of my seat. What the heck is going on? Is she the woman Lucifer said thought I was strong enough? Why is it, this place only provokes more questions than it gives answers?

"Yes." She walks over and sits down across from both of us. Her eyes are dark and restless as she looks over Damien. "I've been worried about you. It took you long enough to come home, son."

Damien nods and my head is doing the swivel routine.

"Will someone explain to me what is going on?"

Auntie J smiles and squeezes my hand. "And look at you, all grown up and taking charge."

"Auntie J, I texted you. I called. I--"

"Had to learn a few truths for yourself before I have been allowed to step in."

The bracelets on her wrists jingle and I watch them, mesmerized as my brain tries to put the facts together. Is it possible a Gorgon demon is more than just a woman of mysteries and wisdom?

"Think about what you've figured out about Damien, Trina." I consider her words. She means he is a duality so complex, he has to balance light and dark.

"He balances to good and the evil. He--"

"He's the instrument that can help stop the apocalypse." Auntie J squeezes Damien's hand and he smiles, but there is a bitterness in his eyes I still don't get.

"I don't get it." I slump on my forearm, defeated. Some people go through life thinking about how they are going to make ends meet or what casserole to bring to the next potluck supper and I'm stuck helping good versus evil find a balance when the big day comes. Whenever that is. I remember my mantra, the one Lucifer seems so keen to keep reminding me of, and I think back to Lowell and Zeke. "Oh my God!" I jump up and Auntie J starts laughing.

"Well, yes. He has something to do with it way back in the day."

"He's--" I point to Damien. "He's the one who can switch the marks!"

Damien taps his fingers on the table. Did he know? Has he known all along and this is all some sort of ruse to bring me into the fold to coerce my cooperation for the apocalypse someday? I glance suspiciously between the two of them.

"Sit down, Catriona. There's still much to explain and no, he didn't know."

I sit on the edge of my seat and peer under the table. Where Lucifer was wearing loafers, Auntie J is

rocking a pair of strappy sandals. The two shoes
dropping couldn't be more different.

"Back in the day when I met his daddy, I was
just a woman," Auntie J begins. She pulls the second
piece of the illuminated manuscript pages out. The
one I haven't been able to decipher. She then pulls a
third piece of parchment from her pocket and places
it on the table next to the script. It's another folio, one
of the missing pages, only this one is of a garden.

"No way." I'm shaking my head.

"Yes, Eden was a beautiful place. I couldn't
have been happier. I shouldn't have been happier.
That was until Damien's daddy came along and
showed me how much more to the world there was."
Auntie J smooths her manicured fingers over the folio
of the Garden.

"J stands for Jezebel, which loosely means,
'where is the prince?' In other words, Satan, the
prince of Hell," Damien explains.

I'm having another moment of what in the
seven sins is going on as the pieces start to click into
place.

"Like, Lucifer said, a little persuasion can go a
long way. When I was first rejected and condemned
by Lucifer's father, the book was re-written. I was the
first 'Jezebel' so to speak," Auntie J continues to
explain.

"You're telling me you are Eve?" I stare at her,
trying to see some mirage or hologram like she's
going to flicker and change, but she remains as solid
and solemn as ever.

"Yes. I go by many names, child. Jezebel, Eve,
Alma…"

I shake my head. This is unreal. "So you took a bite out of the apple, the wisdom fruit, got your in-the-know on, got punished and sent to live here as a Gorgon, a demon of wisdom, all because you and Lucifer ticked off his dad?"

"You certainly have a way of boiling things down to their most primitive meaning, but yes. That is what I am telling you."

I study the folio on the table. It's archaic, but I feel like I can see the animosity between Eve, Auntie J, whoever, and Adam. It's interesting how perceptions can change so easily.

"What happened to him?" It's a personal question, but I suppose it's only fair I get the whole story if they're dragging me into their family feud.

"Ah, Adam. The deal was Lucifer and I couldn't be together until after I fulfilled my promise to Adam. Marriage, that is. Damien was cast out of the house immediately, and Adam and I went on to have more children, Cain and Abel, as I'm sure you are aware. Lucifer filled you in on Cain's whereabouts and I'm sure you can guess where Abel is residing."

"You're telling me the apocalypse has kicked off because you all need family counseling?" I cross my arms over my chest and glare at them. They have family troubles, fine. But why do I have to be dragged into it?

"No. The apocalypse kicked off over something much smaller and innocuous, child. I'm telling you all this so you have an understanding of how grossly misrepresented women are in terms of ancient literature. Have you never wondered why my story wasn't told after the incident in the garden? Nothing is ever mentioned of the deal made on behalf of saving Damien's life. I agreed to resign myself to an eternity down here, never seeing my garden again. Never finding eternal rest if it meant Damien would be spared."

"You were a symbol of purity and your adultery tainted it. I can only imagine the wrath you must have endured," I murmur. I watch Damien's face and he is giving no inclination as to what he might be feeling about all of these revelations. I don't blame Auntie J. Her bed and all, she has to lie in it. I imagine she beats herself up enough for her sins. Much the same way I do? But because we as women sin, does it mean there is some sort of scale determining the severity of the crime? Is there a balance? I've never claimed to be a feminist, but her punishment seems kind of harsh. Although, I guess I'm not the one to judge either. I think the point Lucifer has been trying to make is Heaven and Hell work on a case by case basis, the problem is, they are both inundated with thousands of cases every day.

"Eternity of being imprisoned is a long time. He took the one thing from me Lucifer was trying to offer. Freedom. I can come and go as I please anywhere here in the Underworld, but I am never free to return up above, not even to the human realm." Auntie J's eyes are wet.

I get why she has been so lenient on me. There has been a soft spot in her for the thing I have craved the most since I came here.

"At least you have Lucifer and Damien." I have to say something on account of love. What Zeke and I had may never be classified as love, but I hardly think it is fair for Auntie J, Eve, to have been punished so severely for loving, the very thing that Himself up above works so hard to promote. I get it though. She went about cultivating that love in the wrong way and now she has to pay.

"This is true." She nods her head. "Which is why I'm so keen on you helping my Damien."

"Because he's the light and the dark. He can help fix the areas too caught up in the middle."

"Exactly." Auntie J rises from her chair and walks back to the shadows.

I digest everything she has just told me and I'm about to turn around and ask her how I can possibly help, but like the memories of humans, she is gone into the recesses of the shadows.

"She got a bad rap," I say softly to Damien. He folds his hands and puts his elbows on the table.

"You're so quick to forgive her. What about Adam?"

I sigh. "I'm not saying what she did wasn't wrong. But think about it. For so long what has the joke been? If Eve hadn't eaten the apple. I'm just saying. I get she wanted the freedom of knowledge. And now she has to pay her penance, I also get the punishment fits the crime. Now all the family's secrets are out, supposedly, tell me. Did you know?"

Damien looks out over the top of his hands and he's already shaking his head. "I suspected, but they never confirmed it. Now I understand why. They waited until the opportune moment to tell me everything. I always knew my particular talents were vastly different than anything Lucifer has created before, but I didn't know how he did it. It's not something he conjured up with the supernatural, it's something he created with my mother."

I look at the fruit and the trees on the folio Auntie J left behind. I wonder who scribed these particular pages? And then it hits me.

"Dante!" I rise from my chair and cross the room, pulling open the door. Everyone outside is shivering, but I ignore their discomfort. Knowing the number of lies told to cover up the truth is enough to drive a girl bonkers.

"He said he had to go back," Phil's teeth are chattering.

I nod and turn back to Damien. "Your dad picked him. In exchange for covering up the truth in the Codex Gigas, he gave him a personal tour of Hell so Dante would see the truth himself."

"It can't be. He--"

"Think about it, Damien. Dante was born in 1265. The Codex Gigas was also written in the early 13th century according to dating, but the dates are subjective, aren't they?"

"Ok, I'll buy the theory, but say he was the scribe for my father. Why did he decide to wait over 1300 years to write it all down?"

"Any number of reasons. The written word wasn't widespread until then. The crusades? Maybe he thought the real truth would get out. Look, it doesn't matter. What matters is we have all the bits and pieces, Damien. You know this. You also know the reason I started this sojourn in the first place. Are you going to help me or not? I agreed to rule Hell with you and here we are being given free rein of it to fix the mess your parents made centuries ago."

Damien rises from the chair as the rest of our party looks at us in utter confusion. "I don't know how to switch the marks, Catriona."

"Yes, you do. Think about it. You did it for Marty in a sense." I point to the Hound whose outline has solidified even more. Pretty soon he might even be able to shift back to a man.

The look on Damien's face suggests he is nervous, which is off-putting. "Trina, I only tried it on a dead man's soul and look what happened to him."

Damien points to Marty, but I refuse to look too closely at the gelatinous substance which still clings to him in places. I get if he tries to switch the marks and he botches it, we could end up with two twin puddles of soup, but Lucifer and Auntie J handed us the answers. It sucks not being able to tell anyone else what the answers are, but I get it's for their own good.

"You have to try. Please, Damien. One at a time." I hold the door open and beckon everyone inside. I get the hairy eyeball from everyone, even Phil who looks run down. There's got to be something we can do for the poor kid. I wonder if I'll start looking at everyone, I am around like this. Like I have a purpose and it's to provide them with any reason to feel worth something. "Hang in there kid, it's almost over." I nudge his shoulder as he walks by.

I prop the door with my boot, wondering if I'll ever get the chance to grill Dante about his in-the-know about everything. He practically wrote the baby book about Damien. It's hard to imagine Damien wearing a pair of those knitted booties though. For real, was Auntie J pro pacifier or anti-paci?

Thinking about Damien as anything other than a cataclysmic event is hard to process. Instead, I choose to focus on it because all the other big Q's answered are too much to process right now. I wonder if he ever rode a tricycle around Wrath, the fifth circle of Hell. Ankle bashing anyone with a tricycle is enough to induce road rage. It might explain a few of the less than sweet dispositions around here. I grin. I always knew he had a penchant for getting on people's nerves. If it wasn't so terrifying, it might be kind of fun to be in on the secret.

I'm just about to walk back and sit down when I hear a shout come from outside the doors. I run and slide on the ice as I skid to a halt in front of the bridge. Treachery has many faces and the one I should have been watching out for since the beginning is the evil little smirk of Jeremiah Worthington as he welcomes Zeke and Charles into his ranks. Amongst those ranks, are the hordes of demons we have been waiting on, sent by the uncles he has pissed off. It looks like Damien might have a free pass from mommy and daddy, but the rest of Hell doesn't understand why he's getting away with his coup de grace. I've never been good at subterfuge, and as I watch Zeke shake hands with Jeremiah and Charles' eyes glint back at us in the cold, I kick myself internally, wishing I listened to my gut in the first place.

CHAPTER 19

"Is that your brother hanging on the door?" I point to Judas Iscariot's frozen head, but direct my question at Charles. He frowns and looks confused, answering my question. "Never mind, scratch that. Why did you hop on the bandwagon of betrayal then?"

Charles ignores my question, but everyone is fixated on him, even his double-crossing pals, Zeke and Jeremiah.

"Answer her."

I've never heard Damien's voice be so cold. The menace in it sends a chill down my spine and I kick myself mentally, given after everything I have just learned, I am wondering if Charles can be reasoned with or saved. I never held any hope for Jeremiah and maybe a small part of me did for Zeke, but seeing the look on his face now, I know he's a goner for sure.

"The two of you think you're something special. You talk about changing the system from the inside like you are privy to something the rest of us don't know. Ever since I was put in your little gang, I've faced nothing by restrictions. Did it never occur to you, prince of Hell, I enjoy the dark? I like the way things are run the old way." Charles' eyes are beginning to glow, but the creepiest fact about him is he's openly admitting to enjoying being a predator and hurting people.

"There's a new one. Evil admitting it enjoys doing evil. Your originality is off the charts."

Charles snarls at me and takes a step forward. "I'm going to enjoy ripping out your tongue merely for the fact I won't have to listen to the sound of your voice." His imagery is spot on.

I wonder if he's going to feed it to the wolves so to speak. I look at Marty who is looking a bit peckish, then I shrug. "Whatever. Are we going to do this or what? I've been waiting all damn day for Zeke to make a move, so let's dance and get it over with. You wanted a fight, here it is." Brave words from a woman who is outnumbered one hundred to one at least. I hear Damien clear his throat and wait for his diplomatic approach.

I guess he's done playing the bureaucrat because in the next instant, a wave like a force field blasts through Treachery, knocking everyone including myself over. The effect is the sound of a gunshot ringing from somewhere at the back of the horde and before I can figure out who brought a gun to an explosives fight, the walls around Treachery start caving in. Falling ice spears, the waiting mass of demon bodies below, and it gives us enough opportunity to grab the humans and go.

I launch myself into the fray of confusion as bodies of demons start staggering backward on the bridge. The effect is instantaneous. They freeze in blocks of ice on the spot, giving Damien and I the opportunity to push past Charles, Zeke, and

Jeremiah. I figure if we have any hope, it's to try and save the humans first. I can't help but look back at my girls, who have taken the cue to jump in the fight that has kicked off and try to buy us some time. It won't be long before the other demons realize they are fighting their own, and turn from them to chase us, but without the benefit of Dante and Charles to fly us across the frozen lake, Damien and Phil are stuck trying to fly Lowell and James to the other side, while I attempt to take down the biggest threat; Charles.

It's no easy task either. From the ground, I launch myself onto the shoulders of the nearest frozen demon, which is on all four legs, and I tackle Charles, who has also attempted to fly at Damien and steal James and Lowell away from him.

The best I can figure is he has been plotting with Jeremiah from the beginning and without Charles' help, Jeremiah and Zeke are just two chumps with a dream for freedom. My girls have all shifted and although I can feel the pressure in my spine to go kitty side up, I resist the urge, wanting the takedown to come from my full mental capacity and not the enraged predatory instincts of my inner demon. Charles kicks me in the mouth as I slide on the back of the frozen demon. The cracking of ice sounds like more gunshots, as several demons scramble around trying to get away from the bridge. What I didn't understand and what I am seeing happen now, is the demons who have opted to forgo the bridge and brave the ice of the lake are the ones causing the ice movements I'm seeing and hearing.

Amongst the cacophony of ice sculptures popping up, the souls inside the lake are not at all happy about their slumber being disturbed and let's face it, would you be too if someone walked on your nose to get where they were going? The faces in the ice on the lake are snapping and clawing at the demons and satyrs above them. Judging by the look of surprise on their faces, they never expected the ones they judged and sent here to be frozen to unfreeze and fight back. It's our only chance of ever surviving this attack though. I'm not stupid enough to think the faces in the ice won't turn on my girls and me in an instant, but it's the distraction we need to push through and help Damien.

It's like playing don't touch the floor as a kid, but the object of this game is don't touch the teeth or you'll plummet into the icy depths below. I circumvent the bridge with this tactic and behind me, I hear Tora doing the same thing. She hasn't shifted to a saber tooth yet, and although I'm not sure why maybe she can't handle the shift so soon after the last one, she's apologizing to each face she hops on.

"Sorry, sorry, so--"

"Tora, focus!" I shout at her. I don't want her to get distracted by feeling bad. We've got plenty to feel bad about, but surviving this treachery is at the top of the list in my opinion.

Tabby, Fae, and Leo are pushing through the other demons, who fortunately are so preoccupied with the dilemma they are facing thanks to Jeremiah, Zeke, and Charles, it gives us the opportunity to focus on those three weasels. I see Jeremiah and Zeke crouching next to one of the walls as part of the upper wall begins to rain down in the corridor and I worry there might be a cave in. I launch myself at Zeke and get body checked for my effort. I hit the wall hard as Jeremiah stands and runs over to help my assailant. I just manage to get my hands over my face when I feel Jeremiah's boot connect with my ribs, and I gasp from the pain and dry heave. Charles is the culprit who body slammed me and I look up in time to see him pick Zeke up and begin flying after Damien, James, and Lowell.

Damien's been caught up in some of the demons who can fly and although they are hesitant to take on Satan's son, it seems the area is so congested with demons trying to get above the cave in, they are hindering him from making a clean get away with the humans. I have the momentary thought it was a mistake bringing them here. Of course it was a mistake, but I've never claimed to be perfect when it comes to judgment calls. I'm the queen of hasty, bad decisions. Which also causes me to get another boot to the side because I am so worried about everyone else, I forgot Jeremiah is gleefully pummeling me.

"How'd he do it?" I gasp as I manage to catch his boot before it makes contact with my face.

"Who?"

"Charles. How did he let you know we were here?" I may have caught his boot with my hand, but it doesn't stop the pinky from snapping on my hand and I shriek in pain.

Leo finally pushes through the crowd and pounces on him, knocking him backward as I scramble to my feet. I race toward him as he fights from under a stampede of satyrs who are trying to get out by the elevator. Fat lot of good it will do them if they can only go up ten or so at a time. Even Hell has elevator restrictions.

"Telepathy."

"Makes sense for an incubus. Tell me something. Do you know what I'm thinking of doing now?"

As he freezes and looks around for the imminent danger he's in, I shove him hard. He stumbles backward and trips over a fallen satyr. When he lands, it's with a whoosh of air escaping his lungs, but in the next instant, he freezes. When I mean he freezes; I mean he turns into a solid block of treacherous Jeremiah popsicle. His eyes freeze first, in shock. And then his body begins to slow, like in a slow-mo scene in a bad B-rated movie. He stumbles as he loses mobility in his legs, and then his arms flail like a fledgling duckling as he attempts his first flight, trying to escape his fate. His arms freeze next, the blue tint under his skin creeps up through his arms and fingers, and I shudder as I watch the blue of his veins under his skin in his hands freeze, and so too the rest of him. It's like watching ice form under his skin. It makes me think of the alligators in the south in the winter when the water freezes. I imagine their bodies growing sluggish and then they stick their noses up in the air, just above the ice as it forms around them, so they can remain in a state of hibernating stasis. They know it's coming, so they prepare at the last possible moment, and then they are stuck, nose up past the water level and body remaining frozen in place. Jeremiah, the predator, is no different. He turns his head up in a silent plea to a Heaven that will have nothing to do with him, just as the rest of the ice pushes it's way up through the top of his skull like a weird version of someone blowing their top off in anger in a cartoonish way and steam comes out their ears. Only with Jeremiah, it's icicle shards and it isn't so cartoonish, but silent and creepy. I pushed him onto the bridge he stumbled near.

Without giving him another thought, I turn back around and fight my way through the crowd. It looks like Phil, Tora, Tabby, and Fae have been cornered in one area and are fighting to break through to the back door. Leo is standing guard fending off attacks near the elevator. From the looks of it, she took a satyr horn down her side and it must be deep to cause so much blood, but she'll pull through as long as we can keep ourselves from being torn to pieces long enough to heal. The problem is we are vastly outnumbered. Without the ability to get the word out to the masses we have been given a pardon by Lucifer, we're still considered fugitives until Lucifer has the big powwow with his brothers and the word is sent around to call off the manhunt.

I assess the situation as I punch a demon with a snakelike body and a lion's head. The roaring it is doing while getting all up in my face is distracting.

"To Leo!" I shout to the others and point to the elevator. Fae looks up and begins pushing the group along the wall and they slowly inch their way, but the horde is pressing in on them. I continue to battle with the snake-lion as it slithers back at me, none too impressed with being assaulted by a fellow feline, and just when I think we're all going to go down in the fray, the door we'd come in through bursts open.

In through the door bounds Marty, Dick, and Doug. I'd not considered where he went. I figured he was loitering somewhere near Tabby, but who says you can't teach an old dog new tricks? Marty must have run off to rally his brother Hounds, or Satan sent them to help us, while he goes to the princes to inform them of his hiatus starting as of now.

Marty begins tearing into bodies around him, along with Dick and Doug as they make a path to the Hellcats and Phil. I turn my full attention back to the demon. The closest thing it resembles is a Manticore, and I figure they must be some distant cousins or something, seeing as this whole fiasco is family feud related.

The snake end whips around and just in the nick of time, I grab it before it sweeps under my feet and I yank hard on the massive body. Being a Hellcat comes with some perks, like supernatural strength, but the demon is heavier than the average man, and I only succeed in pissing it off. I see when the attack comes. It strikes like a viper, lashing out and biting, and I dodge to the side in time for the lion's head to hit the ice wall behind me.

I trip and stumble as I make my way to my girls, but the lion's head continues to strike out, crumbling icy faces to the ground each time.

I reach my crew at the same time they break through to help Leo, and Dick and Doug take over the advancing snake demon. One latches on with paws and claws to the lion head, while the other sinks his claws into the scaly tail. It's the most gruesome game of tug-of-war I have ever seen two dogs play. I manage to reach down and punch the button for the elevator, hating the fact we still have to wait for the damn thing to descend.

I look up, searching the ceiling for Damien or Charles, and quickly duck when a spray of ice rains down from the sky. I can't see that high up, but I wonder if either one of them managed to punch through the icy ceiling and escape into the level above. I don't have time to worry about it now, as another satyr jabs at my side with what looks like a halberd. I bring my arm down, forcing the blade to the floor as I hear the ping of the elevator behind me. The doors rattle open and I start shoving my girls into it one by one. They shift, giving room for the next, and a massive pile of bodies presses in as I whistle loud enough for Dick and Doug to hear me.

I feel a hand on the back of my jacket as someone pulls me into the elevator, and I frantically press the button to level one and the button for the doors to close. We all squeeze into the back so Dick, Doug, and Marty can snap at any satyrs and smaller demons who try to press in and prevent the doors from closing. It takes a few minutes for the doors to eventually slide shut, and then we hear the slamming and pounding against it. It shakes the whole compartment, and I'm wondering if they are going to pull the elevator right off the track and send us plummeting to the bottom of the shaft.

The compartment begins to ascend as the cheesy music kicks on while I hear everyone breathing hard and the Hounds panting as we slowly begin to climb. The smell of blood and viscera from the satyrs fills the elevator and I hold my breath, leaning against the back wall, resting for a minute before we face the next onslaught. I have no idea what we will find when we reach Limbo, but what I see when the doors slide open is even more chaos.

Bodies litter the floor of the souls waiting in line. Screaming, panicking people are pushing back to the rivers and even some are escaping through the garage door. I step off the elevator and shout to Leona.

"Grab robes, jackets, anything. Cover up. We're getting out of here."

Leo turns to the nearest Drude and has more brass than I would. She reaches into the haze and grabs onto the robe and tugs. Her eyes widen as whatever horror she witnesses assaults her mind, but she comes away victorious. She tosses the ratty looking robe to Tora who pulls it on, and we push our way through the crowd to Damien and Charles, who are entangled with one another in a battle. I race in, trying to think of how to help, while I hear the indignant cries of people being stripped at the hands of Leo. I scan the room and see Zeke dragging Lowell toward the garage. There's blood gushing from Lowell's head and I wonder how he was injured and how bad. I don't see James anywhere, but he can't be my priority right now. I said one soul at a time and Lowell's soul is about to be kidnapped right out from under me.

I push my way through the crowd, but it takes a long time to get to the doors. I push through to the garage just in time to see Zeke shut the back door of a van parked nearest to the door of Limbo. He must have picked it because it's convenient and Hell gets a lot of bulk deliveries, sometimes straight off the prison yard, so the van, emblazoned with the horned profile of Satan's head, is custom painted on the van.

I sprint after Zeke, but he's already in the driver's seat. There has never been any need to take the keys out of any of the vehicles here in the garage because there has never been anyone stupid enough to steal any of Lucifer's rides. I miss my motorcycle at the moment and I figure without her, I need to choose a different one in order to chase after Zeke, so I hop in the McLaren. I figure if Satan is going to bump up my responsibility around here until the apocalypse decides to throw down, he can bump up my ride when I need him to.

I shove the car into gear and cringe as I race after Zeke. The last thing I want to do is bust up these wheels, but the ride is smooth and I hardly feel the jolt as we smash through the barrier and the portal, ending up on the highway, headed back to Lowell's bar, the Sloshed Sloth.

I shift and pick up the speed. There is no way I am letting the little schmuck get away. Not after everything we have been through this past week trying to right a wrong. The van is no match for the speed of the McLaren and I play chicken with Zeke for the second time as I try to force him off the road. The sun is bright and as I swerve to get Zeke to slow down, I bump the van and feel the scrape of the metal as it connects with the side panel. We come up over a hill at the same time as I hit him and it's just enough to send the van in a roll down the other side. I watch in horror as the back doors fly open, and Lowell's body is thrown from the back. I slam on the breaks and the tires skid along the pavement, just as the van rolls to a stop at the bottom of the hill.

Jumping from the car when I throw it in park, I race to the ditch where I find Lowell, lying limp and unresponsive.

"Lowell! Wake up! Lowell!" I shake him and press my ear to his face. I feel the puff of his breath against it and breathe a sigh of relief. He isn't out of the woods yet, judging by the odd angle of his wrist and ankle, he's got some broken bones. My biggest fear is internal bleeding.

I glance around wildly, but calling for help out here in the dry desert heat isn't going to do me any good. I drag Lowell back to my car, thanking my lucky supernatural stars. It still requires some effort and in addition to being caked in blood, I feel the sweat dripping down my face. I pat my pockets in vain. I'd lost my cell phone out of them a long time ago in the uprising in Treachery. My best bet is to get him to the Sloshed Sloth and call for help.

As I pull past the van, I consider stopping to check on Zeke, but the rattling sound of Lowell's breath is what worries me and I gun the engine. The bar is only a couple of miles down the road and I pull into the parking lot to see the same beat-up cars parked there before, and the doors still standing open. The open sign isn't lit, but I drag Lowell up the steps and into the bar and make a mad dash for the phone and the first aid kit. I dial 911 as tears start to stream down my cheeks. It's been a long time since I cried this much and the thought of losing Lowell now we were so close to saving him, thanks to my stupidity, has finally pushed me over the edge.

"Don't you dare die on me!" I scream at him. I hold his head in my lap and rock back and forth, waiting anxiously for the sounds of the paramedics. I've never been one to welcome the sounds of sirens, but now it seems like they can't come fast enough. I jump when I hear the sounds of footsteps on the stairs outside and I'm about to turn and rage at Zeke for being the reason his brother is on death's door, when once again I am staring down the barrel of a forty-five. The flashback hit's my brain as hard as the coming bullet. It makes me think of black holes in the universe. I have always wondered what is on the other side. Where is the stuff getting sucked up into them go? Is there a massive pile of universal junk and refuse lying in a cavern somewhere on the other side? I guess it's kind of like death. What happens to all the mundane shit we experience every day? Or the drama? The stress and anxiety of life? For most people, staring into a black hole is done with the knowledge or belief there is a light on the other side and all of the crap just drops away into the void of the universe. Maybe it gets recycled back for other souls on the planet to have to experience. Not for me though. That crap stays with me on the other side. I guess it's the Cosmo's big karmic eff-you for not playing the game the right way during life. It's like an eternity of being in the penalty box. You sit there, wanting to be let out and go help the team, help humanity, but for a demon it's too late. It's an eternity of being benched and my ass can't do anything about it. Until I could. Now I'm faced with the same circumstances. Knowing there is nothing on the other side but darkness with only a spark of hope seems impossible to achieve a positive outlook. The light for me comes before the darkness. The light is the realization of all of the things in life I could have had. All of the blessings, the good, and the beautiful and then when the light fades, I know it will be over and there will be despair.

I brace myself, cursing the inner sense of déjà vu. Too little, too late. I made my bed for the second time and I know I'm about to be lying in it. I've gotten comfortable there, until the circumstances with Lowell pushed me to get uncomfortable. I tried to act. To not stand by and do nothing and another big issue with guns is occasionally they backfire. Will I be so lucky for a second chance this second time around? I doubt it. I wonder if Auntie J will be on the other side, waiting for me and giving me her best, "Child you've stepped in it again." Look. I inhale deeply, not needing to but savoring the experience anyway. Hope is one thing I think is inherent in all of us, even when we are presented with odds so drastic, it can be argued we have no business having a sense of hope. But resignation is a different feeling all together. Choices were made. Convictions were upheld. Consequence is a notion inherent to both good and negative experiences and I'm ready to face the consequences of my second go-round. At least, I think I am. Until I see the flash of gunfire blast from the end of the black void and hear the shots of not one bullet being fired from the gun, but two.

CHAPTER 20

I come to and thank my lucky stars the headache is finally gone. In its place though, is the sense something is seriously wrong. I groan and sit up, looking around the bar. The sense of foreboding doesn't lessen any, especially when I set my hand down in something warm and sticky. I pick it up, smelling the familiar rusty scent and see the crimson staining my hand. I blink in confusion and look around, just as I remember the gunfire. Two shots. One between the eyes, blasting away the headache. The other...

I fling myself on his chest and scream as I turn and see Lowell lying in the pool of blood.

"No! Lowell, wake up! Lowell, please!" I pound on his chest before I remember I'm supposed to be doing something in this case. Some human act to help save him. My fists hurt from beating his chest before I remember, and with shaking hands, I start CPR.

I hear shouts and look out the window in time to see Mr. Suit and Tie, along with his two brutes being intercepted by Damien and the rest of the crew. I'm assuming since he is standing there, he laid waste to Charles, and then don't spare the incubus another thought. I press my mouth to Lowell's and breath just as the pounding of footsteps come through the door and the gasps and cries come from Tora and Fae.

"Help me!" I shout at them both and Fae starts compressions as Tora sinks to the floor. The newbie has seen too much this past week. Her eyes glass over and I know it will be a while before she comes out of her shock. I continue the breaths as I hear the sirens in the distance finally, but looking in the dull honey-colored eyes of Lowell, I know it's too late.

Time slows and the sirens become faint and almost like a buzzing as Damien kneels beside Lowell's body. Leo and Tabby are frozen like clay figures running through the door and I see the bodies of the thugs outside the grimy windows where Dick and Doug are standing over them. Marty is crouched low and it's like the whole area has frozen in slow motion and I know it isn't Damien's particular talents, although this time he has been spared the deep sleep the master manipulator can inflict.

"He didn't deserve the mark." I look around for Satan. He appears near the bar, setting a glass of scotch down. "Zeke was the one those thugs were supposed to kill. Please, you have to do something!" I beg, looking up at Satan.

Damien stares at his father, waiting to see if he will interfere with the events.

"I'm afraid there is nothing I can do." Satan crouches, looking over his body.

Damien's hand is resting over Lowell's heart where the bullet entrance is slowly seeping blood.

"There has to be. It was a mistake, a cosmic screw-up. There has to be something you can do." The mark we can all see on Lowell's chest slowly begins to fade. No, no, no!

I breathe into Lowell's mouth again, but it's in vain. I know he's gone as the last part of the light from his soul dims. I watch it as it leaves his body. It floats up like an orb and I wonder who will hold out their hand and collect it. Damien or Satan.

"Please." I breath looking between them.

"They can't do anything, Catriona. But I can."

My head whips around and through the tears I see Phil shrug his shoulders. He looks sad. Like a teenager who has seen too many horrors for such a young age. I frown. What can a fallen angel teenager possibly do to could fix this?

"Phil?" He walks over and crouches down nearus. He doesn't answer me, but instead, he looks at Lucifer.

"Take it. For what it's worth anyway. You can have it and make this right." He points to Lowell and I'm still confused. Lucifer hesitates for a moment and then looks up like he's sending up some vibes to his own father, and then his face flickers as he reaches out to cup the area above Phil's heart.

"What are you doing? What's he doing?" I ask Damien who looks equally confused. I watch as a small, dim light appears under Satan's hand and it comes away with his fingers. Phil sags and breathes heavy, his eyes blink in and out of focus as he watches the small light disappear into Lowell's chest. It's so small, like the taper of a birthday candle, and just as I figure out what has happened, it disappears inside Lowell.

"No! Give it back to him." I touch the back of Lucifer's hand and it scorches my own. I hiss and look at it. There's a red mark on my palm I'm pretty sure will be there permanently, but it doesn't matter now. The mark of the Devil.

I shake my hand and gape at Phil. I've heard of children, en masse and singularly being the most gracious beings on Heaven and Earth. What I have never witnessed is the grace being so readily given by one who has been subjected to Hell. And it's what I am looking at. Phil's grace disappears inside Lowell and the bullet wound in his chest slowly begins to heal and, in another moment, Lowell's eyes blink open and he groans.

"Why?" I plead first with Satan, then with Lowell. He's just a kid. He had a chance to save himself. Redeem his soul where he had fallen, and I don't understand why he would so readily give it up for a stranger, a man with a shady brother and a rocky past.

"Did he never tell you why he fell from grace?" Lucifer brushes a tear away from my cheek as I try to catch Phil's eye. His fingers don't scald me this time, but they are still warmer than a human's hands.

"He fell from grace because he hacked the system and crashed the Wi-Fi for Heaven and Hell."

"What? That was it? The only reason? Your father is punishing a kid who got bored one day and made a stupid mistake? What's the point of working so hard for redemption when something so trivial is the reason people are cast out of Heaven?" I feel the anger pulsing through me as Lowell tries to sit up. Damien pushes him back to the floor as Lucifer speaks again.

"Communication is key. It always has been to

make the system run right. His tampering messed with it and set the motion for the apocalypse to get rolling. By sacrificing his grace just now so Lowell can be saved, he has redeemed himself and stalled the apocalypse, for now."

"You put the weight of the world on the shoulders of a sixteen-year-old fallen angel?" Are the Cosmos full of sick jokes today or what?

"Haven't the humans already done just that with their reliance on the next generation? And yet they sit there chastising his very generation for not being emotionally mature enough to accept such a responsibility. What's the saying? These kids today." The reasoning for the scales to be tipped then balanced is so trivial, it makes my heart ache. How am I supposed to win against odds like this? Life isn't fair, but the judgment day when it ends is supposed to be. It's what we learn anyway. I guess the lesson here is the fairness comes when we make it so.

I have a flash of another child who was taken too soon. A little girl holding a doll who was supposed to save the world with her innovative technology for energy. Would she and Phil have been friends in Heaven? No one will ever know now because, by some design flaw by divine providence, Phil doesn't get to rise up from this. He's made his stand and his time has come. Another youth taken too soon and even in death, he won't find peace save for the knowledge he has saved billions, at least for a time. It should be enough. But it isn't for me. What about Phil? What happens to this one soul now? Do kids slip through the cracks in the after-life like they do in the human realm? It's unfortunate, but just part of the way of things? I can't let that happen.

"If he stays in Hell, what happens to him?"

"I suppose by definition, his sacrifice has earned him privileges. He will be allowed some free reign."

"Me. Let him ride with me and the girls. I'll look after him." It doesn't slip past me. Once again, I am on my knees, begging. But pride be damned. If I can be granted this, maybe as a new co-ruler, I can find the loophole on behalf of Phil.

I look at the melting feathers, which have begun to pool around Phil's feet. He'd been molting for a while now, but the second he made the decision to save Lowell, they fell at once to the floor. I gently touch one. I can't stand to look at his face. The feathers are symbolic of the loss of youth, the loss of life as an innocent. I don't need to see it etched on his face because I'd already seen it. I just didn't know what it was at the time.

"You will be responsible to ensure he doesn't get ahold of anything tech related again. The last thing I need is a bored teenager having the system for fun and starting another apocalypse." Satan's lips twitch and his eyes tell me he knew I would bargain for the kid. Why give me most of the pertinent details of the apocalypse, if the minor ones were going to be left out?

"He won't. I'll make sure of it." Griping about my deal isn't going to do any good now. I have to work with what I have, just as I should have done as a human with my less than stellar circumstances.

"Good." Lucifer stands and glances around the room. "You're going to need to clean the rest of the mess up, Catriona." He gazes down at Lowell, who rises to his elbows.

He opens his mouth, but croaks, trying to ask the question I can't bring myself to ask.

"I suspect you will need a means by which to get there, seeing as you smashed the bumper of the McLaren."

I cringe, but say nothing. I wonder how good his insurance is. He rubs the black and white stubble on his jaw, and walks to the door, looking out over the parking lot.

"I don't know where he is. I left him in the ditch to save Lowell," I admit quietly. Lucifer is adamant the balance is maintained when it comes to the Underworld and the Heavenly realm. He's been denied a soul for Hell and I can only assume he's not at all impressed with the condition I left his car in. But it seems he's not above lending a helping hand, given the circumstances. I reach across and grab Phil's hand, needing to reassure him and myself, although he doesn't get to achieve redemption, it can come in many forms, including the reprieve from eternal torture. I don't know Phil's whole story. I wonder where his family and friends are. I wonder if they are ok and how he died. Did anyone grieve for him? The questions don't need to be asked for me to know it is important to tell him I won't let him sink alone into the abyss. I'll be the someone he needs to hold onto this existence, even as dismal as it seems.

I thought the soul I needed to be saving was Lowell's soul. The funny thing about Fate is it hardly ever lets you know when the curveball is coming. The whole proverb be kind to your neighbor extends to even the people who seem inconsequential. By saving a stranger, one kid has managed to give Damien and I a breather from having to save the world. The apocalypse is coming, there's no doubt about that. The uprising in the Underworld proved the system needs to change, but it's going to come from the inside and with more costs than I care to count right now.

"I can't go there." Lucifer turns to Damien. Wherever the there is he is referring to, I have no idea.

"No, but I can." A familiar voice comes from the back of the room and all heads turn toward it and are greeted with a brilliant white light.

Dante walks around the bar and once again I find a glass of something stronger than coffee being thrust into my hands. Drinking coffee with the Devil and swill with the scribe is something I never thought would happen to me in a million years and yet here I am. I take a drink and feel the burn down my throat. It's long overdue as I think about my last task at hand.

Lucifer raises his glass to Dante, who in turn salutes him, and then time reverts itself to human standards and the sirens draw closer.

As the paramedics pull in, the aftermath of the shootout takes forever to sort out.

"How are you standing right now?" The young paramedic with green eyes stare Lowell down. Lowell shrugs and looks out the window.

"The blood's not mine. There has been a mistake. I think one of the patrons was confused and scared and called it in wrong. The shooter missed me."

"How?" The other paramedic, a woman in her thirties who looks less aggressive and more keen takes in the sight of the blood and then Lowell's shirt. The blood soaking it is going to be hard to explain.

"They hit my dog." The lie rolls easily off his lips and I lean back against the wall, feeling the grime of the day permeating my clothes and skin. There's nothing that makes a girl want a long hot soak or a scalding shower to boil away the sins and stains of the soul. I might not need to take a shower being a demon and all, but I have some standards. Hell might smell like a taxidermist boiling the head of a carcass to bleach and mount a skull, but it doesn't mean I should.

"Really? Where's the dog?" The guy questions him again.

"Out back. Waiting to be buried whenever we are finished here. Clearly I'm not shot and not dead so I'm still wondering why you are here." Lowell's lies are coming smoother than honey. Not that I want him marring his soul I have fought so hard to save the last few days, but I jump on the bandwagon and move this show along. I've got shit to do, tracking Zeke and all.

I walk over to him and put my head against chest, willing the waterworks to start.

"Honey, are we done here. I want to give Zekie a proper burial. He was my favorite good boy! My baby!" I think about Fiona as I wail into his chest. It's the only thing really making me cry anymore. Unresolved issues and all. The female paramedic seems to take sympathy on the situation, although it's clear she isn't buying it. She doesn't have the authority to do anything about it though. The guy on the other hand is clearly uncomfortable. He gives Lowell a sympathetic look like they're bonding over the inability to offer consolement to a hysterical woman.

"Sorry dude." He says and picks up his equipment. Lowell plays along and pats my back, crooning at the top of my head.

"It's cool." To me, "It's ok, Baby. He's not going to suffer now. We'll take care of him. We'll make sure we do him justice" He pats my head and I grimace into his chest. Maybe calling the make-believe dead dog wasn't such a good idea. But it isn't like his acting skills are on fleek and I'm ready for the externals to be wrapped up and sent on their merry medical way. "Sorry for the misunderstanding." Lowell says to them with a finality telling them the conversation is done and they shouldn't let the door hit them in the ass on the way out. They nod and the lady picks up her equipment and walk to the door. As the guy pushes it open, I can see two other paramedics in the parking lot, loading stretchers into the ambulances. The woman turns back one more time.

"I'm sorry for your loss. I just find it strange the shooting happened half an hour ago and yet you've already cleaned up the dog toys, bowls and dog bed? Most people wait a week or two before doing that." Her eyes bore into mine and I slap my mental self so hard with a picture of Fiona in my mind's eye it makes my breath catch and I start wailing anew. Letting myself feel the ache of missing her is enough to start the free flow of tears anew. Not that I want to spank my inner demons and wake them up, but really lady? Give it a rest already.

"How am I supposed to walk past Zekie's bed, Lowell? What does she want from us?" I sob into his shoulder and he pulls me closer. I can feel the tension in his body and can picture the glare he is giving the woman. Yeah, that's right lady. Walk your Medical McJudgy pants the fuck out the door. You're supposed to be assessing medical emergencies, not my blatant insanity. Some monsters wear a smile and a uniform and although I have nothing but mad respect for first responders, if the first reaction is to berate your patients because you don't agree with their pet preferences, get to stepping!

When the emergency personnel leaves with Zeke's former employers in the back of the ambulances, I turn to Dante.

"Where are we going?"

He smiles and holds out his arm. I lightly touch it and in a flash, I feel myself being whipped through time and space as I am transported through what can only be deemed as a Heavenly portal. When I open my eyes, I find myself standing on the banks of the Ogden River in Eden, Utah. Time slowed at the Sloshed Sloth with Satan in residence, but it hadn't for the rest of the world. I hear a crash inside the camp Gigi built and I hold up my hand to Damien, who apparently can come here, despite his mother and father not being permitted back in Eden.

"Zeke, come out now. It's over," I call.

All activity ceases inside the camp and I walk to the door. "Zeke, come on." I reach out a shaking hand and open the door slowly. I should have expected it, but I'm so bone-tired, I misjudged the force of which Zeke comes blasting out the door.

"I don't want to die!" He shrieks as he plows me over. He races around the side of the camp and I scamper after him, tired and sore, but no less determined to see this through.

"Zeke!" I catch up to him and tackle him. We roll down the bank to the river and land in it with a splash. The cool water rushes over my injuries and bathing myself in the waters of Eden somehow seems to lift my spirit. Things didn't work out the way I expected them to, but the more I think about it, they really did work out the way they needed to.

"You killed my brother," he screams and chokes on a mouthful of water.

"Zeke, he's alive." I wrestle with his arms, trying to get him to calm down.

"I saw him. I saw him in the ditch when I drove by. You killed him," he shrieks.

"Damn it, Zeke, he's still alive!" I shout again. I punch him in the nose, grimacing when I feel it crunch under my fist. I think Hell needs to offer sensitivity training and I'm going to ask Auntie J about it when I get back. He continues to struggle, but I see something that makes me stop fighting. Tears are streaming down his cheeks. Is it possible? Is it likely Zeke is capable of feeling some remorse? "Zeke, he has been saved. He's alive and he's at the Sloshed Sloth. I'm telling you the truth."

The tension slowly leaves Zeke's body as the words sink in. I study his face, wondering where the hatred I felt for this man has gone. Is it possible to forgive someone who has committed so heinous a crime as to let their girlfriend be killed? I sit in the rushing cool water of the river and provide the same comfort I gave his brother. I hold Zeke against me, not having felt the humanity in him before now, and I let him cry for all of the things he has bottled up inside which have turned sour.

"I don't want to die," he sobs into my shoulder.

I can't think of anything to say that could possibly make this any better so I shut my eyes and continue to rock him back and forth, like comforting a child.

It's a long while before he calms down enough to pull away. I say nothing as he wipes the tears from his cheeks. How many people do you know who can look at their day of reckoning with complete composure? Everyone, even the bad guys, have a breaking point somewhere.

We climb out of the river and walk back toward the cabin. Zeke freezes when he sees a woman standing next to Damien, talking quietly. Her silver hair shines like the top of the water on the lake. Her skin is so white it is almost translucent, and it looks so delicate, like lace draped over bones that will rip at the slightest touch. Despite the impression of vulnerability, her posture is full of assurance, like whatever she has come for, she has come prepared to stand her ground. I'd expect to see a woman of her age hunched over on a cane, as if the weight of time and responsibility has forced her body to crumple over, but her hands rest easily in her pockets and she stands straight and gazes up at Damien's face which is a full foot taller than her. It takes me a minute to recognize who she is, and when I do, I curse the

Heavens for round three, the final bell tolling as the shock sweeps through me again. I haven't seen her in years. Zeke and I stop at the same time, shocked and awed by her presence. Knowing the polar opposite fate of myself and Zeke, how is she going to receive us. I'm a demon and she, she's always been so much more than I could ever become. My stomach feels heavy, like I've accepted the weight of time that should have been hunching her shoulders over. Maybe it's the way fate works. Going to Hell gives the soul an eternally sick feeling, compared to where she has just come from. Light, airy, without a care in the world. Except if she didn't care, she wouldn't be here, and I know she wouldn't have come all this way for me. It's apparent when she looks our way.

Gigi looks at Zeke with only the look a grandmother can give a wayward grandchild. Most grandmothers I know, or at least I like to think, are the doting kind. Gigi was no exception. So there's this unwritten rule in my book when you piss off Nana, you know you've really stepped in it. Zeke seems to agree with my unwritten rule because the look on his face is a cross between terrified and sheepish. As we approach, I see Damien's lips twitch, but he says nothing and I give him the stink eye. I don't know how many more surprises my psyche can take and if he knows what's going down, he better let on quick.

"You've been up to it haven't you, Zeke?" Gigi's aura glows a little brighter with her irritation and I have to squint and look away. She's like a firefly when her ire is lit up.

"Gigi, I--"

"Not another word, young man. I've just been

conferring with Damien here and he's told me all about it." Gigi is wearing her usual comfortable holiday sweater and stretch pants. I think it might be a grandmother thing, to start wearing holiday sweaters in August. At least, I like to think they do. I never knew a grandma except her.

"Catriona, dear. You've been up to it as well, haven't you?"

She smiles at me and I wonder if a Hellcat is permitted to hug an angel. She seems to think so and it revises my theory about crazy cat ladies because I think reaching level-saber tooth cat lover must be some kind of record.

"They aren't feeding you enough down there." She looks me over and of all the things to comment on, my skinny-ass is the least she should be worried about. Bloodstains and torn clothing would be on any normal person's list of concerns, but Gigi has never been normal, which is why I love her.

"I'm sorry, Gigi," I whisper in her ear. "I tried."

She pats my shoulder and leans back, but the twinkle in her eye suggests whatever tricks she has up her sleeve are about to impress.

"It has been brought to our attention," she gestures to Dante who looks at her with reverie, "there has been some soul swapping and marking is most unprecedented."

I shrug. Where to even begin explaining? She seems to think an explanation isn't warranted though. "In light of recent events, and the knowledge Phil has sacrificed his Grace, we find ourselves disturbed such a sacrifice has been made without a consultation."

"That was done before--" Gigi holds up her

hands before I can finish.

"Damien explained. We were just discussing recompense for it. Heaven was punishing the boy, but we weren't ready to give up on him. We thought a timeout would suffice for his actions, but even that seems to not get through to everyone." She gave Zeke a glare and he had the wherewithal to look abashed.

"What is the proposal to make it right?" I ask, knowing only Damien and I know the system needs fixing to stall the apocalypse.

"It appears as if Hell took three other souls today. Souls that had Hell not interfered with, would have survived a few more months to a few more years." I frown. Three other souls? What souls? Then it dawns on me.

"Mr. Threads and the buffoons?" I slap my thigh. That's right, they'd been caught in the crossfire so to speak. Dick and Doug did their part to ensure they didn't walk away from the bar, but they hadn't even been marked yet. "What does it mean?" I wonder if she is going to reclaim Phil and I hope she does.

"We are prepared to ask Hell to exchange those three for the soul of Zeke."

All eyes turn to Zeke.

"Gigi?" His lips tremble.

How had I not seen the insecurity? Probably because I hadn't been able to see past the despicable creature he built himself up to be.

"I didn't have the opportunity to discuss this with my father," Damien says.

"He's my grandson," Gigi turns on him. Her eyes are fierce and Damien's eyebrows raise.

"Grandson or not, he has no redeemable qualities about him. We saved Lowell, Phil saw to it. Take Phil back if you must."

"That deal is above me, Damien," Gigi tells him. "It's between those two." By those two, I assume Damien's father and grandfather. Which just leaves us standing here haggling over the cost of justice.

Damien looks out over the river and sees the lush greens meet the burnt oranges of the horizon. The river is crystal clear and matches the sky where not a cloud mars the sky. If there is any day where consideration for redemption might be possible, this is the perfect day to do it. Eden is more beautiful than even the Bible suggests. It might seem like just another river with grassy banks and floral horizons, but it's the picture of freedom making it so breathtaking. An apple tree sits at the corner of the lot, the red and green fruit hang from luscious branches, beckoning and calling to those who see it to pick them.

I can see why Gigi picked Eden to build her camp. The camp itself is a simple log cabin like out of a standard mediocre painting, but the simplicity of it is what makes it so charming. I suddenly wonder if Gigi's camp here is intentional. To ensure no one picks the fruit. I'm brought out of my musings by Damien's voice.

"What about Marty?" he asks, but Gigi is already shaking her head.

"You marked him already and he can't face salvation while he's still evolving from what he was to a Hound. He can be considered for atonement after he completes the shift."

Damien nods and sighs and I see on his face the price of haggling over souls is a job he never wanted to do. I never expected to get thrown into this position either. I always assumed I'd bag and tag and be on my merry way. It's strange to think I now have to consider the weight of the soul I am collecting or bargaining for.

"Alright. We will agree to change the books and give Zeke a reprieve, but he needs to prove he is worthy of this redemption. One year to prove he will work to earn it, then we will reassess."

"Five years," Gigi counter offers. "And the Sloshed Sloth becomes neutral territory for Heaven and Hell to meet and converse when necessary."

"Agreed about the bar being a rendezvous point, but one year for Zeke," I say firmly. I figure getting used to ruling Hell comes with the cost of agreeing with my co-ruler sometimes. We might as well find common ground here. "Gigi, he doesn't get any more free passes after this. He has to want to change. It's a choice." I stare at him and he looks away. I wonder if he's capable of it.

Gigi nods and sighs, pulling him into a hug. When she lets go, her eyes are misty as she agrees. "One year. You hear that, boy? If I have to come back down here and haggle for you, you're in for a whooping."

Zeke nods and out of the corner of my eye, I see Dante grow brighter before Lowell appears beside him. He has changed and isn't covered in blood, which is probably good for Gigi's mental state, but I trust she and Zeke will fill Lowell in on the bar being used as a neutral ground.

Zeke's lips tremble again and I nudge Damien, pointing to the bank of the river. We walk off and give them a few moments to let Zeke collect himself. It's not going to be easy and I have every intention of checking up on him like a parole officer on the case of a wayward parolee. After a few moments, Gigi pats his cheek, and I close my eyes as she begins to fade around the edges and glows from within. The light moves Heavenward and we are left standing with Zeke, Lowell, and Dante.

"Are you alright? What about James?" I ask Lowell. He's lost Marty. I can't imagine the pain he must be in. I only take comfort in the fact he might have found solace in seeing Gigi one more time.

"As alright as I can be given the circumstances."

I give him my best smile and then he does something unexpected. He starts laughing. I can't really blame him. I found the funny at the most inappropriate times this past week too. I chuckle with him and see the sparkle in Dante's eyes.

"Well, it's been quite an adventure. I think I have plenty of material for my next novel." Dante looks between us gleefully and I can't help but widen my grin. "Is there anything else you need before I return and sequester myself?" he asks.

I hold out my hand. "As a matter of fact, there is."

***

The mountainside stinks to high Heaven and I wonder if they will intervene to remove the odorous remains. I guess its Lucifer's mess and he should clean it, but I'm just happy Sugar wasn't harmed in the making of this madness.

There're a few rain stains on the leather of her seat along with some pollen and leaves that have stuck to the chrome, but it's nothing a good washing next to the river Styx won't take care of. I slide my leg across the seat and turn the key in the ignition. She purrs to life and I look over my shoulder. Marty is panting happily in the sidecar and Fae is glaring at the line of drool from his jowls down onto the floor. Tabby pops some bubble gum and I'm happy to see Tora has stopped twitching from nerves. She's been given her own bike too. The hearse has been detached and left to grow over like some macabre antique featured in the travel and history magazines. I'll be happy to be back on the highway and breathing in the fresh air as we ride down the road.

Tora took Phil's smaller bike because physically it is easier to handle and Phil pets the new ride under him as he revs it to life.

Leo pulls up beside me on the right and Damien on the left. "Where to, boss?" she shouts over the roar of the engines.

Dick and Doug move in behind Damien while my girls wait for my cue.

I point them in the direction of the highway, and shout, "We're heading home!"

I hear Damien laugh as we pull out onto the highway about an hour later. I direct us to the next portal and we ride biker gang style back on the highway to Hell.

The End

ABOUT THE AUTHOR

Lydia Stevens is a full-time freelance Developmental Editor and Author. Having completed her Bachelor and Master's Degrees in Creative Writing and English, she then pursued an internship with a literary agency, Creative Media Agency and Anthem Press, an academic pressed based in London. Lydia has a passion for genre fiction-specifically fantasy and paranormal but enjoys working with a broad array of genres including romance, mystery, horror, science fiction, thriller, children's books, YA, and speculative fiction. For nonfiction, she enjoys working on memoirs and inspirational novels. She is a co-host of the newly founded podcast, REDinkwriters, where she brings her expertise in developmental editing and creative writing.

When Lydia is not working on projects in the publishing industry, she enjoys spending time in her home taking care of her two "children," her nine-year-old son, and her 86-year-old grandmother; along with her two cats, Sherlock Holmes and Sirius Black, and the newest addition to her family, her border collie mix, Savior.

Lydia can be found at the following social media sites:
Facebook: @authorlydiastevens
Website: Http://www.lydia-stevens.com
Twitter: @Author_Lydia
LinkedIn: www.linkedin.com/in/authorlydiastevens
Instagram: Lydiastevens_author
Pinterest: http://pin.it/gb4bzxzf5rsgzl
Goodreads: http://www.goodreads.com/lydiastevens

REDinkwriters
Facebook and Twitter: @REDinkwriters